A KING'S
RANSOM

A KING'S RANSOM

VICTOR SUTHREN

ST. MARTIN'S PRESS
NEW YORK

Library of Congress Cataloging in Publication Data

Suthren, Victor J. H.
A king's ransom.

I. Title.
PR9199.3.S895K5   813'.54   81-14499
ISBN 0-312-45610-7   AACR2

For my parents,
and in remembrance of
George Bell Dyer

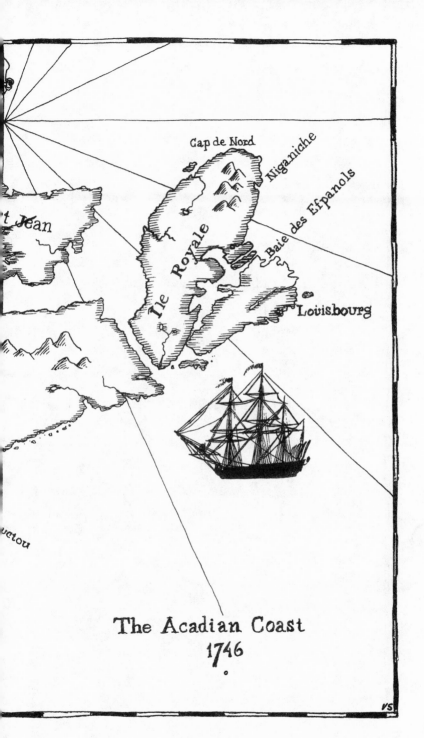

Cap de Nord

Niganiche

Baie des Efpanols

t Jean

Ile Royale

Louisbourg

uctou

The Acadian Coast
1746

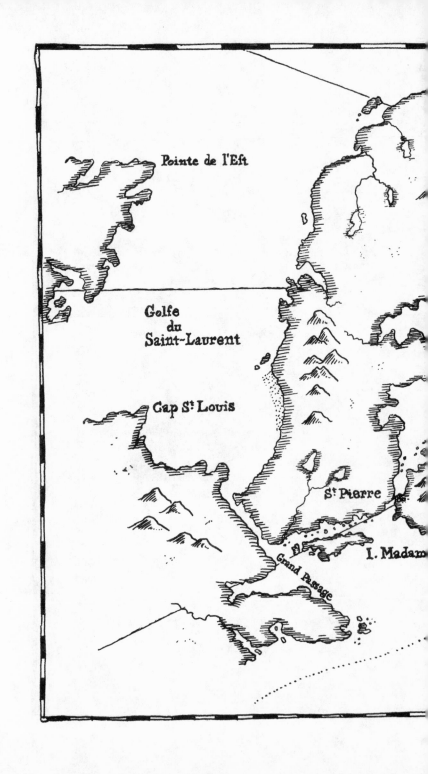

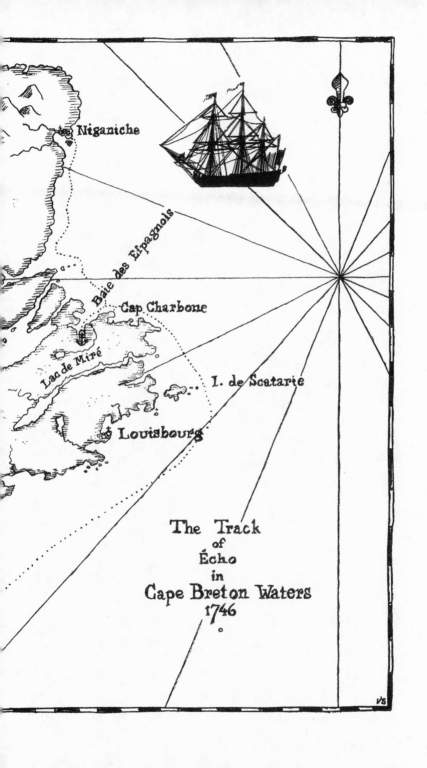

Niganiche

Baie des Efpagnols

Cap Charbone

Lac de Miré

I. de Scatarie

Louisbourg

The Track
of
Écho
in
Cape Breton Waters
1746

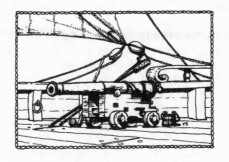

ONE

The sun rose, molten, out of the swirling banks of winter fog that cloaked the dark face of the Gulf of Genoa, the amber light of its rays reaching for its first contact with the French Maritime Alps. Farther to the westward it touched the heights above the great French naval fortress of Toulon. Gradually the great semicircular basin of the Little Roads and Great Roads of Toulon brightened as the sun moved higher into the clear December sky.

Below in the great town the light filtered over the sprawling buildings of the naval arsenal and reflected in the crowded waters of its basins: the old pool of the Vielle Darse and, beyond, the Darse Neuve. Each was crowded with the mixed hulls and rigs of dozens of ships amidst the towering arms of sheer hulks and the clustered little work vessels of the naval dockyard.

The magnificent harbour was really two harbours rather than one, both encompassed by the broad arms formed by the Cap

Sicié Peninsula on the west and Cap de Carqueiranne on the east. From the eastern shore of the Sicié Peninsula the dumbbell shape of the smaller, rocky Saint Mandrier Peninsula jutted into the circle formed by the arms, providing the wider shelter of the anchorage known as the Great Roads, and farther inshore, the opening of the Little Roads. These were beautifully sheltered anchorages, fit to hold a mighty fleet, and as the warm moving light spread over them it revealed that here in the midwinter of 1745 just such an armada was present in them.

Their bowsprits turning to the faint ebb of the tide and the last of the morning zephyrs, the line-of-battle ships and the lesser warships of His Most Christian Majesty Louis XV's Toulon squadron rode at anchor in the Roads. Their hulls gleaming, their masts and yards starkly etched against the morning sky, the powerful vessels of the main battle line lay in a carefully organized anchorage pattern. Randomly anchored among them, like children among parents, rode the smaller hulls of frigates, corvettes, flutes, and here and there an exotic-looking tartan or xebec.

The morning sunlight also touched on the trim blue and tan hull of a graceful twenty-gun corvette that lay anchored off by herself somewhat, in the lee of the Balaguier Tower, on the Saint Mandrier side of the Roads. It slanted in through the broad windows across the corvette's stern into its great cabin, where it spilled onto a paperstrewn desk at which sat the corvette's commander.

Lieutenant Paul François Adhémar Gallant, Chevalier de Saint-Louis, formerly a junior garrison officer of the fortress town of Louisbourg on Ile Royale in the Americas and now commanding officer of the French naval corvette *Echo*, glanced with red-rimmed eyes at the growing light outside. With a sigh he pinched out the guttering candle on his desk. He tossed down a quill on the mass of ledgers and lists in front of him and pushed his chair back, rubbing the back of his neck and closing his eyes to let the images of endless sums and clerk's crabbed handwriting fade from his mind.

Gallant was a tall man, close to six feet, and even though folded into a chair his frame gave evidence of a certain lean strength and military bearing. He was dark, with straight black brows and brown eyes, and a strong jaw line that contrasted slightly with the lines of sensitivity about his mouth. He was deeply tanned in the manner of seamen, and rather than a

12

powdered full-bottomed wig he wore his own hair tied simply back with ribbon. His face was lined with fatigue at the moment, and he scratched at the day's growth of beard that stubbled his chin. Although his face was a study in contrasts, revealing that Gallant could be no more than twenty-five years of age, it was the face of a man used to the command of other men, and, what was more, the command of other men in the severe testing of mortal combat.

While Gallant now sat in the somewhat rumpled comfort of his shirt and breeches, other articles of clothing draped over the one other chair in the sparse cabin and a settee under the stern windows revealed that he wore the indigo blue and grey-white uniform of the Compagnies Franches de la Marine, the independent companies of naval infantry who served as marines in the warships of Louis XV and also garrisoned the colonial bastions of France overseas.

Gallant was an Acadien, a native of the Americas who had won his commission in the garrison of the fortress of Louisbourg through a combination of personal zeal and the influence of his uncle, a merchant in the town for the Compagnie des Indes and a member of the powerful Du Pont family. But when he had proudly stepped out on the Louisbourg place d'armes in the uniform of the Troupes de la Marine, young Enseigne Gallant had no thought that he would one day several years later be sitting in the captain's quarters of a corvette of the French Navy, at anchor in the harbour of Toulon, with the responsibility for working and fighting a warship on his hands rather than the simple command of ragtag infantry in far-off Louisbourg.

The scuff of shoes sounded outside Gallant's cabin door and he heard his marine sentry clump to attention. A knock sounded.

"Come", said Gallant. He looked up to see the burly form of *Echo's* first mate step in through the door and duck in under the low beams.

Théophile-Auguste Béssac was a muscular and weather-beaten Minas Basin man whose career had taken him from the flatlands of his home into most of the world's seas. He was barely literate, an enormously resourceful professional seaman whose skill had come instead through the surer school of experience. When *Echo* had plied her trade in the great Atlantic commerce triangle between l'Orient, the Caribees and Louisbourg under her merchant captain, Béssac had worked the ship and her crew into a capable efficiency rare in the world of merchant shipping.

"Still and yet, capitaine? Not yet done with that clerkish henscratching?" said Béssac, slumping down on the settee under the stern windows.

Gallant snorted. "Not by half, mon vieux. God's Teeth, but this is a tiresome business!"

Béssac turned his hat in his hands and grinned affably. "Sometimes it helps to not be able to write a lick", he said.

"Indeed?" said Gallant. "What was it you wanted, then? You didn't come in here to gloat about being illiterate."

Béssac jabbed a thumb toward the side of the ship. "There's a boat alongside. The duty lugger. There's two hands and a coxswain who says you're wanted ashore."

"Says? They've nothing written?"

Béssac shrugged. "No, m'sieu'. I was about to tell 'em to shove off when the coxswain spelled out your whole name and said, very businesslike, that His Excellency the duc d'Anville, Lieutenant-General of His Majesty's Marine and not a gentleman whose messenger should be told to bugger off wants to see you in his quarters at" — and here the mate squinted out through the windows for a moment — "the turn of the glass."

Gallant sat up. "D'Anville? What in God's name does he want to see down at my lowly level for? Christ, he barely talks to a chef d'escadre. And last I heard he was in Versailles. But if he's here in truth. . . ." He slapped a hand to his forehead. "The turn of the glass! Béssac, that's half an hour from now!" He rose and kicked back the chair. "I've got to shave. And you'd better get the longboat off the boom and in alongside. . . ."

Béssac raised a calming hand. "There's an off-duty lad from the larboard watch bringing a bowl o' hot water from the galley right now. And the coxswain of the lugger says he's to wait and take you. He's hooked on at the starboard fore chains enjoying the bottle I swung down to them."

Gallant raised an appreciative eyebrow. "You're in the wrong trade, Béssac. You should've been a country housewife."

Ten minutes later Gallant was eyeing his reflection in a small steel mirror hung behind his cabin door. His hair was retied into a neater queue with a black bow, and on his head, perched at the correct angle over his right eyebrow, sat a gilt-

14

trimmed black tricorne, a large black cockade of silk ribbon above the left eye. Over the shirt and close-fitting stock he wore a dark blue vest and breeches, buttoned in brass, and dark blue hose reaching down to buckled black shoes. Over the vest he wore, unbuttoned, a grey-white coat with blue lining and large turned-back cuffs of blue, again heavy with brass buttons. Secured around Gallant's neck by a blue ribbon was the sign of a Compagnies Franches de la Marine officer on duty, a half-moon shaped gilt gorget bearing the arms of France. To complete the uniform a buff waistbelt under his coat supported the scabbard of a slender dress sword, whose tip protruded out through the part in the full-skirted coattails.

"Looks all right", he said to Béssac. Did the coxswain say where His Excellency has his lodgings?"

Béssac nodded. "Between swigs. He's at number twelve, Rue Traverse-Cathédrale. A stone's throw from the cathedral."

Gallant grimaced. "Not a religious zealot. I hope."

Béssac guffawed.

When Gallant reached the deck and walked down into the waist of the ship, the morning sun was strong and bright, and he delighted in the feel of the cool air after the long night in the closed cabin. He clasped his hands behind his back in the manner he favoured while on deck and cast a proprietorial look over his ship.

For all that Béssac was making much of ignoring the paper imposition of naval standards on the running of *Echo*, the ship looked every bit a miniature man-o'-war wherever Gallant turned his eye. The decks gleamed from the morning's holy-stoning, and here and there the small bits of brightwork about the ship gleamed in evidence of the application of brick dust and effort. Aloft, the black yards were swung square and level, the sails rolled tightly and lashed down with their gaskets to the yards at regular intervals. The ship's running rigging was tightened up enough to give her a clean look, and at the fiferails and taffrails the coils hung below their pins in neat symmetrical rows. Amidships, the eight nine-pounder guns that now thrust their red muzzles out through the waist gunports were securely and carefully set up, the breeching lines at just the right tension and hang, the falls of the gun tackles hooked to the ringbolts on either side of the ports neatly cheesed on the bone-white deck. The piece of each gun had been painted a glossy black, except for the red muzzles, and this contrasted pleasingly with the deep ochre of the gun carriages themselves.

Even the hands working at their duties on deck and aloft, Gallant noted with pleasure, looked cleaner and more smartly turned out than he had ever seen the knockabout Acadiens look before. One of Gallant's first actions on arrival at Toulon had been the purchase of a number of bolts of strong blue cloth and white canvas, to give the ragged men of *Echo* a chance to repair the damage long toil had done to their clothing. Now he was noticing that the men had made an effort at some kind of uniformity, and that although most had reverted to multi-coloured shirts and stocking caps, they were largely wearing white breeches and large, full-sleeved seacoats in either white or blue.

Then Gallant's eye was caught by the little party drawn up at the entry port in *Echo's* rail.

"Well, I'll be damned, Béssac", said Gallant to himself.

On one side of the port the ship's boys were drawn up in a line. Beside them, a bos'n's pipe held to his lips and a look of immense importance on his face, stood Bédard, the stoic helmsman Béssac had made coxswain of the ship. Ranged across from the boys stood the six-man squad of Compagnies Franches marines that *Echo* now carried, under the glowering command of a mustachioed sergeant named Garneau.

As Gallant approached the port, Garneau snarled at his men and the muskets moved smoothly into the Present, the marines' white-gaitered legs snapping back in well-drilled unison.

Gallant raised his hat and bowed slightly while Garneau performed a graceful salute with his halberd, all the while beaming in pride at Gallant. The marines had come aboard the corvette a sullen and dispirited lot, certain they had been drafted to a backwater existence in a miserable little merchantman. Béssac had soon displayed that, notwithstanding his old seacoat and jocular ways he ran a tight and efficient ship, and the military hearts of the marines had warmed to that.

But it had been Gallant himself who had unlocked the reservoir of loyalty in the marines. Not only did he make a point of remaining in the uniform of an officer of the Troupes de la Marine when the right was his to dress as a naval lieutenant; there was something in Gallant's character that these men had not seen in an officer before. Gallant cared for his men; he looked them in the eye and talked to them as men and not as slaves to discipline; he explained things to them, and made it clear that he believed in them to do their very best for him, as he would for them.

Gallant paused at the rail and lifted his hat toward the stern where the broad white Bourbon ensign curled lazily on its staff. He squinted against the flickering points of light reflecting from the wave tips as a breeze ruffled the harbour surface.

"Keep your powder dry, capitaine", said Béssac at his elbow. "I'll have the longboat waiting at the curved steps of the Vielle Darse for you."

Gallant nodded, then winced involuntarily as Bédard let out an ear-piercing blast on the pipe, obviously intended for a salute.

As Gallant went down the battens into the sternsheets of the lugger, Béssac's voice followed him. "Think we'll suffice as a naval vessel, capitaine? How about that pipe, eh?"

Gallant looked up, deadpan, at the mate who was now looking over the rail above. "A disgrace to the Service."

Béssac chuckled loudly and lifted his hat. "À vos ordres, capitaine", he laughed.

In a few moments the lugger had dropped out of *Echo's* lee and was reaching in over the dark wavelets toward the inner harbour.

Gallant swivelled in his seat, unable to resist the universal sailor's compulsion to stare back at his ship at anchor while going ashore from her.

Echo's trim and ducklike hull, her lines and beautiful sheer a tribute to the French logic and clarity of her design, lay mirrored in graceful beauty in the dark water.

As Gallant watched over the widening distance he saw figures moving on the foredeck, Béssac's burly form among them. The mate had mentioned he was going to freshen the hawse, which meant to ease or haul in the great cable slightly so as to shift the point of wear against the lip of the hawse pipe.

Gallant smiled to himself. No man could fail to be proud of that ship. Nor of any man in her.

"So you are the renowned Lieutenant Gallant, who tweaks the noses of Englishmen and Moors alike. The pleasure of the meeting is mine, Gallant. Take a chair for a moment."

Jean Baptiste Louis Frédéric de Roye de la Rochefoucauld,

duc d'Anville, Lieutenant-General of the Marine, grasped with a long, strong hand the one Gallant extended in surprise and gestured to a chair at one side of his broad desk. He then turned back to a slimly elegant aide with whom he had been talking when Gallant had been ushered in.

"As to the music, see to that yourself. But a good string quartet, mind; none of your damned tootling oboes. And I want Lully, perhaps Rameau as well. *Les Indes Galantes* is Madame DesHerbiers' favourite, particularly the first movement, and she'll twit me all night about it if she doesn't get it."

The aide bent in a stylish little bow and left. As he passed Gallant his pale eyes swept over the Acadien from head to toe, a split-second gesture of dismissal.

Gallant ignored the look and concentrated his attention on the figure of the duc, who was carefully arranging papers about the desk. D'Anville had a long, handsome face centred by a thin, hooked nose and lit with very bright and very black eyes. Above a wide and patrician forehead a wig of the latest cut flowed in smoothly combed waves down to his shoulders. From behind his neck the broad black bow of the wig's queue framed the white stock of laced linen which gripped the duc's throat. Over a vest of crimson silk the nobleman was wearing a full-cuffed uniform coat of deep red, the great rolled cuffs and the buttonholes looped in gold lace. His wrists were heavy with lace.

The two men were seated in d'Anville's rooms, which were large and airy and looked out through flung-back doors into a delightful small garden. The exterior of the housefronts had deceived Gallant as he approached them from the street; he had not expected a suite of such size and elegance to be hidden behind the modest facade.

Nor was he prepared for the purposeful bustle and activity he found himself amidst. While impassive, heavily armed sentries of the Gardes de la Marine watched at every doorway, an array of sober-faced and intent naval officers were at work about the chambers.

It struck him with some awe that preparations of enormous importance and scope were underway here, in absolute seriousness, and that those preparations were drawing their power and purpose from the desk of the man before whom Gallant sat.

The marine was now receiving a level, appreciative look

from this renowned nobleman who, at the age of thirty-seven, was already one of the most powerful and influential men in the French Navy, not to speak of Versailles.

D'Anville set a last sheaf of documents to one side on a delicate chinoiserie table and smiled again. "There we are. How fortunate for me I was able to tear you away from your duties, Gallant."

Gallant inclined his head, gravely. There was very little of the fortunate in responding to a direct order.

"Your servant, Excellency", he said.

"I am familiar with your exploits, may I say. M'sieu' the Comte de Maurepas was so taken with your report he showed it to me personally. You appear to be an officer of great resourcefulness."

"Your Excellency is too kind", said Gallant.

"My Excellency knows what I read. You needn't play the cagey courtier with me, Gallant. You're here to talk business."

Gallant, taken unaware, pursed his lips. Then he caught the reassuring warmth in d'Anville's eyes. "Very well, m'sieu'. Thank you for the compliment at any rate."

D'Anville waved a hand. "I'm not a seaman myself, Gallant. Never been afloat, really. But I respect men who have been, and who do it well."

D'Anville rose and paced to the far end of the room, his heels ringing hollowly on the cool tile floor. He looked out for a long moment into the shadows of the garden.

Unexpectedly he said, "You are aware, Gallant, that the English are able to keep well over one hundred and fifty warships at sea against us. An overwhelming preponderance."

"I knew the figure was something like that, yes, m'sieu'," Gallant replied.

"And that this, therefore, requires that we husband our ships and resources to carry out whatever tasks we have set for us at sea. Carry out the mission, no more."

Gallant was silent.

"Silence, Gallant? Do you object to something I've just said?"

Gallant took the bait. "If you please, Excellency, I realize you have just enunciated the prime philosophy by which we are meant to carry out our duties. But. . . ."

"But?"

"It's rubbish, m'sieu'. We are giving the seas to the English with that kind of thinking."

"Dangerous talk, Gallant", said d'Anville. "But go on."

Gallant swallowed down the sudden tightness in his throat.

"The English prowl the seas in their worm-eaten hulks and bottle us forever into the harbours for one reason, Excellency, and that reason isn't the relative strength of our fleets, with all due respect."

"Oh?"

"No, m'sieu'. Our ships are faster, better designed. Our weight of broadsides, gun for gun, is heavier than theirs. A French seventy-four can crush two English third-rates with ease if she's well fought."

"And?"

"And nothing, quite simply, Excellency. The British whip us and send us back into our harbours to lick our wounds more often than a courageous man can admit with any peace. The rosbifs sit off out there at sea and literally become extensions of their ships, continually learning and testing themselves, while we lie in our snug coves, do some little sail-handling drills, run the guns in and out, and remain forever nothing but damned amateurs!"

"I'm not for a moment saying I agree with all this, Gallant", said d'Anville after a long moment.

Gallant's neck tingled but he pressed on. "We have the goal of getting somewhere or delivering troops or some court ninny's luggage off to a far coastline, and we dodge out of the Englishman's way as if he were a pack of wolves. We insult ourselves. As seamen and as Frenchmen."

D'Anville paced back from the window and folded himself into his chair again, his eyes unswerving from Gallant.

"Do you realize the cost of keeping the navy at sea, Gallant?" he said. "Do you realize that the Comte de Maurepas estimated last year that it would cost him twenty million livres to run the Marine, the colonies, the galleys and the ship construction programme, and that the King granted him merely six million? How can we prowl at sea for long periods with that kind of budget, hein?"

Gallant set his jaw. To hell with the balancing of their damned books.

"We shall lose the seas to the English, Excellency", he said slowly, "unless we seek them out. Seek them out, engage them, fight them to the last man if need be. And defeat them." He shook his head. "If we do not, France will lose all need for a navy, m'sieu'. There will be nothing left to defend across the oceans."

D'Anville stared at him for some moments, silent. Coolly, Gallant returned the stare, recklessness and pride victorious now over the fear he had felt when he began to speak.

Then a sudden smile broke across d'Anville's features. The nobleman thumped a fist on his desk top.

"By God, Gallant, that was well said. The kind of thing I was hoping I'd get from you."

Gallant's face was flushed. "Excellency?"

D'Anville was out of his chair again. "What do you know of the supposed expedition to retake Acadie?"

"Very little, other than lower deck rumour, m'sieu'."

"Such as?"

"The Toulon fleet is to attempt to get to sea when the winds are northerly and work out past Gibraltar. Attempt some kind of embarkation of troops on the Spanish coast."

"The Comte de Maurepas is no more seaman than I. Did you know that, Gallant?" The duc was at the windows again.

"I know very little about him, m'sieu'."

"M'sieu' de Maurepas has said that the loss of Île Royale and its fishery is more of a loss than the mines of Peru might be. Do you agree?" D'Anville had spun on his heel and was looking at him intently.

Gallant thought for a moment, choosing his words. "Of course, Excellency. And both the East and West Indies trade depend on Louisbourg as an entrepot, a transshipment point. And as for the defences of Québec and Canada, there is no question that to lose Louisbourg is to lose. . . ."

"The key to America for us! Very good. You agree entirely with M'sieu' le Comte."

To say nothing of the poor wretches who called Cape Breton home and who have lost it all, thought Gallant with a pang of sadness.

D'Anville had resumed his seat.

"I am ostensibly meant to be assembling a fleet to aid that disastrous fellow Charles Edward against England, Gallant. But between you and I, my ships will sail against Louisbourg and Acadie, or I haven't read the cards correctly." He pursed his lips. "And you shall be part of it."

Gallant's heart bounded. At last, the confirmation of endless suspicions.

"It will be a prodigious undertaking, Gallant. Over fifty ships. Ten of the line, three frigates, two other corvettes, at least two fireships, a hospital ship. And troops. Fifteen troopships, and nineteen storeships in addition to all that. I shall be setting up my standard at Brest next month, and the vessels will begin assembling with a view to a rendezvous in March."

D'Anville's carefully manicured fingers moved in patterns over the desk top. "We'll convoy off the Isle d'Aix and set course for the harbour at Chibouctou, in Acadie. Do you know it?"

Gallant nodded. "Yes, of course. Very deep, with a basin at its farther end. Good firewood and water on its shores."

"Exactly. It is the intention of the Chevalier d'Estournelles, my second-in-command and myself that we use Chibouctou as a base for the reduction of Acadie before we bring our forces to bear on the routing out of the damned Bostonnais . . . as I believe you call them . . . from Louisbourg."

D'Anville sat back with a gleam in his eye. "We'll have some of the finest King's ships afloat, Gallant. The *Mars*, the *Argonaute*, even the *Renommée*. My flag will be in *Northumberland*." Then he paused.

"I want you to use your apparent skills to carry out a task for me", he said, after a moment. "A task of the utmost importance to His Majesty himself."

D'Anville drew from a desk drawer a broad chart, which Gallant recognized at once as being that of the Caribbean Sea and the Atlantic Coast of the Americas.

D'Anville motioned to Gallant to come closer, while he himself rose and bent over the chart. "Think back to what you know of the movement our brave Spanish allies make of all their American plunder to Europe each year. It almost always follows the same pattern." He gestured with a long finger at the chart. "The Manila Galleon puts in to Acapulco with her China cargo, and it is then hauled over to Veracruz on the Gulf of Mexico side. Meanwhile, down here," said d'Anville, pointing to Darien and below, "the real treasure, all that is left of the Peruvian bullion and the Potosi silver is shipped to Panama and muleteamed over to Portobello. Then the Terra Firma Fleet puts in from Cartagena, picks up the bullion and sails for Havana, where it is supposed to join the New Spain Fleet from Veracruz."

"Supposed?" said Gallant.

"They sometimes miss their rendezvous. But at any rate both fleets convoy back to Spain from Havana."

Gallant grunted. "And get plundered by the English and the boucaniers all the way."

"Exactly", nodded d'Anville. "But they're fairly safe so

22

long as the convoy can hold together, and not spill its guts all over one of the Bahamas.'' The nobleman pointed at a position just north of the island of Lucayos. "At about this position one large vessel, about the size of a third-rate, left under sealed orders the main convoy group to make her way north. She was the *Santa Maria de la Vela*.''

"Where was she ordered to, Excellency?"

D'Anville smiled. "Why, to Louisbourg, my dear Gallant."

"Louisbourg!"

"Indeed. And to the great consternation of a great many influential people, she failed to arrive", said d'Anville.

"I see.''

"Do you?" said d'Anville, with a small smile. After a pause he went on.

"You know, naturally, that until last year France was not officially at war with the damned English, although we certainly carried on as if we were. Four years of fraud, during which we rendered some quite valuable assistance to the Spaniards. All that was not simply out of a desire on the part of His Majesty to help propagate the Faith or smite the rosbifs, Gallant. Deals were made. And our missing *Santa Maria de la Vela* figured very prominently in such an arrangement, of vital importance to the Royal purse.''

Gallant was becoming more and more fascinated by the tale at each of d'Anville's words. "How so, Excellency?''

"Quite simply, Gallant, she and the contents of her holds were to be a personal, *personal*, mind, gift from the King of Spain to His Most Christian Majesty. It consisted in part of a magnificent Madonna cast in Manila, perhaps a century ago, about three pieds in height. Cast in solid gold, I should add.''

Gallant gaped. "In gold, Excellency? Three pieds? My God!''

"In addition", said d'Anville smoothly, "she is encrusted and worked with a prodigious quantity of jewels and precious stones, of a wide origin: Mindanao, Canton, the Celebes . . . which is not to mention the figurine's interior. That bears its own cargo. Uncut diamonds, I'm told.''

Gallant stared, fascinated.

"There was a certain quantity of gold and silver ingots with the *Señora*, as the figurine has come to be known. Properly she was entitled Nuestra Señora de la Concepciòn.''

Gallant shook his head. "And . . . the value?"

D'Anville thought for a moment. "With the *Señora*, the

cargo is worth perhaps two million livres", he said evenly. "She alone is worth at least one million, Lieutenant. Give or take a few hundred thousand."

D'Anville went on. "The *Santa Maria de la Vela* was reported at one point, however. A Breton fisherman spoke her about ten leagues southward of Cap de Sable. She was standing on to the northward under plainsail and appeared to be in no trouble."

"So she therefore may have come to grief somewhere along the Acadien coastline between Sable and Louisbourg", said Gallant.

D'Anville's eyes brightened. "Precisely."

"One question, Excellency. When did she speak the Breton?"

"In early March. The convoy had been meant to sail from Havana the September before. The pox had hit them."

Gallant thought. "March", he said, after a moment. "But the New Englanders hadn't arrived at our doorstep then. She should have made it, particularly a vessel that size. Provided no pirate picked her off, of course."

"Indeed", d'Anville nodded. "The possibility of her falling prey to the pirates is a real one. They continue to infest the shores of the Americas in spite of the war. "So therefore, Lieutenant, we have that as an added complication to our question: what has happened to the *Santa Maria de la Vela*, to the bullion, and, most importantly, to the remarkable Señora?"

D'Anville rose and moved to a sideboard where a tall decanter of brandy stood with several glasses. He poured two strong measures and handed one to Gallant.

For a moment both men enjoyed in silence the fiery path of the brandy down their throats.

Then d'Anville looked Gallant directly in the eye. Calmly he said, "I want you to find the answer to that question. You will take your corvette and sail within the week for America. And somewhere between Cap de Sable and Louisbourg, the English or pirates notwithstanding, you are to find that ship. Further, you are to undertake to restore its cargo, most importantly the Señora, to His Majesty."

Gallant heard d'Anville's words echoing round the room as if they were gunshots.

"You will have several months of time ahead of us on that coast, Gallant. I shall expect you to be either at anchor in

Chibouctou when I arrive, or to report to me there when you have anything to report." He smiled and sipped the brandy. "With luck you'll rejoin us in time for the assault on your own Louisbourg. And you needn't look so glum, Gallant; if the ship's been a wreck there'll be little you can do about it."

"And if it hasn't? If she's been taken?"

D'Anville's reply was even. "His Majesty is unswervingly concerned with the successful resolution of this task. Therefore, my dear Gallant, if someone has the King's property who shouldn't, you will relieve him of it. And restore it to His Majesty."

On impulse Gallant drained the brandy in one gulp and gasped as it seared its way down into his vitals.

D'Anville turned back to the decanter. "Another touch. And this time for success." He refilled Gallant's glass to the brim.

Raising his own he said, "I sail to take back part of a continent, Gallant. You sail to recover a lost lady and her immensely valuable dowry."

For a moment d'Anville's eyes wandered to the open window. "A king's ransom, one might almost say", he murmured. The glasses clinked together.

"May God grant we both succeed", said d'Anville.

Amen, thought Gallant, and threw the brandy down his throat.

Lieutenant Anthony Robinson, Royal Navy, and newly appointed to the command of His Britannic Majesty's Ship *Salamander*, 28 guns, tugged at the tight stock which was constricting his throat. He loathed formal clothing, and longed for the ease and comfort of his rough sea-duty shirts. The little waiting room in the Admiralty building, Whitehall, was hot and stuffy. He had been there for almost an hour, and the other occupants of the room, two men with the look of Post rank on them, had coldly ignored him in their conversation.

At last there was a sound of pump heels echoing on marble and the attendant appeared at the waiting room door.

"Lieutenant Robinson? This way, please."

Robinson rose to his feet, and followed the man down a long and echoing portion of the great hall.

Unexpectedly the servant stopped at the foot of a wide staircase, opened a door into a large room, and stood to one side.

Robinson strode in and then stopped short, as he realized where he was.

Robinson was standing in the Board Room of the Admiralty, the scene of the Navy's most critical decisions and the source of its most far-reaching orders. Decisions and orders reached and decided upon at the enormous and gleaming table that dominated the centre of the room, surrounded by chairs, three of which at the far end occupied by gentlemen of a very naval, very correct and very senior bearing.

The gentleman in the middle motioned Robinson forward. "Come, come, Lieutenant. Pray be seated."

Robinson swallowed and moved to the proferred chair, the heels of his dress pumps echoing hollowly on the floor. They were black, and very tight, with small silver buckles over his toes and a slightly tapered heel, high in the French style. Robinson despised them with a passion.

The three men who were regarding him with appraising stares were dressed in the fashion of senior naval officers of His Britannic Majesty's Navy, which is to say that in contrast to the more logical French, who wore a common uniform at every rank level except that of common seaman, they were resplendently attired in varying forms of vaguely military dress. The officer on the left, a thin, hook-nosed individual with piercing eyes, was all in brilliant scarlet and gilt; the gentleman on the right, shorter and heavyset, was in a russet-edged green silk.

But it was the central figure to whom Robinson's gaze remained directed, and found a reassuring, cool and steady look in reply. Almost as the even, handsome face below the beautifully powdered full wig registered in his memory, Robinson knew he was in the presence of one of the King's ablest sea officers.

George Anson's name was never far from the lips of every officer who valued seamanship and competency above glory and promotion. In command of the *Centurion* he had made an epic four-year circumnavigation, returning two years ago with his ship almost awash under the weight of Spanish booty looted from the Pacific. A year later, in 1745, he had been made Rear-Admiral of the White, and now only a year later it was virtually certain that he was to be named Vice-Admiral of the Blue. Tall, guarded, a disciplinarian and an administrator *par excellence*, he was as much a master of the King's Regulations for the Navy as he was of his own distant and reserved spirit, and it was said by his enemies that he often confused the two. But it was certain to all who cared about such things that the arrival of George Anson in the Board of Admiralty augured well for the immediate future of the Royal Navy. Below a spotless white stock Anson wore a striking uniform of a deep, inky blue coat, edged with gold lace, and under it, to judge by the waistcoat, white small clothes fastened with brass buttons.

"Aye, aye, sir", said Robinson, and folded into the chair, his hanger digging into his ribs.

"Captain Trowbridge, Captain Bayne. This is the young chap I was telling you about. The one Fitzsimmons brought to my attention."

Robinson started, taken unawares by Anson's words. He bowed slightly, remembering at the last moment to mumble "Your serv'nt, gentlemen."

"And yours, Lieutenant", said the hawk-nosed man, not unkindly. He evidently was Trowbridge.

Anson picked up a be-ribboned sheaf of correspondence from the table in front of him and set a pale gaze at Robinson over the top of it.

"You've just taken over *Salamander*."

"Sir."

"Where is she lying?"

"The Nore, sir. I read myself in during the Forenoon, yesterday." The first act of a commanding officer taking over a new command was that of reading aloud his commission to the assembled ship's company and thereby formally taking possession of his vessel and her men.

"I see", said Anson, after a moment. "Ready for sea?"

Robinson shifted in his chair. He had been up all the first night aboard studying the ship's documents and records and talking with his First Lieutenant and his other officers, but he was still uncertain of *Salamander's* real state of fitness. But he could get to sea.

"Would be in three or four days, sir. I'm short powder and ball, and fresh water."

"*Salamander*. Twenty-eight?" interrupted Trowbridge. "Took the *Héroine* and two luggers off Ushant three months ago, what?"

Robinson nodded. "Yes, sir. Off Penmark, actually."

Trowbridge grunted. "Good. Damn fine little ship. Fast. You were lucky to get her."

"So I've been told, sir", said Robinson.

Captain Bayne, who had been sitting quite still on Robinson's side of the great table, swung round to fix a cool blue eye on the young man. His cheeks and nose were etched with the red lacework lines of a certain overuse of wine and spirits.

"What do you know of the North American station, Robinson? Any service there?" he said.

"Some, sir. I carried out dispatches from Gibraltar to Vice-Admiral Townsend off the Virginias in the fall."

"Were you inshore?"

Robinson shook his head. "Hardly at all, sir. We spent time at anchor in the James River while I went inland ashore to the capital, Williamsburg, to deliver a sealed dispatch to the Governor's secretary."

"Ah, Williamsburg", said Trowbridge. "Bloody hot little town. Where'd you stay?"

"The Raleigh, sir", said Robinson, surprised. "Duke of Gloucester Street."

"Umf. Only damned decent lodgings there."

Anson's voice sounded from the head of the table. "I think we need pursue Lieutenant Robinson's American experiences no further. The reports of his superiors speak for themselves as to the nature of his service record."

He looked coolly at Robinson while still talking to the other two men. "What we are looking for is a fast vessel commanded by a man who demonstrates the right sort of attitude and initiative. I think Robinson satisfies those needs."

Robinson flushed slightly, pleased. Then his eyes rose to Anson's, doubt circling in his mind.

"In answer to your unspoken question, Lieutenant", said Anson with a slight smile, "we have it in mind to send you on a task of some independence, requiring thereby a corresponding degree of initiative on your part."

"Sir?" Robinson's heart began to beat faster.

Anson tapped the fat dossier before him.

"You are aware, Mr. Robinson, of the difficulties the Crown has been facing with Charles Edward and the Scots, and the efforts of the French to support him."

Robinson nodded. It was easy enough to be aware of a narrowly averted French invasion scheme, and the hair-raising successes of the Young Pretender's clansmen against the King's regiments of Foot in the north. Robinson's service had in the last four years been entirely on the Mediterranean station,

28

but he knew how tension had run high and was still high over the bitter Scots uprising.

"I have learned this morning", went on Anson, "that His Majesty's troops under the command of His Grace the Duke of Cumberland have inflicted a crushing, and it would appear final, defeat on Charles and the Jacobites. The slaughter of the Scots is said to have been quite remarkable."

Robinson jerked up in his chair. "That's extraordinary news, sir!" he burst out.

"Now if only Billy can do that in Flanders . . ." said Trowbridge under his breath.

"Quite", said Anson, dryly. "Nonetheless the Duke's victory has presented some rather surprising problems for us elsewhere."

Anson rose and began to pace up and down the Boardroom, his hands moving as he spoke.

"One of these problems, gentlemen, involves a certain sum of money, of rather startling size, which we have learned the Spanish had arranged to pass directly and quietly into the hands of King Louis. The Bourbon Compact at work, I'd think."

"The money, gentlemen, would appear to have been meant as a bribe", Anson went on. "A bribe meant to ensure that Louis would see to it that the French Navy would support their allies the Spanish in the latter's misadventures in the Americas and elsewhere. Support beyond what they have given to date."

"Was it a large sum, sir?" asked Robinson.

"Rather", said Anson. "One could buy the entire Dutch line of battle with it."

Captain Trowbridge picked up the narrative after a glance at Anson. "You see, gentlemen, the Dons' usual fleets or convoys from the Americas had, in one instance, an extra vessel added last year. It was very likely carrying the monies to be used in the bribe. And although we knew of its existence almost as soon as our agents in Portobello got word to us, we have held back from interfering with it."

Robinson scratched a fleabite under his waistcoat. "But why, sir? Isn't any effort at co-operation between the French and Spanish something we would immediately try to prevent?"

Anson sat down again and answered Robinson's question. "Of course. Except when one wants the French to be under strong pressure to go hounding off in support of the Spaniards, in place of being at our throats while the Duke dealt with . . . er . . . 'Charlie', as I believe his Scots call him."

A light flicked on in Robinson's mind. "Ah", he said, quietly.

"But this recent news from the north changes things, somewhat, Mr. Robinson", Anson went on. "We might have even wished the bribe to go through and be successful, before; but now that we've slapped Charles' wrists it is certainly not in His Britannic Majesty's overseas interests that the money reach Louis' hands."

Anson shook a fly off one heavily laced cuff. "We are not certain as to the exact value in sterling of the bribe hoard, which our Portobello agent said was shipped in an armed merchantman named", and here Anson glanced at the dossier, "the *Santa Maria de la Vela*. We learned from another source that its track was to be from Havana to Louisbourg to L'orient, and that it left Havana, was spoken off southern Nova Scotia, but failed to reach Louisbourg."

Trowbridge leaned forward and rapped ring-laden knuckles on the oaken table. "That haul of bullion or plate or whatever it is may be enormous, Lieutenant. And if we can put our hands to it, it may solve other problems in the bargain."

Anson spoke in reply to the puzzled look Robinson turned on him. "Captain Trowbridge is referring to the colony of Massachusetts, Mr. Robinson. The good burgers of Boston Town put their colony heavily in debt to fund the successful siege of Louisbourg last year. Now they want His Majesty to make good the expenses, and between the caterwauling in Parliament and the King's other preoccupations it's damned unlikely the money can be found quickly to pay them!" Anson sat back in his chair. "If the hoard is of sufficient value it might go a long way to pacifying the colonists' General Court as well as replenishing the Household coffers. Not that the colonists don't deserve every penny."

A peculiar premonition was crawling up Robinson's spine. "Sir, is it that you want me to . . ." he began.

"Exactly", said Anson. "Find the damned stuff, Mr. Robinson!"

Robinson sat up. "In earnest, sir? My God, it could be anywhere from Hatteras to Newfoundland!"

Anson smiled. "Not entirely. The most recently arrived letters from Commodore Knowles at Louisbourg indicate that the wreck of the vessel has been tentatively identified on the lower Nova Scotian coast. Commodore Knowles intends to send *Magnet*, 36, under Captain Rand, out to investigate."

Robinson pursed his lips. "Then what would my task be, sir? If *Magnet* is going to be on the scene."

"Your responsibility would be to take possession of the hoard, if Rand in fact finds it. Knowles, however, needs every vessel that he can muster, and if Rand hasn't found it, he will return to Louisbourg and you will do your best to find the ship and its money, or whatever, and return it to England."

Anson's face sobered. "Knowles needs Rand, Mr. Robinson, because we have been lax and allowed a sizeable French fleet to escape into the Western Ocean, bound for Nova Scotia, or even possibly the New England colonies themselves. We must also consider the possibility that the *Santa Maria* has been the victim of pirate actions. The preoccupation of the West Indian and American squadrons with the conduct of the war, and the proliferation of privateering colonial vessels under letters of marque has provided an opportunity for renewed pirate activity, I'm afraid. They are at sea, in strength, and neither we nor the French can spare a hand to lift against them. It may well be these outlaws with whom you will have to deal."

"I see, sir", said Robinson. The seriousness of the task he was being given was growing on him minute by minute, and in particular now that he knew *Salamander* would be sailing alone into waters which were also the goal of an enormous French fleet.

"There's one other thing you should know, Mr. Robinson", said Anson, after a moment.

"Sir?"

"Rand will have no way of knowing this, unless my letter reaches Commodore Knowles before *Magnet* sails. But we believe the French have sent out a fast vessel under a capable man to recover the money for themselves. Therefore your presence will serve to make more likely the probability — if the Frenchman gets anywhere near the money before Rand or you do — that it ends up in British hands."

Anson rose unexpectedly, signalling that the interview was at an end. He acknowledged Robinson's angular bow after the latter had risen to his feet. "You'll finish storing your ship and get her to sea as soon as you can. I believe the Frenchman has been already at sea for some time, but the peculiar weather may have held him back somewhat. You've no time to waste!'"

31

TWO

It was the twentieth day of May, 1746, and *Echo* was pitching into a heavy grey swell from the northeast, the steady and bone-chilling wind that blew above the sea driving curtains of rain pattering across the corvette's deck, to mingle with the salt spray her passage was throwing up over her rail. The little ship was close-hauled on the larboard tack, working out into the miserable wastes of the cloud-overhung Atlantic off the southeastern coast of Nova Scotia.

Echo had made landfall at Cap de Sable after a gruelling transatlantic passage, and now had spent days working with agonizing care round the myriad headlands that thrust into the sea from the maze behind Cap la Heve eastward to Cap Rosse. It was slow and man-killing work, endless sailhandling, endless bracing. The leadsman was kept toiling in the chains until he became incoherent with cold or fatigue and another would take his place, the line arcing round and then swinging out ahead, the chapped and cold-blistered hands overhauling the dripping line, the voice monotonously tolling, "Five . . . five . . . and a half . . . six . . ." Slowly Gallant had worked the ship along the shore this way, in a dangerous and exasperating search, the eyes of the lookouts in the tops who searched the shores joined by others that watched nervously to seaward, ahead and astern, for other vessels.

Gallant's eyes roved the shore, but almost every second minute he swung his gaze along the seaward horizon, scanning for the hurrying dark shadow of the killer squall that could drive *Echo* ashore to her death in almost seconds. More than once a strange sail had shown hull-down to seaward or appeared round a headland, and then Gallant had worked the ship with suicidal determination into narrow coves and inlets where *Echo* would lie, her men eyeing nervously the weed-coated cruel rocks that lay visible below her until a lookout clinging to the maintruck would report the coast clear.

Now Gallant stood on the windward side of the quarterdeck, legs braced against *Echo's* pitching, huddled into a heavy woollen boatcloak that reached to his ankles.

He looked over at the helmsman, sodden and pale-faced at the wheel. The man's hair was matted in streaks across his forehead from under the limp stocking cap, and his mildew-blotched seaboots were spread wide on the dark, wet deck.

"Mind you don't stiffen up, Chouinard. Let the ship talk to you. The best windward course isn't a straight line. Watch your topsail luff and keep her way on accordingly. Follow?"

"M'-m'sieu' ", nodded the man. He was shivering from the cold, like a dog kept out on a doorstep too long.

"Deck, there! Deck! Strange vessel!" The fore-top lookout's voice echoed down, urgent and strong, out of the haze aloft.

Gallant started, a cold knot in his stomach, the frightening image of a British ninety-gunner emerging out of the mists under a full press of canvas leaping into his imagination.

He cupped his hands. "Deck aye! Where away?"

"Inshore, m'sieu'! Well into that bay that's opening abeam of us now! Saw it in a break of the mists, capitaine. An Englishman, I'd swear!"

Béssac was clambering up the quarterdeck ladder, pulling on the familiar old seacoat, his pipe puffing a blue-grey trail behind him. "Another one, by Christ. I don't know if I can take much more of this damned cat and mouse business."

Gallant ignored him, cupping his hands again. There was

a peculiar premonition tingling the nape of his neck. "What kind of ship, man? Is she a fisherman?"

The lookout's shaggy head appeared out over the edge of the top. "A small ship, capitaine. But a warship for sure! Sloop of war, maybe a small frigate. She was clewing up her canvas like as to come to anchor!"

Gallant narrowed his eyes in thought. As *Echo* beat out to sea it was Cap Rosse from which she was drawing clear, opening the broad mouth of Baie Mohone on her port quarter. The English were making some tentative effort at settlement along this coast. And the ship might have been just a fisherman, a reeking Massachusetts schooner putting in to scour out her fish tubs.

But a warship?

"Prepare to come about, Béssac", said Gallant briskly. "Starboard tack. Your course is," Gallant eyed the masthead pennant and then glanced at the binnacle, "nor'nor'east by north. Bear in where the lookout sighted that vessel." He took off the tricorne and slapped it against his leg to rid it of some of the water it had collected. "I'm going below for a moment to look at the chart."

Béssac nodded, the pipe clamped in his teeth at a jaunty angle, as a buzz of excitement went through the watchmen on *Echo's* deck who had overheard Gallant. "Oui, m'sieu'!"

Gallant clumped down the ladder leading to the passageway which led aft to his cabin. A strange excitement was bubbling in his mind.

Calm down, you fool, he thought. You're ready to jump at straws.

But the excitement kept humming in his mind, and as Béssac's voice generated a tumult of activity on deck and *Echo* dipped round with squealing blocks and thumping sails to her new tack, Gallant was staring at the small chart which was spread out on his desk, weighted down in a somewhat theatrical manner by two delicate flintlock pistols. They were Boutets, a gift to Gallant from d'Anville.

Echo was standing in now on a course a shade off dead north. And when she had come about she had been, Gallant decided after a moment's thought, no more than three leagues at most off the bay.

Dipping a shortened quill into his inkwell Gallant penned in *Echo's* reckoned position when she came about. He thought again for a moment. The corvette would make eight, perhaps ten knots under this kind of wind. Certainly that if he got the topgallants set. Then there was the alongshore current, which seemed by observation to be setting southwestward at about two knots. That would give *Echo* on this course a possible track of . . . . Bending over the chart he used a slim mahogany rule to pen in a delicate line running almost dead into the mouth of the bay.

If *Echo* were able to make good a true course within two or three cables of this course she would pass hard along the inlet-laced edge of Mirligueche, on the bay's western cheek. There was a broad channel, about a league in width, between its heavily shoaled waters that ended at an islet called Petit Canard, and a ledge that bore east by north from it. Then, farther in at where an imaginary line would cross from the jutting shore of Aspotogan on the bay's eastern cheek to the western, the bay mouth was blocked by four islands arranged almost in the form of a diamond, and marked in what looked to be warnings about treacherous shoal water.

Gallant pursed his lips, steadying himself against the deck edge as *Echo* lifted and then thumped down over a particularly heavy swell. Had it been against one of those four islands the lookout had seen the English vessel?

He examined the four islands closely. In the diamond formation the northern, eastern and southern islands were relatively small; but the fourth, the western island, was a good-sized chunk of land as big as the other three combined. It had a vaguely fishhook shape, with steep shores shown on its seaward face, the southern, and in the bight of the fishhook, on the eastern face, there seemed to be a sheltered anchorage and circular beach. Gallant squinted at the island's name which was hard to make out in the dim light from the lantern above his cot. Isle Tancouque.

Echo's track would take her through the main channel deeper into the bay, leaving Tancouque to starboard. And then would come the mass of islands that formed the northwestern and western shore of the bay. Gallant shook his head. In the cluster of islands and channels you could hide ten *Santa Marias* carrying bullion and treasures like the Señora. And ships could pass two leagues away and not know the difference.

It was time to get aloft and see what the lookout saw, islands or not. Clamping his hat down over his eyes, he was soon back on the weatherdeck.

Béssac met him at the foot of the mainmast.

"Starboard tack, nor'nor'east by north, capitaine. No more'n two leagues off that western headland."

Gallant blew a drop of water from his nose and pointed upward with his chin at the foretop lookout's perch. "Any further word from the lookout?"

"A little. Just before you came on deck he called down that the Englishman, or whatever it is, had gone in behind one of the islands in the bay."

"What? Damn!"

"But he says he can still see the t'gallant truck of it."

"Ah. Anything else round the horizon?"

Béssac shrugged. "Nothing. Nothing this minute, that is."

"All right", said Gallant. "I'm going aloft. Keep an eye on the bearing of that low island—there, off the starboard bow—that's well to seaward. The rosbifs call it Pearl Island. The chart shows a ledge midway between it and Mirligueche."

Gallant slung his cloak over the foremast fiferail and in the next moment was clambering up the shaky ratlines of the starboard foremast shrouds, which were wet and tarry. Several seconds later he swung up from a frightening hanging scramble around the futtock shrouds to the foretop, where the lookout knuckled a forelock at him, immensely pleased that his captain had come to join him on his windy and sometimes precarious perch.

Gallant grinned at the man. "All right, Busque. Where in hell's your Englishman?"

Busque pointed shoreward with a tar-blackened finger. "Just fine on the starboard bow, m'sieu'. She was clewing up as she stood in, and then she made a turn to starboard, right round the larboard end of that island. But I can see her main t'gallantmast long pennant flash every now and then."

Gallant braced his back against the topmast and snapped open the little glass. And, as Busque had said, there was the white, distant tendril of the Englishman's commissioning pennant, drifting in the air and apparently disembodied above the spiky dark green hedgerow of trees on the land before it.

That's it, thought Gallant. He's gone in behind the first island.

"You've got fine eyes, Busque. Like a bloody hawk. And you're right about what the ship's done. There's two islands, and she's gone round the first and looks to be at anchor off the second."

Busque grinned back at his captain with gap-toothed pleasure. Then his face sobered.

"There's another odd thing, m'sieu'."

"What's that?"

Busque snuffled and wiped his nose with his cuff. "Maybe that glass'd bring it near, m'sieu'. But I think you can see a good bit of the larboard half of that island. The second one, I mean. She's got a steep shore all along the seaward face. At least what you can see."

"And?"

"There's something against that shore, m'sieu'. I may be wrong, but I think it's a wreck. A big one."

His neck tingling again, Gallant snapped open the glass and swung it up, looking now to the left of where he had been watching the English pennant. The steep shore was not very distinct through the mist and rain.

Then he saw it. A broad, bulky shape, flattened in the field of the glass. The shape of a heavy ship's hull, masts gone, driven high and careened on to its side against the shore, which looked as if it fell off quickly into deep water. The hull's stern was visible: a high, ornate sterncastle from which gilt glowed dully, the intricate baroque carving just discernible and incongruous against the brute shore.

"Good Christ!" breathed Gallant. "It's her. It's the damned Spaniard, or I'll fry!"

"M'sieu'?" said Busque in puzzlement.

But Gallant did not hear him, for he was already out over the futtock shrouds and bounding down the ratlines, heedless of risk. As his shoes slapped down on the deck a savage anticipatory joy was bursting in his chest.

"Béssac!" he roared, and he bounded like a tiger up to the quarterdeck as the mate turned to stare at him, a glint already in his own eyes. He had seen Gallant act this way before. "I'll have the courses, t'gallants and flying jib broken out and set if you please! And lively!"

Within minutes *Echo* began to accelerate as the extra canvas rippled and thumped before arcing to the power of the wind. As she gained in speed, knot by knot, the swells rolling in from the windward beam lifted her but could not make her roll as the straining canvas kept the ship stiff and driving on with only a slight heel to leeward. Gradually the roar under her bows and along her sides to her counters built until within fifteen minutes of Gallant's command she was driving like a greyhound through the mist and rain toward the gloomy and foreboding shore.

Gallant looked ahead over the bows. They were closing the inshore water rapidly. It was time to prepare *Echo* for what Gallant sensed awaited her in there.

"Holà, Béssac! Send the hands to Quarters, if you please!"

At a bark from Béssac the duty boatswain's mate sounded a piercing blast on his pipe and began moving down through the bowels of the ship, baying in his turn. "Take heed, there, aloft and alow! Hands to Quarters! Hands to Quarters!"

Again the months of training told their tale. *Echo* drove on toward the bay, its waters now only a league away. And as she did so the feet of her men pounded on her decks and worked up the rigging as each man moved swiftly and surely to his assigned action post. Gun crews, fo'c'sle party, topmen, waistmen, afterguard, all moved with a resolution and surety in their preparations that was not lost on Gallant.

Below on the gundeck, Akiwoya's voice boomed out over the clink and scuffle of work as the long eighteen-pounders were readied. Without seeing what was happening, Gallant sensed from the orderly, brisk movement, unmarked now by chatter amongst the men, that the training and discipline had taken root. On the weatherdeck the crews of the smaller nine-pounders were working with a similar speed and efficiency. The drizzle was easing, with signs of stopping altogether, but Akiwoya had still given orders for waterproof canvas vent shields to be lashed on each weatherdeck gun. Kept on until the last possible moment, they would guarantee the greatest possible chance that the nine-pounders would fire even in the wet conditions.

There was a creak of blocks aloft, and Gallant looked up to see the topmen slinging into place the broad net that would hang over *Echo's* deck, to catch the rain of falling debris from aloft the fighting might produce, and which might otherwise smash down on the men working below. And now up the hatchways the offwatchmen were appearing, their hammocks lashed in neat rolls which they bent into a "u" shape, curve uppermost, and wedged side by side into the nettings that circled the weatherdeck like a fence, affording a sort of extra shelter barricade. Then the men moved quickly off to their own action posts.

There was a flash of uniform blue and grey-white from the midships companionway, and Garneau and his reduced squad of marines doubled smartly aft up the the quarterdeck, where they fell in.

With a rush the final pieces of *Echo's* readying fell into place, and now as she surged in toward Baie Mohone her hull was lined with the red muzzles of her guns in the opened gunports. Above Gallant's head the enormous white Bourbon ensign streamed as if in intensified pride.

Béssac appeared up the quarterdeck ladder and cocked his head at Gallant, a pleased grin on his face. "Ship's company at Quarters, capitaine, as I have the great honour to report."

"Very good", replied Gallant, with an answering smile. The marine pondered for a few moments, hands locked behind his back, listening to the rush of *Echo's* hull through the sea, the plaintive cries of a circling gang of seagulls sounding down from where they hovered above *Echo's* stern.

"When we get in close to that Englishman, Béssac", Gallant said finally, "I intend to attack his vessel immediately. No pause, no hesitation. Right for the throat."

Béssac pursed his lips. "Why so quickly, capitaine?"

Gallant pointed inshore. "The Spaniard's wreck is there, I'm sure of it. And I have the oddest feeling that the rosbif might just be putting in on the same business we're on." He tapped the rail with his knuckles for emphasis. "So we'll take him right out of the picture. And right now."

"Deck, there!" The foretop lookout's voice rang down through the sea noise and the cries of the gulls.

"Deck, aye!"

"The angle's opening on the island, m'sieu'! That small island isn't obscuring the bigger one any longer, and I can see the Englishman at anchor!"

Gallant drew a deep breath. "What ship is she? Can you tell what type?"

There was a pause before the reply. "Bigger'n a sloop, m'sieu'. I was wrong. She's a frigate. Thirty guns or more!"

Oh, Lord, thought Gallant. Would *Echo* ever fight an opponent equal to her in size and power?

But *Echo* was going in to the attack nonetheless. There would be no turning away. He pursed his lips and tried to picture mentally the chart in his cabin. So the English vessel was a frigate. Therefore, she drew too much under her keel to anchor right in the midst of that half-moon cove. Out from the cove, a little less than half a league, there was a small unnamed island. The chart showed a depth of eight, maybe nine fathoms between it and the cove at low water. The frigate might ride in closer, up to the four fathom line, but likely no closer.

Gallant ducked to look out under the broad curve of the main course and saw that *Echo* had worked in quickly; Petit Canard was barely a third of a league off the larboard bow, and Pearl Island was drawing abeam quickly far off to starboard.

He paced the windward side of the quarterdeck, the captain's private domain, his mind racing. The frigate lay in Tancouque's southeast cove, head to eastward. *Echo* was reaching in hard past Petit Canard into Baie Mohone, the treacherous shoal waters of the bay's western shore flecking white in the distance to larboard. If the corvette kept this point of sailing—and did not run up on some damned unmarked ledge—the frigate's watchkeepers would have to see her; but then, surprise might well be a lost thing already. If *Echo's* lookout could see the frigate, then her men aloft probably could not have missed *Echo's* shape against the seaward skyline as she swept in. There was already only one option open to Gallant, if he did not turn tail and run: get in and deliver a telling and incapacitating blow.

Gallant leaned on the rail and stared at the water boiling past the corvette's side. So then what if *Echo* churned into the bay on this reach until she put the southernmost island of the diamond, a low and flat island, dead abeam to starboard? The corvette would then be out of sight from the frigate, and the mass of Tancouque would prevent *Echo* from being seen. The Englishman might decide she had passed on in toward the head of the bay.

But if the wind held easterly, *Echo* could turn smartly up to starboard and work up past that sheer south face of Tancouque, tacking briskly in short boards past the Spanish wreck until she burst round the south head of Tancouque, fell off onto a reach and ran in for the clinch with the frigate.

Gallant spat into the sea and wiped the back of his hand across his mouth. But could *Echo* manoeuver in that unknown anchorage? Could she haul the wind, tack up past the frigate's bow, athwart her hawse, and rake her as she passed? Then tack smartly to fall off and run back for another rake or boarding, without taking the ground in the cove? Or would she fail to make the crucial tack, and grind to her death on the rocky ledges that projected from the cove's northern point?

The questions and arguments began to snowball in his head. And what if the frigate had already seen *Echo*, and was planning to break her anchor free, swing outbound for a broad reach to seaward between Tancouque and the flat island, and would appear across the corvette's bows just as *Echo* was tacking up toward her? Then it would be *Echo* that would take the terrible raking fire, and leave her bones on the steep Tancouque shore beside the wreck she had come to find.

Enough! Gallant stopped his whirling mind and stared forward. One could go on asking "what if" forever. He would attack as he planned. And to the devil with the consequences.

He turned to Béssac, who was nearby still.

"We'll reach in until we're hidden from her by Tancouque, Béssac. Then we'll tack up, work round the point, and hit her while she lies at anchor. Rake her once, twice, larboard and starboard batteries in broadside. Then we board and take her. Clear?"

Béssac grinned at him like a fiend, rubbing his pawlike hands together in anticipation. He swung round impetuously, his enormous voice booming across *Echo's* decks.

"D'ye hear that, lads? Better say your *Aperi Domini* while you've got a chance! We're going to board the Englishman! Board, by God!"

A roaring cheer burst from *Echo's* men, catching Gallant by surprise. He looked round at their eager faces, seeing the expectant and ready light glint in their eyes.

Christ Jesus, don't let me bungle this, he thought in quick and urgent inner prayer.

Gallant touched Béssac's elbow. "This isn't going to be easy, Béssac. You know what the English are like in a fight." He pointed forward with his chin. "Have Akiwoya send the gun captains to me. I'll be wanting the cutlass barrels set out as we planned, one for each pair of guns. And have the two wooden chests from the magazine brought up to me."

"Oui, m'sieu' ", said the mate, and moved off forward.

Gallant turned to Chouinard and the other man at *Echo's* wheel. "Steady as she lies now. We're almost abeam that island there, Petit Canard. We'll be hauling wind in about half a glass, and that'll mean tacking right round to starboard till we put her on the larboard tack. Then it'll be short boards right up to the turn round the island, to close with the rosbif." He spat over the side and smiled slightly at the two men. "So you'd better steer like hawks."

41

Both men laughed, reassured by Gallant's easy manner. The marine turned forward to see Akiwoya's gun captains clustered in the waist, the two heavy chests on the deck before them. Gallant went down the ladder and joined them.

"Right, then, M'sieu' Akiwoya. Open those chests up, would you?"

Each chest was filled with rough muslin bags about the size of a sailor's ditty bag. Gallant lifted out one of the bags and carefully took out its contents, which were a fat earthenware pot about the size of a grapefruit, and what appeared to be an ordinary powder flask.

Gallant hefted them, one in each hand, and looked round the faces of the gunners.

"These are a little surprise I had the gunners' stores make up. And you're going to tickle the rosbifs' fancy with them today."

The gunners looked at each other meaningfully as Gallant lifted up the earthenware pot. "A bad smell, messieurs. A 'stink pot', quite literally. Crammed with saltpetre, sulphur, the filings of horses' hooves; a rare concoction that when put to fire throws out a lot of thick smoke and a smell you'd kill to get away from. The fuse is put in . . . here . . . and when lit you hurl it over the rosbif's bulwarks and watch the fun."

He set the pot down and hefted the flask. "This is just an ordinary powder flask, hein? Up to the nozzle with powder. You add a fuse, like so, light, and toss it like the pot in amongst the poor sods." He sniffed. "Guaranteed to upset them more than a little."

The gunners laughed in delight.

Gallant showed his teeth. "We'll be going in fast. First one battery will get a chance for a raking broadside, if we're lucky. If we're doubly lucky, the other battery will get their chance for the same thing. Then we slam in alongside her. The battery on her side fires a last broadside, point-blank. Then you let them have the pots and flasks, particularly you nine-pounder captains up on the weatherdeck. And then . . . ."

"The cutlass, capitaine?"

"Exactly. Larboard battery, both decks, board her aft, about even with her mizzen shrouds. Starboard battery crosses at her bows. Then you work in toward her waist."

Gallant indicated Béssac and Akiwoya, who had come up now behind the men. "M'sieu' Béssac will command the party crossing aft; M'sieu' Akiwoya, those crossing forward. I'll follow with the topmen amidships.''

"That's if we leave any rosbifs for you, capitaine!'' The cry from among the men set off a general roar of laughter that ended the explanations.

"Very well", said Gallant, grinning widely. "Back to your guns. We'll be on the bastard's flank within the glass!''

Gallant watched as the gun captains took up the muslin bags and dispersed to their guns. He turned back to Garneau, who stood cradling his halberd beside the silent little line of marines.

The marine-sergeant stiffened to attention as Gallant moved to him.

"I'll want good marksmanship, today, Garneau. You'll be responsible for the Englishman's quarterdeck. Put a ball into every man you see.''

An odd light flickered in the sergeant's dark eyes. "And when you board, m'sieu' . . .?''

Gallant grinned. "Hell, man, a Compagnies Franches officer can't go boarding an enemy vessel without some staunch Franche bayonets beside him, can he?''

Gallant left the squad elbowing each other in glee and went below to his cabin, where he took down the slim infantry hanger and its belt from its hook above his bunk. As he buckled it on he glanced once more at the chart.

Just there, he thought. Maybe half a league away from the Señora and all that preposterous loot. Loot that maybe the Englishman has already had his hands on, and for which I'll have to fight him. God, I hope he's well into a bottle of port and not expecting us!

Gallant picked up one of the delicate Boutet pistols. Reaching under his hard mattress he pulled out a pistol case, from which he took a small powder flask and other materials. Very carefully he loaded the pistol, in a process not unlike a miniature of a ship gun drill. Then when he had eased the pan shut and set the pistol at half-cock, he thrust the weapon into his waistbelt, under his uniform coat to shelter it from the sea damp.

He glanced at his watch. It was time to begin *Echo's* beat up past Tancouque. Gallant regained the quarterdeck, the impatience on Béssac's face there evidence that the mate had the same thought.

Gallant winked at him. "Tack ship, old friend. Larboard tack. Your course'll be almost dead on east sou'east.''

As *Echo* turned fully into the wind, its raw chill struck home all the keener, and Gallant found himself missing the sodden boatcloak. The delicate pistol suddenly felt like a cold stone against his body. The rain had ended, and *Echo* settled into her first tacking board under a sullen sky below which dark, twisted wisps of broken cloud raced. There was little swell, and the corvette worked rapidly along, the shoal waters lying a half-league before Flat Island looming near uncomfortably soon.

Within minutes Gallant was bellowing forward to Béssac.

"Tack ship! Starboard tack, M'sieu' Béssac! Your course'll be nor'east by north!"

Again *Echo's* men threw themselves into the hauling, and with a thumping and creaking aloft the corvette swung round onto her second tack, her bows now dead on Tancouque's steep shore and, below it, the hulk of the Spanish wreck, if that was what it was.

Gallant raised his glass and soon found the wreck. He was barely able to stifle a gasp as the huge ornate sternworks filled the field. And there, in broad chiselled and gilt-overlay lettering across the stern below the shattered gallery windows, he read the ship's name, *Santa Maria de la Vela.*

"Sweet, loving Jesus!" he breathed. "I knew it was her. Right from the beginning!"

Béssac had regained the quarterdeck, and met Gallant's gaze when the latter lowered the glass. "Time to go about, capitaine? We're only a quarter-league off that wreck."

Gallant nodded. "Right. Tack ship again, if you please. We'll put her on sou'east by east, or about the left-hand edge of Flat Island."

Echo once more put her flank to Tancouque and, pitching lightly over the short inshore swells, moved rapidly on past the steep island shore. With some surprise Gallant realized that his eyes, like almost every other eye in the ship, were scanning the green-black forest edge, looking for some kind of movement. Looking, in fact, for the English.

Behind Gallant, Garneau's halberd butt thumped on the deck. "Carry your arms", said the sergeant. His command was the only other sound to join the rush of the sea along *Echo's* flank and the creak and work of her rigging.

"Prime and load", ordered Garneau.

"Support", said Garneau, as the ramrods slid back into place.

Gallant had been so engrossed in watching the drill that he jumped at Béssac's voice in his ear.

"We should tack again, m'sieu'. Hold this board a cable more and the frigatemen'll see us for certain!"

Gallant squinted shoreward, his stomach performing a sudden and alarming leap. *Echo* was coming up rapidly to a line due south of Tancouque's south head. And Béssac was right: it was tack now or come into view of the frigate while almost a half-league toward Flat Island.

"Right as usual, Béssac." Gallant filled his lungs. "All hands, tack ship!" He turned to Chouinard. "Down your helm!"

Her broad ensign rippling proudly behind her, *Echo* swung round with graceful speed, and aloft and alow the men worked her with quick and intense effort. They knew that this was the fateful final tack.

The corvette surged in toward the shoal water off Tancouque's tip, the bottom of the reversed comma. At a word from Gallant, *Echo* hauled the wind a trifle, pointing up so as not to take the ground in the shallows projecting from the point.

The island mass rushed nearer, and beyond the point the view was opening. Gallant bit his lip. Ten minutes more and they would be out of the cover of the point. Ten minutes until the Englishman would be fully in view.

"Another pull on the fore t'gallant lee brace, Béssac! Keep her speed up, damn it!"

Blocks squealed briefly aloft as Béssac's men hauled beside the rail. *Echo's* speed was very evident now as she swept into the point, making for her sudden pounce round its tip on her prey.

Gallant glanced quickly round the deck, feeling the old familiar dryness in his throat. The gun crews were crouched by their guns, motionless and waiting, faces taut and serious, a few lips moving in prayer, all jocularity gone. Behind him Garneau's marines listened to the blood pounding in their ears and hugged the heavy muskets a shade closer, as if to find comfort in their steel and wooden bulk.

Five minutes now. Tancouque loomed up on the larboard bow, and Gallant could see the tree-tops ashore bending in the wind. In the chains the leadsman had begun to chant now, his voice regular and monotonous in the tense waiting. The sea rushed and hissed under *Echo's* bows, and the little ship moved in under the loom of the island.

Scant minutes, now.

Gallant swallowed. His throat felt like raw leather. Had he forgotten anything?

"There she is! Sweet Christ, look at her!"

The shriek of *Echo's* topman ringing over her decks, the corvette boiled along with tremendous speed past Tancouque's point, the shoal water glimmering tea-coloured under her rushing hull. The broad cove opened with dramatic suddenness before her, and Gallant's eyes widened at the sudden scene.

"Up helm! Five points! A fast reach, Chouinard!" barked Gallant. *Echo's* yards squealed round anew and the little ship lunged across the wind with new speed.

Echo had done what he wanted, by God! She had surprise as her ally. Dead off the larboard bow, looming impossibly close and large, the broad flank of the English frigate lay in clear and startling detail; a big vessel, well over Busque's estimate of thirty guns. In a split-second Gallant's eyes took in a hundred details: the heavy cables, fore and aft, showing the frigate was moored; the gunports mostly shut, a few open as if to ventilate; mainyard canted overside, offloading a ship's boat; figures moving up ratlines, others aloft on footropes passing gaskets on furled canvas; a brilliant British ensign rolling and flicking at the stern staff; the long white commissioning pennant from the maintruck, drifting delicately; another ship's boat heading into the cove beach; other figures on the beach, waving and gesturing frantically now; the blue and white form of an officer pacing the quarterdeck. The hull was a mustard colour, with trim in black except for the red of the open gunport lids.

Dear God, thought Gallant. She's huge!

Gallant cupped his hands to shout aloft. "Make ready, there, in the tops! And aim truly!"

There was an answering shout from the marksmen, and levelled muskets appeared out over the edge of the crosstree platforms.

Gallant stepped up to the waistdeck rail in time to see Akiwoya thrust his head up through the midships companionway.

"Akiwoya! Batteries ready?"

"Oui, m'sieu'!"

"Good! After I give the first order fire as you bear! One

round, then man the opposite battery guns! We'll be across her bows in two minutes!''

Echo rushed in toward her target.

Gallant spat and looked once again round the corvette's deck. The gun crews crouched by their guns, eyes white now with tension. The sailhandlers clustered, poised for action, their eyes on Gallant and Béssac, who stood at the mainmast foot.

"Steady, lads!" Gallant called. "But a cable or two and we're on her!" He whirled on Chouinard. "Larboard a point! Another!" he growled.

A sudden gust struck *Echo* and she heeled briefly, a roar sounding from the water that boiled along her leeward side. God, the little ship was flying!

There was a sudden rush of movement on the frigate's fore-deck, and then unexpectedly there was the brilliant pink flash of a gun, and as the sharp report cracked in Gallant's ears he saw a gout of white smoke whip up and back along the frigate's deck. There was a sound like ripping canvas in the air over his head, and Gallant spun round in time to see a huge, fin-gerlike geyser leap up in the sea astern of *Echo*.

Gallant bellowed upward. "Tops, there! Give fire! Get me that damned gun crew on her foredeck!"

"Fire!" came a shriek from the foretop, and from the lev-elled muskets a ripple of pink flame lanced out. Almost immediately the maintop sharpshooters fired as well.

Gallant was beside Chouinard now, orders curt and sharp on his lips, correcting *Echo's* course to clear the angling hawser line off the frigate's bows.

"Fire!" came the cry from aloft, and again the muskets barked out. At this range it was hard to guess their effect. Then the maintop muskets spat and Gallant saw a figure writhe up above the frigate's bulwark, arms flung high in agony, to topple back out of sight.

Fifty yards. The frigate was alive with movement now.

Gallant slapped the rail in almost unbearable strain. "Come on, come on!" he muttered.

The frigate's bowsprit loomed high ahead. *Echo* swept in toward it, her run-out guns thrusting their red eyes out like the face of a hideous sea-creature.

Gallant winced as a flicker of musket fire showed along the frigate's rail and balls thumped and whizzed around him. A young seaman holding the rammer of the forward nine-pounder on the quarterdeck gasped and toppled backward in a sprawl, a gaping hole where one eye had been.

"Béssac! Another man to ram for this gun!" Gallant barked. He looked up as another patter of musket shot slapped into the deck around him.

"Fire, Akiwoya!" Gallant roared.

Echo dipped and heeled by the bow of the frigate, the sea between the two ships suddenly a leaping cauldron of foam. The men on *Echo's* foredeck stared overhead in disbelief as the great jib-boom of the frigate passed its shadow over them, impossibly close to the corvette's rigging. The air was filled with the bark and rattle of musketry, and Gallant realized that Garneau's men had already fired three sharp volleys and were reloading for a fourth.

But then, almost as Gallant's words had left his mouth, *Echo's* guns spoke. Forward on the weatherdeck the first nine-pounder banged, the 'huff' of flame up from its vent spurting high in the air, the men serving it leaping close to reload almost before the gun had halted its recoil back on its breeching line. A huge ball of smoke suddenly had appeared at *Echo's* rail, to sweep over the bows of the frigate. Then a split-second later the next nine-pounder fired. Then the third. And from below on the gundeck the big eighteen-pound guns began their roar.

In split-second precision the guns crashed out in a deadly rhythm, each gun vomiting its hail of shot and fire as it bore on the frigate's bows. Again and again the tremendous concussions sounded, as *Echo's* main armament punched round after round at its target as the corvette sped by.

Gallant gripped the waistdeck rail, his feet wide spread, ignoring the hail of flying shot. He stared in disbelief as he watched the effect of *Echo's* guns. Point-blank they poured their destruction into the frigate, one after another.

As each gun fired, the bows of the frigate visibly shook with the impact of the shot. Great fragments of wood and gear were flung up or simply disintegrated. At the first shot from the eighteen-pounders the gammoning of the frigate's bowsprit was cut as if with a knife, whiplashing and curling back as the great spar broke free of its restraint. On the next round the figurehead shattered into a radiating halo of splinters, a gaping hole suddenly smashed into the fo'c'sle bulkhead aft. Another round, and an enormous section of rail cartwheeled back along the frigate's deck, scything down half a dozen men into mangled heaps as Gallant watched.

Echo's gunners were yelling and shouting now, the voices incoherent in the tremendous din of the guns. And Garneau's marines were baying like hounds as volley after volley burst from their levelled muskets. Pots arced down from *Echo's* tops and burst with dirty gouts of choking smoke over the frigate's foredeck.

Echo swept on. With something like awe, Gallant stared as suddenly an explosion of fragments leaped from the base of the frigate's mizzenmast, the pulped body of a seaman amongst the flying debris. The mast swayed, tottered, and then with an enormous rending crash toppled in slow motion back over the stern in a welter of snapping and whiplashing rigging.

"Dear God!" breathed Gallant.

In the next instant *Echo's* guns abruptly fell silent, as the corvette swept past the frigate's bows. Gallant saw the crews leap across to the starboard battery, and he could hear Akiwoya's voice bellowing from below.

"Secure those guns! Starboard battery, lads! Run out! Prime again, if you have to!"

Gallant stared around the deck. Other than the man who had fallen to the musket ball *Echo's* men were untouched. He spun round to see Garneau's marines, lips black from the powder of their cartridges, feverishly reloading, teeth bared in fierce grins of delight and satisfaction.

He looked aloft, then forward. *Echo* had to come about now, or die on those rocks ahead.

"Tack ship, Béssac, tack ship! Down helm, Chouinard!" Gallant barked. "Helm's a-lee!"

"Up tacks and sheets!"

Smoke tendrils still drifting from the muzzles of her larboard guns, *Echo* swooped up into the wind with a rush as Chouinard slapped the wheel over. Aloft, the canvas rippled and shook with demonic violence, and the air was alive with whiplashing lines and banging blocks. *Echo's* headsails cracked like gunshots in the bows as the corvette swung.

Gallant bit his lip, staring out over the bows at the rocky shallows of the cove's northern shore. They were far too close for comfort. Had he turned too late?

No! *Echo* pitched round into the eye of the wind, no hideous crunching announcing from beneath her hull that she had taken ground.

"Haul mainsail, haul!" Gallant roared.

Echo began to swing round now on to the larboard tack, and Gallant spun to squint at the frigate.

His lips were bone-dry. Christ, for a mouthful of brandy!

The frigate's decks were alive with movement. Gallant could see men moving, working, the flash of axe blades in the brightening sunlight as overhead the haze and cloud began to burn off. There was a glint from brass and bayonets. The wreckage of the mizzenmast lay in a black snarl over her stern, and forward the bowsprit was canting up at a strange angle.

Echo was round. "Let go and haul!"

To the music of squealing blocks and the grunts of the men hauling at her lines the corvette leaped ahead on her new tack. Within seconds she was rushing in at her waiting prey again, the waters of the cove boiling under her forefoot.

Gallant threw a glance at the cruel rocks of the point astern, feeling the cold sweat in the middle of his back. That had been a near thing, by God.

He spun back to stare at the frigate as *Echo* rushed at her. Now the real test was coming.

"Ready the boarders!" Gallant barked, and heard the order passed on rapidly. "Grapnels, pots and flasks, lads!"

He whipped the hanger out and glanced back at Garneau and his marines.

"Ready, marines?"

"Oui, m'sieu'!" breathed Garneau, eyes aflame.

Echo rushed in again with the same breathless speed, and this time the musketry from the frigate was strong and intense as it began. Amidst the popping of the muskets Gallant heard the sonorous *ftoom* of a swivel, a deadly weapon that spewed a hail of almost any missiles that could be imagined for it. Balls began to hum and thump into woodwork around them, and then with a sudden shriek one of Garneau's marines spun round, grabbing at his neck. A bright arterial stream of blood squirted from between the man's fingers and painted an arc over the deck as he sprawled forward in front of Garneau.

Gallant ignored him. "Ready, Akiwoya!" he roared. "Béssac! The grapnels!"

There was an answering wave from the mate, half-hidden behind the mainmast. They would be ready.

Again, now, the bowsprit of the enemy vessel loomed above *Echo's* own. The sea boiled along *Echo's* leeward side as she swooped in again for the second blow.

"Fire, Akiwoya!" Gallant cried, as the corvette began the pass. "Ready for the hard turn to leeward, Chouinard!"

The guns of the corvette blasted again. In the same deadly rhythm the nines and eighteens pounded at the frigate, and this time the shot was aimed higher. Gallant winced as he saw a redcoated knot of British marines on the frigate's foredeck suddenly be smashed back and away like twigs under an axe. On the next round a gun on the frigate's deck was pitched over backward as if by a hand, and Gallant heard the agonized shriek of the men it crushed as it toppled over. *Echo's* guns were producing an enormous cloud of smoke, and already the frigate was shrouded in it, making a hell of flying slivers and splinters, darkness, screams and destruction.

Echo's decks were still leaping to the thundering when Gallant fought his way past Garneau's marines to the wheel.

"By God, Chouinard, now! Helm up hard!"

Echo swung in toward the smoke-wreathed frigate, another point-blank blast of an eighteen-pounder impossibly loud in the grinding abyss that suddenly came into being between the ships. *Echo* turned her stern to the wind and ground down the frigate's starboard side, the corvette's yards, tightly braced for the reach, entangled in the frigate's own spars.

The din of musketry and the roar of the guns were indescribable. A terrific bang from the frigate and a leap of the deck under Gallant's feet signalled that the frigate had begun using her own guns. And those twenty-fours would pound the corvette to fragments in minutes.

"Clew up, Béssac, clew up! Grapnels!" Gallant bellowed. He saw stinkpots arcing through the air, and great curls of foul black smoke began to envelope the frigate's deck. Gallant saw pink flashes flickering in the smoke as the powder flasks began to explode. Screams and curses reached his ears over the terrible din of the guns.

Echo's grapnels hurtled through the air, and almost as they hooked in the frigate's rigging the lines were hauled taut, binding the two ships together.

Gallant pointed his sword. "Come on!" he shrieked.

Behind him, Garneau's marines let out a blood curdling bay. And out of the corners of his eyes Gallant saw Akiwoya's gun crews streaming up from below, their cutlass blades gleaming evilly in the peculiar smoky light. With a rush the men made for the foremast and mizzenmast ratlines.

"Topmen, with me!" Gallant cried, and with a bound he

was up on *Echo's* rail. For a split-second he paused over the terrifying chasm of leaping water and smoke between the ships, and then he was over and clinging like a squirrel to the frigate's side. With fanatic energy he flung a leg up over the rail and rolled over it to land on his feet on the frigate's deck.

He struck out blindly ahead of him with the hanger, and a shriek rang in his ears, hideous and agonizing. He jerked back the blade, now crimson, to see a blond seaman in a checked shirt topple forward, eyes goggling, clutching at his pierced throat. Unheeding, Gallant struck at the man with his free hand and then was gazing wildly around for a new assailant.

In the next instant a terrific blow on the side of his head crumpled his knees, and he crunched to the deck, lights flashing in front of his eyes. He looked up to see a British marine, his tall mitre cap askew, teeth bared, raising his musket and bayonet for a killing thrust down at him.

With savage anger suddenly in his throat, Gallant lashed out with his foot and caught the man hard in the groin. The Englishman gasped and dropped the musket, staggering. Then in the next instant one of Garneau's men levelled the man with a sweep of his musket butt before stepping on over him.

Gallant rolled to his feet. Two seamen locked in fearful struggle rolled against him and he fell against the frigate's rail. He looked up to see a huge Englishman in a seacoat and dog-eared tricorne rushing at him with a cutlass extended. At the last possible moment Gallant brought up his hanger to parry the blow, only to have the cutlass smash through the slim blade like a reed. Gallant stared in horror at the stump of blade.

"Have a taste o' good British steel, ye damned Frog!" snarled the Englishman, and lunged. Gallant dodged to one side and grappled with the man, the anger rising again in his throat. Gallant began to roar incoherently. He smashed his fists into the man's belly, once, twice, three times. Then with an overhand blow he drove the man to the deck.

He looked up. In a struggling knot of men he saw Béssac locked in desperate struggle with two brawny Englishmen, and for all his strength, getting the worst of it. Gallant saw a knife flash in the hands of one of the seamen as it lifted to plunge into Béssac's back.

"Béssac!" Gallant bellowed. The Boutet pistol was suddenly in his hands, and he lunged forward and shouldered into the man with the knife, thrust the pistol into his stomach, and jerked the trigger. The blast crumpled the man like a rag doll, his gargling scream dying in his throat. With a vicious back-hand cut of the sword stump, still in his other hand, Gallant cut the man to the deck. At his side, Béssac broke free of his assailant's grip and began driving powerful blows of his fists into the man's face, the Englishman buckling his knees under the onslaught.

Then there came a sudden silence. The smoke curled away, and Akiwoya appeared a few feet away, his cutlass running scarlet.

It was over!

The smoke lifted more, revealing a hellish scene of heaped and bloody bodies. Blood in hideous dark pools spread over the decks.

Gallant was shaking uncontrollably as Béssac abruptly appeared at his elbow.

"Mother of God, capitaine, they've done it!" the mate said hoarsely. "They've taken her!"

Gallant tried to slow his breathing. His throat was burning with thirst. And if only his damned knees would stop shaking!

Echo's men were moving swiftly about the littered deck, herding the English back against the frigate's rail in a group. The English were a powerful, beefy lot, their faces startlingly pink in contrast to the darker complexions of Gallant's men.

Gallant narrowed his eyes. "Béssac, there's hardly fifty men there! A frigate this size carries a bigger complement than that. There had to be more men aboard!" He looked round for the companionways. "What about below decks?"

"Just a few, capitaine", said Béssac.

"Then where in hell . . . . ?"

Akiwoya had overheard as he strode up. "The rest are ashore, capitaine!"

Gallant squinted shoreward, and his eyebrows lifted in surprise. Men were rushing out of the woods onto the beach, and already there must have been fifty clustered at water's edge, shaking their fists in helpless anger toward the two ships in the cove. Many seemed to be carrying tools.

"A working party, for God's sake", muttered Gallant. "What in . . . ." A chill ran up his spine, and he spun on Béssac. "The longboat! Did it get ashore?"

Béssac spat heavily over the side. "Non, m'sieu'. A ball shattered the one they were lowering. And the other's along-side, aft there by the battens."

Gallant nodded, relieved. "All right. Load one of the nine-pounders and train it on those bastards on the beach. And keep lookouts on them every moment. I wouldn't put it past the rosbifs to try and swim out here to get at us!''

Béssac nodded and moved off as Gallant turned to Akiwoya. ''Many of our lads hurt? No, never mind a count now. Just get 'em back into *Echo* so you can get a look at them.''

Gallant glanced at the mob of prisoners, guarded now by the bayonets of Garneau's small squad. ''And just what do we do with that lot?'' he mused.

Akiwoya sucked a tooth noisily. ''I've one answer, m'sieu'. Something we did in the old Channel lugger I was in once.''

''What's that?''

''We battened 'em below with a gun facing the hatch. Just a swivel, mind, but it kept the rosbifs below until we decided what to do with 'em.''

Gallant nodded. ''All right, why not?''

Akiwoya grinned, teeth white in the strong ebony face. ''À vos ordres, capitaine!'' He strode off, bellowing for Garneau.

Gallant was deep in thought when Béssac reappeared, with images of the Señora whirling in his mind. Was it for that and the plunder with it that the English had gone ashore?

He looked sharply at the mate. ''I've yet to see an officer among these English, Béssac. Were there none in her when we boarded?''

Béssac clapped a hand to his forehead. ''Sweet Mary forgive me, I forgot! We found the commanding officer still in her!''

''What? For God's sake, Béssac!''

''I know, I know. He was felled cold by one of our lads with a cutlass hilt at the very start. We found him a few minutes ago under that pile of bodies I've got the lads heaving out through the forward gunports.''

Gallant shuddered involuntarily. ''Well, where is he now?''

Béssac grinned. ''Chouinard's cleaning him up. Figured you'd not be interested in exchanging gentlemanly salutes with him looking like a slab of raw meat, capitaine!''

He pointed with his chin behind Gallant. ''Look, he's got him now.''

Gallant turned on his heel to face Chouinard, who was supporting the ashen-faced figure of a British naval officer, his head swathed with an enormous bandage. Chouinard released his grip on the man and stepped back a pace.

''The rosbif capitaine, m'sieu' '', he said.

Gallant looked keenly at the man, and found the Englishman's grey eyes, though clouded with pain, were looking level and direct into his own.

Gallant thought over his English vocabulary for a moment, and then stepped forward to the man.

"Are you able to stand alone, sir?" he asked evenly.

The Englishman nodded, making an effort to square his shoulders.

Gallant raised his hat. "Lieutenant Paul François Adhémar Gallant, commanding His Most Christian Majesty's Ship, *Echo*, corvette, at your service, m'sieu'. And who may I have the honour of addressing?"

The Englishman made an effort to bow, paling with the exertion. Teeth clenching in self-control, he replied in a hoarse whisper.

"Ca. . . Captain Richard Allen Rand. His Britannic Majesty's Ship, *Magnet*. I have the honour of presenting my swor. . . ."

The Englishman had made to pull his dress sword from his waistbelt, but suddenly went sheet white and began to weave on his feet. Gallant stepped forward in time to catch the fainting man before he fell headlong to the deck.

"He's unconscious, capitaine", said Béssac, who was holding the man now as well.

Gallant smiled grimly. "Not surprising. All right." He motioned over to two seamen standing nearby. "Take this man to my cabin and put him in my bunk. And treat him with every courtesy. Make sure he keeps his sword with him."

He pursed his lips in thought as the men carried Rand away. "I have a feeling that Captain Rand and I may have a great deal to talk about."

He looked round the frigate, seeing now for the first time in clarity the grinning faces of *Echo's* men as they watched him, pride and exultation shining in their eyes.

"Béssac?"

"M'sieu'?"

The marine smiled. He would have to go below now and see what papers and documents Rand's cabin might contain. But there was something he had to say.

"You can tell the lads that no ship's company ever fought better than they have today. None! So make brandy all around, hein? Double issue!"

With the whoops and cheers of *Echo's* men ringing across the decks of the two ships, Gallant made his way below to inspect the prize their valour had won.

THREE

"But tell me, capitaine, were you at anchor long before we came upon you?"

Paul Gallant had set down his brandy glass on the desk and looked at the man propped in his bunk with as neutral a facial expression as he could muster. He already knew the answer, of course, to that question.

Captain Richard Rand held one hand to the bloody bandage over his temple. With the other hand he raised his own glass tremblingly to his lips.

"Perhaps half a glass, Lieutenant. No more", he said presently.

"On a task of some importance, I imagine."

Rand raised a hand in protest. "Merely woodcutting and watering parties."

"Over seventy men?" said Gallant.

"We had much to cut. So much that I had far too many men ashore when you and this—this little ship of yours appeared." Rand sipped at the brandy, eyeing Gallant over the rim. "Else our positions might have been reversed."

"Ah. But they are not, Capitaine Rand", said Gallant, rising. "Look, your ship is unfit for sea. You've lost the mizzen, sprung the bowsprit, parted much of your standing and running rigging, and your hull is a mass of shot damage. Thirty of your men are dead, another forty or more lying with their wounds in your gundecks, and besides the men I have under guard below your ship's company is lodged ashore, helpless."

"Spare me the . . . ."

"Spare be damned, Rand!" snarled Gallant. "Now I want facts! I want to know what you were doing here! And I want to know it now or . . ." Gallant snorted. "Or to hell with your gentlemanly pretensions. I'll burn your ship where she lies. With your wounded in her."

Rand's eyes flicked open, stunned. Aghast, he lifted himself on his elbows and stared at Gallant.

"You couldn't do such a . . . a despicable act!"

"No?"

"You're a gentleman, for God's sake!"

"I'm a man at war, Rand!" roared Gallant. "At war! And by Christ I'll do what I have to, to find out what I need to know!"

Rand fell back on his pillow, lips working. He coughed and whispered, "You . . . cowardly . . . murderous . . .!"

Gallant snorted. "Save your insults. Listen, Rand. Tell me what I want now and I'll see that your men are put ashore safely. I'll leave you most of your ship's provisions. A boat when we leave. This is an English coast. You'd be found in short order."

"And *Magnet*?"

Gallant shook his head. "She burns in any event, Rand. I can't take a prize now. And you'll not have her back."

Gallant leaned forward again. "You have no choice, man. None." He moved closer to the bunk. "Now, for the last time, tell me. What were you doing here?"

Rand set his lips in a tight line, and Gallant could see a turmoil of conflicting emotion raging behind the Englishman's eyes.

"Were you salvaging from the *Santa Maria de la Vela?*" Gallant shouted.

"Yes! Yes, you damned hound, I was!" Rand fell back, hands clutched at the bandage.

"I see", said Gallant, in quiet triumph. "Very well. And what had you found?"

There was a long pause as Rand recovered his self-control. When he spoke, his voice was the flat monotone of a man who has admitted defeat.

"Nothing. Nothing at all."

Gallant stared. "What do you mean, nothing? Are you aware of what she was carrying?"

"Over a million pounds of Spanish loot from the Americas."

"That's right. Now what in hell do you mean by saying you found nothing?"

Rand reached compulsively for his brandy and threw it down his throat. "We've been in the bay here for three days, Gallant. Second time at anchor in this cove. We've been all over that damned wreck round the point. And she hasn't a single bloody piece of eight in her!"

"What?" Gallant raised a dubious eyebrow.

"It's true, for God's sake!" snarled Rand. "She'd been gutted out! Emptied!"

"If that's true, what were you . . .?"

Rand shook his head. "I thought there might be a chance it had been buried ashore by survivors or plunderers, or both, on the island." He sighed. "We were about to do one last search when you had the indecency to interrupt."

"Did you plan to look anywhere in particular?"

Rand shook his head. "No, damn it, I had every inch of that island crisscrossed soon after we first arrived! There's not a trace of diggings ashore. I was giving it one last go."

The Englishman's voice faded, and his head lolled back against the pillow. Clearly he was exhausted and dangerously weak.

"All right, Capitaine Rand. Thank you", said Gallant, and he lifted his hat from the small desk to move toward the cabin door. "You had best attempt to rest."

Rand's whisper was faint. "My wounded people . . . your part of the bargain . . ."

Gallant paused, a small smile on his face.

"War causes us to say and do many terrible things, Rand. But the murder of defenceless men is not a thing I have stomach for. Your men would have been safe enough regardless of what you might have said.''

Rand's eyes burned at him from the shadows of the bunk. "You're . . . an unprincipled son-of-a-bitch, Gallant'', came his whisper, after a moment. "But I thank you.''

Gallant laughed. "Rest well, Rand'', he said, and closed the door.

In the passageway outside Gallant found Béssac, an expectant look on his face.

"Et bien, capitaine! Did he say anything?''

Gallant nodded. "Yes. And no. They were hunting for the loot, all right. But it's gone.''

"Gone!''

"Not in the wreck. Not buried on the island. Rand says there's not a coin to be found. Anywhere.''

"Sacristi!''

Gallant's mind was racing, grasping on a sudden thought that had risen of its own accord out of his memory.

He gestured upward with his thumb. "What's the situation up there?''

Béssac wiped his mouth with the back of his hand. "We're moored, fore and aft. Wind's hauling round, probably be westerly again by tonight. Sky's clearing.''

"The wounded?''

"Ours are fine. We lost seven men killed in the boarding. Akiwoya's made the English as comfortable as he can on their gundeck.'' He shook his head. "They're in a bad way, capitaine. Little water, no leeches . . . .''

Gallant cut him off briskly. "Watch the wind, Béssac. And watch the tide. As soon as the wind's gone fair I want us out of here. Tonight, if we can.''

Béssac looked at him in some surprise. "Leave? But the wreck . . .?''

"To hell with the wreck. I think Rand's telling the truth.'' Gallant took the mate by the elbow. "Man a gun or two for cover and then ferry the English wounded ashore under a white flag. Have Garneau's bloodhounds stand off in a guard boat. Ferry the prisoners—bound, of course—ashore as well, with as many casks of biscuit as you can from the frigate's stores.'' Gallant hauled out his heavy brass watch and snapped it open. "I want it done by the change of the First Watch.''

Béssac gaped for a moment, and then snapped his jaw shut.

"All right. We've done miracles before. But what about the frigate?"

"She burns. When we leave."

Gallant watched Béssac pad to the ladder and make his way up to the weatherdeck. If the mate knew what Gallant was planning he might not have got on with his duties with so little complaint.

There was one chance, one way to find out what the *Santa Maria* might have done before she wrecked on Tancouque. A wreck was usually a messy business. And something of the hoard should have been in evidence if it had been in the ship when it struck, looted afterward or not. The wreck's hull was just in too good a condition for it to be otherwise.

But Rand had said it. *She hasn't a single bloody piece of eight in her.*

Gallant sucked a tooth. But what if the Señora and all that treasure had been taken from the ship before it ran up on Tancouque? In another port, another cove, off another island? The hoard could be anywhere, if it was not securely tucked in the hold of a pirate vessel at sea, in which case it was gone for good.

Nonetheless, there was one possibility that might lead to clues.

In the sheaf of documents d'Anville had given him in Toulon Gallant had found a sealed letter in the nobleman's own script. A letter that said that if all else failed, there was a contact that could be made within the occupied fortress of Louisbourg itself, the Señora's intended destination. A few of the French inhabitants of the town had elected to stay when the New Englanders took possession. And the contact, Nicolas Morin, was one of these: a mysterious and shadowy figure whose official income as an admirauté clerk had been augmented by his secret pay as an agent and informer for the Minister of Marine.

'Morin will be Aware of what course the Ship will have been ordered to Take', d'Anville's letter read, 'for he is en-trust'd with much of the Scheme's lowlier Work & Executions & particularly as concerns the itinerant Sea folk of the Harbour.'

The letter had listed Morin's address, a quiet lane of low houses that Gallant half-remembered lay at the foot of Rue du Scatari, in Louisbourg.

The task was clear, and as it took shape in his mind Gallant felt a cold wash of apprehension spread up his spine. But there was no other way.

He would go ashore. *Echo* would land him somewhere on the Cape Breton coast and he would make his way alone to the fortress town. Somehow he would slip into the town and find Morin, and with luck learn either what had happened to the *Santa Maria de la Vela*, or what was supposed to have happened.

Gallant grunted. It was grasping at straws. But Gallant had only one straw to grasp, and this was it.

He turned back to his cabin door and opened it.

"Do you have any items in your possessions you must needs keep with you, Capitaine Rand?" said Gallant. "We'd best have them sent for. In a short while you shall be needing them ashore. . . ."

The black ship, hidden as it was close against the face of the small island that was one of many deep in Baie Mohone's western curve, was indistinguishable against the dark evergreen shoreline. It would have required a sharp eye to have seen its dark shape, and the hideous black flag that curled in evil languor at its stern staff.

But there were sharp eyes aboard that ship; eyes that watched with hot interest the distant cannon smoke rise above the melded masts visible behind the distant hump of Isle Tancouque, and ears that listened to the rumbling of cannonading.

The ship's rail was lined by its crew, who were to a man silently watchful of the distant fight, stirring only to spit derisively into the sea, or snort with mocking laughter. They were a wild and menacing lot, in queer and flamboyant clothing, with an aura of unfettered brutality about them. It would not have taken a glance at the black flag their ship wore to identify them with the hated name of Pirate.

Two men, set more apart from the others, stood on the quarterdeck, and nodded with a knowing look at each other as the distant gun noise faded away.

"Ha! That's done fer 'im, Ned, me lad!" said one. "The Frog's gutted 'im, sure!" The speaker was a figure that might have stepped out of a merchant captain's nightmare. He was tall, well over six feet, and dark in a swarthy, almost Latin way. Below dark, glittering eyes and a hawk's-beak nose the man flashed a wolfish, gapped smile that split a monstrous, tangled beard. His clothes were all in red: a heavy coat, stained and rum-splotched, with dirty lace at wrist and throat; tight corduroy breeches stuffed into high sea boots; and around his waist a broad crimson sash into which a brace of Sea Service Tower pistols had been thrust.

The second man grunted. "Aye. Mayhap. Just as long as the buggers don't see us, is all." He spat heavily over the rail. He was tall as well, but with a dark cloak that hung round him to his boot tops covering a powerful frame. Below blond hair, hatless and clubbed with a simple seaman's rattail, his ruddy and lined features were marked by cold, ice-blue eyes under overhanging brows. His voice was broad and nasal, the unmistakable tones of a Yankee. And he spoke with a slow and deliberate emphasis, as if a man much given to leading others.

"See us?" snorted the man in red. "Damn me, they'd be provident t' clap lights on us from a cable off, so snug we be in 'ere!"

The man called Ned nodded, listening to the voices now of the watching men at the rail. "Belike. What's afoot ashore? The lads got it all down the shaft yet?"

The man in red, who was known in the ship by the name of Ben Spooner, spat out through a gap in his teeth with expert care. "Aye", he said, wiping his mouth. "Thirty cases o' ingots, and all them sacks o' coin. And that damned statue! They've got to take 'er by 'erself, it's so damned weighty! Christ! I'd never seen the like o' such a haul since I went on th' account!"

His companion grinned without mirth. "Hell, Ben, I could've told you that Spanisher was a-brim with swag! Alone an' scuddin' fer cover like she was. We wouldn't 'ave needed Monsieur Nick to twig us about 'er, if we'd cross't 'er track by ourselves."

Spooner cleared his throat. "Well, aye, but we didn't, did we? It was old Nick what got 'er for us, like 'e's done all them others. I for one thinks 'e's earned his divvy." He picked his nose and wiped the results on his coat front, sniffed and spat again. "You ever take a haul like that afore, Ned? You can't fox me that old Ned Salter, a Yankee o' the Brethren an' on th' account fer belike five year or more, 'as not seen swag like that, now?"

Salter narrowed his eyes, watching the distant clouds of gunsmoke slowly disperse to seaward over Tancouque. "Oncet only, Ben. I was in the *Hawke* brigantine, out o' Boston Town. *Privateers* we were, right proper with a Letter o' Marque 'n' all, under Cap'n Edward Fennel, God rest his Christian soul. By Christ's guts, we cruised to th' south'ard, 'n' took three Spanishers inbound to the Havana from Campeche. That'd be in '42, maybe '43. Jesus, you'd a-watered yer jaws at *that* prize, Ben! And the women! Oncet you boxed 'em into sweetness they were properly a-commodatin'. Aye, sir. A-commodatin'!''

Then Salter checked himself, as if struck by a sudden thought. "Be the statue gone over th' side yet? T' be took ashore?''

Spooner shook his head. "Not quite, m'lad. She's a good three feet o' gold an' jewels! Hell, I'll be needin' a whole boat's crew to get 'er overside and ashore! Why, she'd . . . .''

"Never mind. I'll keep 'er, belike, for a while in the great cabin. So as to admire, y' might say.''

Spooner's eyes flashed a warning. "Watch yer helm, Ned. The mates'll think you've gone agin th' Articles. Fair and square share, all alike! They'll vote ye out as Cap'n, to be sure, an' ye'll get a slit gullet fer your trouble . . . .''

Salter bared his teeth. "Steady, Ben! She'll be there for all t' see! You know it's agin the Articles fer me t'lock the cabin, eh? Well, there ye are. It'll be theirs as much as mine, now, and ye may lay t' that.''

Spooner shifted his hat over his eyes. "That's as may be. Only tread easy and steer small, is all.''

"I mark that'', said Salter, with a nod. He squinted up at the brightening sky. "I'm damned glad *Pearl* was up to nor'ard when that King's ship put in, and the Frog after 'im. D'ye think there be any other Brethren in these waters, 'sides we?''

A snort. "Like as not. We be three ships only, and able t' slip by amidst the privateersmen. Hell, there be a hundred o' them cruisin' twixt 'ere an' Boston alone. *And* th' King's ships. And the damned Frogs!'' He sucked a tooth. "Nay. The lads'll be snug aboard Hispaniola, or be it Puerto Rico if the whoreson *guardas-costas* ain't been paid off. Belike a few'll cry privateer and berth into New Providence, like th' old days. But they'll all be in warm waters, I'd say.''

"Aye'', said Salter. "We've needs to be glad there be a war on. No place better t'hide than in a battle, I says.''

Spooner's grin was broad and repulsive. "An' to haul in

swag the like o' this! But where be the main haul buried? Th' one Monsieur Nick's been buildin' up fer all these years, or so he says? Once we digs that up n' steer for th' Indies, we'll be Kings, lad. Kings!'' His dark eyes glimmered in anticipation.

"That be what we needs Monsieur Nick for, then, ain't it, ay? He's kept a proper record o'it all, says he. Charts an' instructions, neat n' tidy, clerkwise. Oncet I gets back in an' can get thick again with 'im, he swears he'll have it out from where 'e hid it. Then, by Christ, you bring *Pearl* and the *Heart's Delight*, an' that new other prize, 'round 'ere to collect us, an' we'll go an' dig it up. And Kings it'll be, certain!''

There was a muffled wail from below decks in the black vessel that set several of the men at the rail into sneering laughter.

"The Spanishers are restless, again'', said Spooner, licking his lips. An odd light had come into his eyes. "D'ye think we should . . .?''

Salter's eyes hardened. "How many of the buggers are left?''

"Nought but ten o' th' men. Th' one who had 'is nose cut off by Bill Tewke died in the first.''

Salter nodded, and scratched at a fleabite.

"Kill 'em'', he said, after a moment. "But no guns. They're foulin' the hold, in th' bargain.''

"And th' women? There's three still alive. The young ones.''

"Fair and square share, all alike, ain't it?'' said Salter, baring his teeth. "Give 'em to th' lads. But I want 'em gutted and over th' side when they're done with 'em. No waste o' vittles, ay?''

Spooner spat. "Aye. You want one?''

Salter nodded. "I do. The youngest one, in the fancy dress. She'll do fer me.''

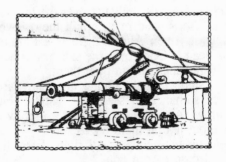

FOUR

The predawn light along the eastern horizon was a dark orange band between the inky blackness of the sea and the only slightly less dark mass of the overcast sky. It cast no warmth over the frigid, tossing ocean waste, nor the shadowed hump of the land off which *Echo* lay pitching.

Shivering in the bone-chilling wind, a little group of *Echo's* men were clustered in the corvette's waist, eyes on the pitching longboat which had been lowered away minutes before and tied on at the lee forechains.

The men were heavily wrapped in watchcoats against the sea chill, and most were wearing solid shoes over their usually bare feet. Over their shoulders were slung rough canvas bags, with a few personal belongings hastily crammed inside. It mattered little to the men that they were carrying meagre enough supplies to set foot on a rough wilderness shore. They had been the fortunate ones but a half-glass ago when Gallant had stunned *Echo's* crew, letting them draw lots for the chance to be set ashore on Île Royale and seek out homes and families long since lost or cut off by war.

Gallant stood with Béssac on the quarterdeck, muffled against the chill by a great black boatcloak.

"You're taking a risk, capitaine. You know that, hein?"

Gallant glanced at him before looking back at the small knot of men at the rail.

"I know, mon vieux", he said quietly.

Béssac shifted his pipe and spat over the lee rail.

"They're all Île Royale men, aren't they? Two from Port Dauphin, at least. Even Augier there is a Lorambec man." He shook his head. "Once over the side you'll never see 'em again, even if the English don't get them."

"Perhaps", said Gallant, after a moment. "But I had to give those men a chance, Béssac. The rest are abiding by the luck of the draw. And you'd have had a mutiny cruising on this shore without letting them try it."

Béssac held up his hands. "All right. Have it your way. But don't say I didn't warn you!"

Gallant went forward and down the ladder to the waist. As he reached the rail the men clustered round him.

"Listen, lads", said Gallant. "You're going off now. It's about a twenty-minute pull in, and you'll have to be damned careful, because the boat will be overloaded. And for God's sake don't tempt the poor bastards in the boat's crew to go with you."

"Where are we, capitaine?" said a man at Gallant's elbow. "That headland . . . ."

"That headland is Cap Charbone, and just to starboard is Baie des Espagnols, opening inland. Stay off both its arms, as the Bostonnais fishermen like to water in there. For the love of God remember to stay off the coast paths and use the inland trails, and remember too that the English will likely have parties out at least three days' march from Louisbourg. So keep your heads down!"

There was a silent moment as the men stared at Gallant, the respect his hardbitten earlier ways had produced touched now with a mute appreciation of the chance they were being given, and the trust Gallant was demonstrating. In an age when many a ship-of-war's commander kept his complement together with the lash and the bayonet, Gallant's gesture had raised the young marine's value in their eyes beyond measure.

"Remember. *Echo* will be here in two weeks' time, right

to the hour, if she can. She'll be off this coast like this in anything but a heavy gale, and if she can't risk coming inshore she'll be here the next day, or the next. If you're there, show two fires, side by side."

He paused for a moment. "I know you'll all be there if you can", he said evenly.

Before the men could reply, Gallant spun on his heel and cupped his hands at the quarterdeck.

"Béssac!" he barked. "Away your seaboat's crew! Get these homing pigeons ashore!"

For a long moment Gallant watched the boat pull in, lifting and vanishing over the swells, oar blades flashing golden in the yellow light.

After some minutes Béssac appeared beside him at the rail.

"We'll have to pay off and put her underway soon, capitaine. We're making more leeway than I thought."

Gallant nodded. "All right. How long?"

"Twenty minutes, perhaps? No more'n half a glass."

"All right". He looked at the rising sun. "Now that we're visible I don't think we should stay on this lee shore in any event. One sighting by that English squadron at Louisbourg and . . . ." He did not finish.

"That doesn't give you much time."

"Exactly. Get Akiwoya and meet me in my cabin."

A few minutes later Béssac and Akiwoya stepped in through the low doorway to Gallant's cramped cabin, and found him gathering a sheaf of documents together and slipping them into a leather pouch.

"Good. Come in", said Gallant.

The cabin was dimly lit by the small lantern over Gallant's bunk, but there was light enough to see that the marine had put off his usual shipboard dress and was attired in readiness for quite different work. On his feet he wore a heavy pair of common soldier's shoes. Covering these, and rising to several inches above the knees, Gallant wore a pair of black-painted canvas gaiters.

Tucked into the leggings Gallant was wearing a wine-coloured pair of heavy ribbed corduroy breeches, and above those he was wearing a heavy shirt and the dark blue full-sleeved waistcoat of his work uniform, wearing it now like a coat. Around his neck he had wrapped a woollen scarf, which was tucked into the waistcoat, and on his head he wore a plain black tricorne decorated with a single seagull feather.

Around his waist Gallant wore a russet-coloured infantry-man's belt, with a bayonet and evil-looking tomahawk thrust into its frog. Slung from his left shoulder to his right hip was a bulky Compagnies Franches cartridge box, and under his right arm, on its own thong, hung a small powder horn of priming powder. His equipment was completed by a heavy canvas haversack which hung on his left hip from his right shoulder, and a bulky blanket roll over the opposite shoulder. Against the bulkhead behind him leaned a gleaming three-banded model 1728 infantry fusil with a protecting cloth bound round the lock.

"What the devil are you staring at?" said Gallant.

"Nothing, capitaine", said Béssac, chuckling. "You just look more like a trapper than a King's officer."

Akiwoya could not keep his surprised silence any longer. "Capitaine . . .!"

"Yes?"

The big African scratched his head. "No disrespect, capitaine, but if you've told M'sieu' Béssac here what's going on, you certainly haven't told me!"

Gallant laughed easily, and tossed the packet of papers across the desk toward Akiwoya. "My apologies, my friend. But I didn't have time to tell all of you what I had planned." He gestured at the papers. "In there are the ship's key documents. Commission, orders, the lot. All you need to take command of *Echo*."

"Command!" Akiwoya was incredulous.

"Exactly. What I decided to do, Akiwoya, once we had found out from that Englishman Rand that the wreck was stripped, was to fetch up here and get into Louisbourg myself."

"What? That's suicide, capitaine!" said Akiwoya.

"Peut-être", nodded Gallant. "But there's a man there, one Morin, who was the only man in Louisbourg who knew what was happening—or would happen—to the *Santa Maria*. And he stayed when the English took the place."

Akiwoya picked up the documents and hefted them. "So you've deduced that the best course is to go in and get the bugger."

Gallant grinned his reply.

The African sighed, but an answering smile spread over his strong features. "All right, capitaine", he said. "What do I do?"

The marine's face hardened. "You take command of *Echo*,

68

here and now. Get her out to sea and keep out of the hair of the English. Our freshwater casks are low so you can try watering farther north, where you'll be less likely to run into a Bostonnais cruiser or an Englishman. Try up here", he said, tapping the chart that lay unrolled on his desk, "Niganiche, past Cap Enfumé. Good anchorage there, and a few habitants-pêcheurs if they haven't been burnt out."

He looked up. "Then you bring her back here and heave to off this head two weeks to the day from now. Watch for two fires ashore and send in a boat for whoever is there. Take 'em off and get to sea. If I'm not among them . . .", and here Gallant smiled and pointed to the sheaf of documents in Akiwoya's hands, " . . . the detailed letter in the first envelope will tell you what to do."

Before Gallant could go any further Béssac harrumphed. "Pardon, capitaine. Not that I think that Aki here can't handle the ship, but just what the hell am I supposed to be doing while . . .!"

"Sorry, Béssac", said Gallant with a steady look. "I've changed the plan somewhat. You're coming with me ashore. Now."

"What!"

Béssac stared at Gallant, and then at Akiwoya, who was restraining his laughter with difficulty. The big mate's mouth gaped for a moment, and then it snapped shut and he bolted out the door.

Gallant looked back at the African. "Keep her well, mon ami. We may be in desperate straits when the two weeks are up, so don't fail us."

Akiwoya squared his shoulders. "We'll be here."

"And if you must fight, get to sea and fight there! And if you do, remember everything we've learned and practised, hein?"

The African's smile was strong and reassuring. "Count on it, m'sieu'."

Lieutenant Anthony Robinson of His Britannic Majesty's Ship *Salamander* looked slowly round his maindeck at the attentive faces of the duty watchmen, and then up at the quarterdeck rail, where the swaying line of the mitre-capped marine squad made a reassuring sight. He hefted his hanger in his scabbard and looked back at the ragged figure who stood at *Salamander's* entry port.

"Let me be quite clear about this, Mr. Bishop. You say *Magnet* was attacked and defeated by a Frenchman and then *burned?*"

The ragged figure, which on closer inspection revealed itself to be a dirty and windburned boy in the remains of a midshipman's coat, nodded and wiped its nose, snuffling.

"Aye, aye, sir. More'n a fortnight past. Captain Rand had most of the watches ashore on that island digging for the . . . for the. . . . "

"Yes, yes. I know what for", said Robinson testily. "But what happened, boy?"

"The Frenchman caught us at anchor and half ashore, sir. We'd barely taken up a mooring when he came boiling round that point—there, sir—and crossed our bows twice. Raked us both times and then boarded."

Robinson's eyes narrowed. "How big a ship?"

"A . . . a twenty-gunner, sir. I think the French call 'em a corvette . . . ." The boy's voice trailed off miserably.

"All right, lad. No need to look so downcast. What of Captain Rand and the others? My coxswain says you were the only man he could find."

"There's only me, sir. It was me that lit the fire you saw."

"Well, what the devil has happened to the rest? And where's Captain Rand?"

"He . . . the Frogs sent him ashore before they burnt *Magnet,* sir. He was wounded in the head."

"And?"

"When he came round presently, sir, the corvette'd gone and *Magnet* was a big torch, yonder in the cove."

"Why are the others not here?"

The lad wiped a sleeve across his runny nose. "Captain Rand took ten hands and the officers in the longboat, sir. Was going to work southward, down Mirligueche and La Have way, and hope for an English vessel."

"The rest? You had no officer left?"

"No, sir. Me 'n' the rest of the lads were told to wait on the island, but most of 'em decided they'd cut logs and raft to the mainland.

"Why didn't you go?"

"A wounded boatswain's mate, Jenkins, was why, sir. He couldn't be moved. I volunteered to stay with 'im." The boy's face sobered. "He died last week."

"All right, lad. You'll tell me the rest later. Mr. Hawkins! Get this young gentleman some clothes from your gunroom. And then see that Mr. Bishop has some supper!"

"Aye, aye, sir!" The respondent, a cheeky-looking lad of fifteen, fixed a not unkind smile on Bishop and led him off.

Robinson turned to his first lieutenant, who had been standing attentively nearby throughout the interview.

"My God, Tom, did you hear that?" said Robinson, under his breath. "Rand must have lost his mind!"

"Never heard of a ship's company being abandoned like that, sir", said the first lieutenant, whose name was Morgan.

"Nor I. Very melancholy indeed." Robinson glanced up at the streaming mainmast pennant. "Take her out, due south. I want to get clear of this cove. Stand out until we get a nor'east by east bearing on that next headland. I want to get clear of this damned coast for a while!"

"Very good, sir. And after?"

"We'll shape our course for Louisbourg, long as this wind doesn't turn foul. I'll dump young Bishop off with the Commodore and he can scribble the report to Their Lordships. Admiral Anson will not be pleased."

"Sir?"

"No matter", said Robinson, walking up to the weather rail. "Unless the Commodore has other ideas, Tom, I'm going to beat back south to Sable and work up this damned coastline, every inch of it. That Frenchman obviously did it, and so can we. And he's off somewhere, hot on the trail of that same bloody plunder. If only we knew what Rand told him!"

"The boy mentioned the French ship's name, by the way, sir", said Morgan.

An odd premonition tingled in Robinson's spine.

"What was it?" he said.

"*Echo*, I think, sir."

A vision flitted across Robinson's mind. A vision of a cocky little French corvette brought to surrender in the Bay of Algiers by the British squadron that included Robinson's own bomb ketch. A corvette later seized and sailed away in a daring escape by the same Frenchman who had surrendered her.

"God's Bowels. It's the same man!" breathed Robinson. "It has to be!"

Robinson settled his hat over his eyes and spread his feet a little wider on the planking.

Beware, my Froggy friend, he thought. I shall find you, and that damned pile of plunder we both seek. And I shall be the one who carries off the prize, or our bones will lie together at the bottom of these damned chilly seas!

Gallant and Béssac were standing together in the shadows of a small knot of jackpine that crowned a tumble of rock at the sea's edge, the dark surf washing over the green seaweed fringes scant feet below their shoe-tips. They were oblivious to the threatening wisps of foam that lapped at them, however, their eyes fixed instead on the small dwindling shape of *Echo*, far out to sea.

"Sweet Virgin, capitaine", said Béssac, "I'm sorry to see her go off without me. Without us." He was leaning morosely on folded hands atop his musket.

Gallant nodded, wordless.

"All right", he said, finally. "We'd better get going, old friend. Even our landing might have been seen."

Béssac raised an eyebrow at his younger companion, and scratched at the stubble on his chin. "Capitaine, I'm too old to be doing this sort of thing. You know that, hein?"

Gallant clapped him on the shoulder. "Come on, Béssac. Think you're doing it for God and His Most Christian Majesty."

Béssac rolled his eyes in mock anguish. "You hear, Lord? You hear the man you fated me to follow? He talks about the King, for God's sake!"

Gallant laughed and slung his musket over his shoulder, looking here and there for an entry into the forest mass.

"That way", he said finally, and they were off.

The European experience of wilderness rarely prepared men for the nature of the primeval forests they found when they came upon the dark and haunted shores of America. For there was no equivalent to the endless stretching carpet of gigantic trees that went on without halt to the horizon, day after day wherever men walked. And the forest made the discoverer's world of North America one of shadow; darkness and shadow so profound and filled with real and imagined menace that the settlers struggled with grim strength to gain sunlight. The first tools their hands took up, eyes agleam with purpose, were the axes, to hack away at the towering barrier that enclosed them, kept them locked in the shadow of the forest floor without break save in the winding silver rivers or sundappled lakes. They cursed and swore and hated the forest and the black nightmare shadows of its depths, and they were faced by it in the earlier days with three choices: to destroy the forest, and plant anew the ordered parkland of Europe; to admit defeat, and leave the leafy giants to their domain; or to let themselves be drawn within it and meld with its rhythms and its purposes, as the brown men they alternately fought and befriended had done for thousands of years.

For Paul Gallant and Théophile Béssac, their racial seed planted in the soil of North America only a scant century, the natural path came as the third choice, for there was something in their calling as seamen that brought to them an equal ability to navigate this dim ocean of shadowed forest floor and animal trail. Had they grown in the sturdy sabots of farmers' sons, their impulse would have been to curse the tangled dark and long for axe and plough to bring light and order from a hated primitive chaos. But both men had grown to manhood shaping their life courses across the sea, and being thereby shaped by it. They comprehended a larger power, an element beyond them in scope and tenacity which they learned to navigate for the reasonable and hoped-for purposes of their lives; the sea could not be axed, hewn, farmed, tamed, fenced, or ground down. Both men accepted the nature of their home element and worked as far as they could in harmony with it. And so it was that they came to move into the green swells and billows of the forest instinctively, seeking its calms and eddies, respecting its turbulences and rages, insinuating themselves through it as they might their ship through the sea.

With quiet watchfulness they marched through the shadows of the great trees, keeping the sunsparkle gleam of the sea visible from time to time, but ever careful not to step out onto the open shore.

The closeness of the forest made the march difficult work nonetheless, with the endless stepping or vaulting over toppled logs, ducking beneath deadfalls, and pushing through knots of clinging bracken. When Gallant squinted up at the forest roof high above and judged by the shafts of sunlight that it was time for a noonday pause, both men were wringing wet with sweat, and their faces were dotted with the bloody marks of blackfly bites.

Gallant swung up on a moss-laden boulder and used his shoes to stamp down the heavy ferns that grew in a hollow on its top. He looked round carefully, noting thick tree masses on three sides and a glimpse of the sea to the fourth.

"Here", he said. "Long as we do without a fire we can lie up here and not be seen by anyone ten feet away."

Béssac threw off his blanket roll and slapped at a mosquito on his neck. "Damn these pests! They'll have no trouble finding us!"

Gallant laughed as he shucked off his gear. Squatting down, he began to rummage through his haversack.

"The Micmac have a cure for the flies, Théo", he said. "Only it's a fat coating of animal grease over your skin."

"What? Faugh!"

Gallant tossed over a brick-hard ship's biscuit and a piece of the fire-spiced garlic sausage that seemed impervious to sea rot.

"Ho! That's better!" said Béssac, and letting his kit tumble off him where it fell the burly mate hunkered down on his heels, drew his knife and began to hew off great chunks.

As the noonday sun gradually shifted the slanting beams that lanced down to where the two friends lay, Gallant and Béssac sprawled in rude comfort in their temporary lair.

"How far do you think we've come?" said Béssac. He had stood up and was puffing industriously on his stained little clay pipe, having discovered that it kept the hovering insects respectfully at bay.

Gallant rinsed out his mouth with a final swig of wine and spat. "Two leagues. Maybe more."

Béssac spat and knocked the dottle out of his pipe against his shoe, grinding down the ashes into the wet until they were out. He struggled into his kit and was about to sling his heavy musket over his shoulder when Gallant stopped him.

"Not now, old friend. No slinging. Check your priming. Then carry it this way. Or this, in open spaces."

The first way was horizontal, trailed beside Gallant's thigh, the musket grasped in the middle by the marine's right hand. The other way was across Gallant's body, cradled in the left arm like a baby.

"Either way you're ready to use it, hein? Keep the pan tightly closed. And put the piece at half-cock."

74

"So we're into dangerous country?"

Gallant smiled. "Were from the start. Now we start being ready."

Over the next few minutes Gallant instructed Béssac in some rudiments of forest fighting. He showed him how to walk on the outside edges of his shoes, to avoid sounds. He taught him two or three hand signals for communicating to a visible partner. He rearranged the mate's kit so that nowhere did metal clink on metal. And he taught him how to heft and cut with the wicked-looking tomahawk.

Several minutes later the two men checked round their little camp for anything forgotten, and then set off, Gallant once more in the lead.

The afternoon lengthened, and gradually Gallant and Béssac worked their way round the south eastern bulge of Cape Breton toward the distant Louisbourg, the cool tingle of the sea air reaching in through the trees to their left cheeks.

Finally Gallant stopped, to stand resting on his long musket, his breath coming like that of a man at the top of a particularly long flight of stairs. Béssac stepped up beside him and set down his own weapon.

"By the Virgin!" Béssac breathed, "I'm glad I don't carry one of these things for a living, like some poor bastard soldat. I'd have arms ten feet long!"

Gallant suddenly stiffened, his eyes widening. "Quiet!" he hissed.

"Quoi?" said Béssac.

For a moment there was only the harsh jeer of a bluejay, shrill over the whisper of the winds in the pine boughs. Then Béssac heard it, loud, and very clear.

One shot, and another. A third, all the heavy boom of muskets echoing and re-echoing through the forest. And then the piercing scream of a woman.

"That way! Come on!" Gallant sprang off ahead, ducking wraithlike into the shadows toward the sounds. Béssac spat and loped after him.

The two men moved rapidly through the bush, their path, as the minutes passed, climbing inland, slanting away from the sea. The great trees were not nearly so close-spaced here, and Gallant and Béssac wove and dodged past them at a dog-trot, eyes straining ahead, breathing deep and impossibly loud in their own ears.

Then more muskets sounded; three, then a fourth. And again a scream, terrifying and disembodied as it echoed round them.

Gallant slammed himself up against a tree trunk, his musket held vertically close against his chest. An instant later Béssac was at his shoulder. Both men dripped with sweat.

"It's no more'n a long musket shot ahead, Béssac!" Gallant whispered between heaves. "The Micmac are sometimes on these coasts after the seals. Like as not a camp of 'em has picked up some unwelcome company!"

"English?"

"Who else?" snorted Gallant. With a grunt he struck out again, and in a minute they were stumbling in a crouch off through the sunlight-shafted groves.

Without warning the distinctive click-blast of a musket roared out ahead, so close that Gallant and Béssac flung themselves into the ground and lay there, chests heaving and hearts pounding in their throats. Then a babble of voices suddenly sounded amid the trees, and one voice, thick in drink and tinged with a cruelty that sent a shiver up Gallant's spine, rose in mirthless laughter. A girl's wail, piteous and rending, followed.

The two men rose to their knees and found they were behind a final row of thick bracken edging a rough clearing in the woods, in a grove of white birch. The clearing held three broad, conical huts of birchbark slabs laid over sloping poles, and several smoky cookfires, overhung with iron kettles on tripods. And it also held several crumpled and bloody bodies in buckskin and trade cloth, surrounded by the rubbish of ransacked possessions.

Gallant swore under his breath. On the far side of the clearing three tall and heavy-set men, two in rumpled tricornes and one in a raccoonskin cap, were pulling together in a blanket a little pile of items they were obviously plundering from the camp. And cringing at their feet, her long black hair twisted in the cruel grip of one of the men, an Indian girl in moccasins and long dark-blue robe lay, sobbing bitterly and reaching out toward the bloody-faced corpse of an old man that lay several feet away. As Gallant watched, one of the men barked something at the girl in English and callously kicked her arm away.

Beside him Béssac swore under his breath. "Peste! Who are those whoresons?" he hissed.

"Bostonnais! Militia garrison out of Louisbourg, likely. Out for a few days to pick off what they can. From old Micmac men and helpless women, God damn them!"

Béssac pulled his musket up beside him. "Shall we . . .?"

76

Gallant shook his head. "No! Too far away. The third man might get us. Or the girl'd get it." Gallant pulled his legs round and rose slightly for an instant's clearer look, and then ducked back down.

"The trail out the other side of the camp goes up a hill on the other side. Likely the way they'll go." He pointed with his chin off to the right. "I'm going to try and get round them up the trail. You wait here and . . . ."

"Damn it, don't leave me out!"

"Listen! You wait! Until they start to move off. Then go straight in from this side and as soon as they're strung out on the path get the rear one. We'll trap 'em between us!"

"And what if they don't leave? The way they're eyeing that girl . . . ."

Gallant wiped his mouth. "If they pin her down and start taking off their breeches, I'll make a front-on rush. Yells, everything. When they go for me you hit from behind."

The mate nodded, eyes wide with excitement. "Bon!"

Gallant left the mate and, heart pounding in his ears, plunged silently off to one side in the trees, watching to see he stayed well out of sight of the clearing. Working in a great semi-circle, he worked up the face of the rise, his shoes slipping over the needles and moss, sweat stinging in his eyes. He ducked under branches and vaulted over logs, sure the crunch and crackle of his movement was carrying to the ears of the three New Englanders.

Then suddenly the narrow footpath was in front of him, and he looked both ways along it. As he did so a shout sounded from the clearing below that sent his heart pounding.

"Harkee, Isaac, I be goin'!"

Gallant shifted his musket and glanced round for cover. In a moment he was sheltering down behind the tangled shoulder of an old uprooted elm. Ignoring the cold seep that began to work up through his breeches and gaiters, he loosened the tomahawk and bayonet in their belt, and then, reaching into his waistcoat, drew out a long, slender sheath knife, which he slid into his belt.

He settled his hat down over his eyes and hunched well down behind the root tangle, resting the musket on it for steadiness. His line of fire was dead on a broadening of the trail, and the Bostonnais would have to pass through it mere yards from the muzzle. He eased the hammer forward, checking the angle of his flint, and after looking to see that the pan was properly primed he slowly drew back the hammer to full cock, the double click-click loud against the backdrop of his own deep breathing. His hands were trembling slightly.

Then, without warning, the voices of the marauders were carrying to him along the trail, thick-sounding as if from drink. The men were cursing and giggling as they crashed along the trail from the camp toward him, heedless of stealth or concealment. One bayed in coarse laughter, and with a chill Gallant heard a fourth voice, the girl's, cry out.

So quickly that he almost took Gallant by surprise, the first man had materialized out of the trail's shadows, tall and red-faced, a rough brown coat in the English style hanging loosely about him. He was in muddy boots, and wearing a plain tri-corne set with a red cockade. The man was cradling a heavy dragoon pistol.

An officer, by God, said Gallant, and squeezed the trigger.

The weapon's deep-throated report echoed through the trees, and as it bucked against Gallant's shoulder the officer howled and was pitched backward by the ball's impact to the ground, legs flailing.

There was a startled yell from the next man and a musket flashed, the ball humming past Gallant's ear. The smoke of the two rounds thick and blue amidst the trees, Gallant only glimpsed three figures: one pushing a smaller one roughly aside and crouching; a second dropping a heavy sack and sprinting with frightening speed toward him.

Now!

Gallant flung aside his musket and vaulted over the root tangle. The gleaming knife seemed to appear by its own volition in his left hand, the tomahawk in his right. With a growl he leapt forward.

The musket of the further man flashed, pink-flamed in the smoky gloom, and a searing pain lanced through Gallant's left arm. Then suddenly in front of him a tall, pale-faced man in black, eyes wild and staring, was raising his musket like a club, his gap-toothed mouth contorted in a snarl.

Gallant ducked the whistling blow and drove his shoulder into the man, hearing him grunt with the impact. The two men crashed to earth, the man's hands clawing womanishly at Gallant's eyes.

A red rage seemed to flood Gallant's head, and he fought free of the raking nails. Ripping out of the man's grip, he swung the tomahawk down in a short, vicious arc. The man's

78

mouth twisted into a quick, choked scream as the blade bit deep into his skull with a horrid sound.

Obeying some animal fighting skill that was driving him now, Gallant rolled instinctively away from the plunging bayonet that was driving for his back, and rose catlike to his feet, hat gone now, to meet the third man.

The last Englishman was shorter, in seaman's clothes, blond hair hanging in greasy rattails from under a raccoonskin cap. He had pale blue eyes, slitted now with rage, and as he swung the musket's bayonet to centre on Gallant's throat he was mouthing a stream of obscenities.

For an instant the two men froze, eyes locked. Then the sailor lunged.

Gallant twisted, feeling the bayonet stab through the bulky cloth of his waistcoat, a whisper away from his skin. The man muscled into him, his foul breath of rum and rotten teeth enveloping Gallant sickeningly. Gallant saw his opponent's eyes goggle as the marine clutched the man to his chest and let the momentum of the sailor's rush carry them over backward. As his back thumped into the earth Gallant drove his knees up sharply, and the Englishman toppled over into a sprawling somersault. Gallant kept moving, rolling on his own shoulders until he was atop the man. Then with every ounce of his strength he gripped the long knife and thrust it to the hilt hard into the man's belly.

The sailor shrieked, a short, cutting outburst of agony, his hands clawing at Gallant's. Then he slumped, still.

Gallant jerked out the scarlet knife and slowly wiped it on the man's coat, as if in a dream.

"Capitaine!"

The mate appeared up the path, moving quickly. He froze as he saw the three bodies.

"Mon Dieu. You got all three?" he said in a whisper.

Gallant nodded, looking at his aching arm. The cloth was ripped away, but all he could see was a massive and growing bruise, with no blood. His voice was hoarse when he tried to speak. "By luck. Where the devil were you? I thought you were going to attack from behind . . . ."

"There was a fourth one in one of the huts. He . . . he'd had his way with another woman and then cut her throat." The mate's face was black with contempt. "I got him when he came out at your first shot. Lucky I heard him, the bastard!"

Gallant shook his head, stunned, feeling his stomach surge

anew. God in Heaven, what manner of men were these?

The girl!

Gallant kicked aside the clump of tall fern he remembered seeing the girl thrown into. She was lying in a tight ball on her side, almost like an infant. Her long blue robe, which he could see now was really one of the traditional Micmac long dresses, was torn and dirty. The moccasins on her feet were holed and disintegrating at the heels, and the girl's small clenched fists were dark with grime. She was lying with her face turned downward, and her hair, which was long, was spread in tangled and matted ebony waves over her shoulders.

Béssac came up as Gallant knelt over her. The mate was wiping his bayonet with a handful of moss.

"Poor creature", he said. "Is she dead?"

Gallant shook his head. He touched the girl's neck with his fingers. "Good heartbeat. But I don't understand it. The Englishman didn't put her down that hard. And look at her clothing!"

"What about it?"

Gallant looked up at him. "It's filthy. Her dress is like a rag. Micmac women just aren't like that, Béssac! They smell of spruce gum and woodsmoke, and a good womanly musk, hein? But they're never dirty. Not like this!"

With great gentleness Gallant turned the girl over on her back. Her face was caked with dirt, streaked with tears, and her hair wisped across in a touching elfin way. Although it was difficult to tell with the soot, she appeared to have small, even features except for broad cheekbones and a full, sensual mouth. The girl's eyes were closed, and she was breathing quickly and shallowly.

"Sacristi. She's burning up with fever!" said Gallant, laying a hand to her forehead.

Béssac stepped back a pace. "The smallpox. Get away, capitaine! She's poxed!"

Gallant shook his head. "No. Doesn't look right, Béssac. There's something else. If only I could think . . .!" With a sudden movement Gallant seized the girl's dress at the neck and ripped it open.

"I knew it, Béssac!" Gallant grunted. "Look at these red marks, all over her breasts and stomach!" He closed the ripped garment. "She's got the typhus!"

Béssac stared. Fever was fever to him. What did it matter if you split hairs about its name. It all killed one equally well.

"How do you know?"

"Saw it before. On the next farm to Philippe's—my brother's—on the Miré. Almost took a whole family. They got it from a filthy peddler."

Béssac was sweating. "Capitaine, you've got to . . . to leave her before she plagues you!"

Gallant looked up at him, eyes full of emotion. "Béssac, I've just killed three men in so brutal a fashion it makes me sick to think of it. That clearing down there is full of death. This one is alive, hein? Alive!" He looked down at the girl. "The Micmac are good people. They helped me once, when I was a lad."

He stood up. "This is a chance to repay that debt. Now. Here."

"All right", sighed Béssac, shaking his head. "But for God's sake I hope you realize what you're doing!"

Gallant nodded. "So do I, mon vieux. Now sling your musket and help me with her."

The girl was so small and light that the two men soon had her settled in Gallant's arms. He moved toward the clearing as behind him Béssac stripped the dead Englishmen of their weapons and packs.

Gallant's eyes hardened as he moved into the clearing. There were four bodies in Indian clothing; three old men and an old woman. From their dirty and dishevelled state they obviously had been terribly ill, too, helpless as the brutal New Englanders had descended on them.

Sweet Mary, what a filthy business is war! thought Gallant.

At the low entrance to one wigwam the fourth marauder sprawled, a wide look of surprise on his stubbled face and blood seeping through a neat triangular hole in the chest of his fringed hunting shirt. Gallant stooped to look inside, and then backed out, a wave of revulsion overcoming him. The girl had been barely a child, and lay naked and spread-eagled amidst the ransacked rubbish of the shelter, a great crimson gash across her throat.

He straightened, lips white, and carried the girl in the blue robe over to one side of the cluster of wigwams. He laid her down gently, and then turned to Béssac, who was fingering the dead officer's dragoon pistol.

"Light a fire, mon vieux", said Gallant.

"Should we show one, capitaine?" said Béssac. "What if . . .?"

"You forget the delightful quartet we just rid the world of, Béssac. They were meant to be out doing dirty deeds. So we'll do it for 'em."

The marine pointed to the bodies in the clearing. "We'll put them all into this one, hein? With that poor wretched child. Fetch down her killer's comrades as well from up there." Gallant's eyes burned with purpose as he spoke. "Kick down the other shelters except one, and pile the wood and bark on. Then we burn everything the Micmacs touched. Particularly clothes, or blankets. Anything the Bostonnais left around, too!"

Gallant smiled without humour at Béssac. "Then we strip, old friend."

"What! Now, wait a minute, capi . . .."

"We hang our clothes round the fire. Bake 'em till they're too hot to touch. Was that a rum bottle clinking in that rosbif's pack? Good! Dig it out. We'll use it to wash our hair." He pointed to the girl. "And I'll do the same for her."

Forty minutes later Gallant and Béssac were squatting naked in the glare of a blazing column of flame that leaped and curled skyward from the pyre they had made. The clearing was wide enough and the wind still enough that it was unlikely they ran the risk of kindling the whole countryside; nonetheless the intense heat of the fire caused both men to squint away from it, and their bodies soon were running with sweat.

Between them, her nakedness covered by a cool blanket of moss Gallant had gathered, the girl lay trembling in the depths of her fever.

"God's Bowels", said Béssac, his face dripping, "I'm going to melt and flow away! How much more of this must we have?" He winced as the great fire popped loudly and spat out a shower of glowing embers.

"Till we're well toasted, old friend. And till she breaks out into a sweat. The fever's got to break, or she'll die."

The sun slanted down through the great trees in glowing shafts in the drifting smoke. Gradually as the day lengthened the fire died, and as dusk approached and the shadows within the birch grove deepened, the flames faded into a wide ring of glowing embers.

Through the afternoon Gallant had tended the girl, periodically peeling away the moss and wiping down the girl's hot skin with the ripped tail of his shirt, soaked first in rum and then in water. His heart softened as the girl moaned softly under his hands, her face moving into expressions of fear as if her feverish dreams were filled with the forms of the marauders, still pursuing her. His hand worked over the smooth contours of her slight body, and slowly the heat of the fire joined with his touch to bring a sweat all over the girl, and she fell into a deeper sleep, less troubled and more peaceful in her breathing.

Gallant sat back on his heels, exhausted, as Béssac threw his clothes at his feet.

Gallant pulled on his breeches. "I think she'll live, mon vieux. The fever's broken." His voice was hoarse with fatigue.

"Thank the Virgin." Béssac smiled. "She's a pretty thing, hein?"

"Yes", said Gallant, staring down at her. "Damned pretty."

Béssac touched his elbow. "I've got the blankets inside the remaining shelter. And all our gear. Shall we . . .?"

Gallant shook his head as if to clear away an unwelcome thought. "What? Yes. Let's move her. Gently, now."

With infinite care the two men cleared the moss from the girl's body, and as Béssac cradled her head like a child's, Gallant brought her robe from where it had been stretched before the fire and dressed her. In spite of himself his hands trembled as he closed the bodice over the girl's round and softly tipped breasts.

The girl lay still and delicate in Béssac's lap, her eyelids fluttering every now and then. "Poor petite", murmured the mate.

"Hold her while I pick some more moss for a bed for her. Sleep is what she needs, now."

Some minutes later Gallant returned. He bent over and lifted the girl up with ease in his arms and strode over to the wigwam. Stooping inside, he laid her on the spruce boughs and moss he had collected. Then he picked up his blanket and laid it over her, tucking it gently under her chin.

Béssac entered, and both men sat back on their heels and stared at the sleeping girl.

"Water's short. I'll get some from that little creek again", said Béssac. "What else do we do now?"

Gallant thought. "One of us has got to hunt in the morning. We'll need fresh meat. And Christ knows how long we have to keep her still."

"Aaaaiieeee!"

The war shriek rang out, piercingly loud and blood-chilling in the dusk light. Then in the next instant three muskets blasted at the clearing's edge.

Gallant had leaped out the doorway at the shriek. Now his hat went spinning from his head, and the brass pot he still carried leaped away with an echoing *spang* as a ball slammed into it.

"Jesus Christ!" he breathed, and dropped into a ball, rolling for the wigwam door and the muskets that lay inside it.

Béssac swore luridly and scooped up the dead Englishman's dragoon pistol. As Gallant tumbled in the doorway the mate snapped off a shot in the direction of the shriek, the pistol's report sharp and deafening.

The hidden muskets barked again, and the shot whizzed and splintered through the wigwam's birchbark scant inches over their heads.

Béssac swore, feverishly reloading the pistol. "Who in hell is that? By God, I'll wager it's more damned English come to . . .!''

"Quiet! Listen!" Gallant hissed.

Béssac froze. He could hear voices.

"Micmac!" breathed Gallant. "By Heaven, Béssac, they're Micmacs!" Gallant cupped his hands and shouted out the wigwam opening.

"*Jiksutaan! Wigumadeek!* Do not fire! We are French!"

There was a moment of silence from the trees, and then a deep man's voice sounded, full of caution.

"*Wenooch?* Frenchman? You are not of the *Bostonka-waach?*"

"*Mogwaa!* No! We travel here as brothers, not your enemies! We are caring for one of your women we found here! The English had attacked the camp!"

"Wenooch! Show yourself! You and all with you!"

Gallant looked at Béssac. "Do as he says", he whispered. "And keep your hands in sight, and open."

Béssac's eyes were still aflame. "Could be a trap, couldn't it? They might just shoot us down!"

"They can do that anyway, even if we get a few!" Gallant replied. "Come on. We can use their help if they'll trust us." He cupped his hands again.

"*Ankaptaan! Nayaase!* I'm showing myself!"

The marine stepped out through the entrance way and raised

84

his hands, palms open. Béssac stepped out beside him.

"*Ootetaum*. I am here."

There was a tingling moment of suspense when there was no movement or sound from the shadows. Gallant's spine suddenly shivered with the thought that he had miscalculated, that in the next instant the muskets would boom and he and Béssac would pitch back in agony, clutching at bowels torn by flying lead.

But instead the leaves moved, and three figures stepped forward. They were tall men, about Gallant's height, the dark Indian features and strong jaw lines set off with glittering black eyes. They wore loosefitting buckskin shirts and fringed leggings, and on their close-cropped heads they wore round seal-skin caps very like Béssac's own. The shirts were beaded in bands across the chests, and round the men's necks they wore beaded amulets against which small pewter crucifixes gleamed. All three were armed with short hunting fusils, far lighter than the heavy military weapons Gallant and Béssac were carrying.

Fusils ready, the three men padded toward Gallant and Béssac noiselessly on moccasined feet, the piercing black eyes never leaving the white men's faces.

The two men remained motionless as the Micmacs approached, and then stopped a few yards away. The Micmacs' eyes took in the burnt circle of fire, and then exchanged glances.

The foremost man, who had an older air about him, pointed at Béssac with his chin. "You. Are you both *noojematunaaga?* Warriors?"

Béssac nodded, lips a tight line, as the Micmac used both French and Micmac words.

The dark gaze turned to Gallant. "Where is my family? My lodges, *Wenooch!*"

Gallant spread his hands. "I am sorry, m'sieu'. The anglais were here. They killed all but one girl, whom we saved."

The warrior's eyes flashed. Gallant saw his jaw muscles suddenly clench, but his face remained impassive. There was a tinge of hoarseness in his voice when, after a moment, he spoke again. "Which girl?"

Gallant indicated the wigwam. "In there. She is small and beautiful. And she has the fever of the body lice, as they all did. *Wiskuswokun tan kesusooa'dasik.*"

The black eyes lightened. " '*Ntoos!* It is my eldest daughter.

And does she yet live, *Wenooch?''*

"Aa", Gallant nodded. "Yes. She lives, but must be cared for if she is to recover."

The warrior gazed at the burnt circle. "And all the others?"

Gallant lowered his hands, as did Béssac. "There were old people, and a younger girl. We burned them, as we did the English." He looked toward the wigwam. "Your daughter lies asleep, now, surrounded with the arms and possessions of the *Inglunkawa* killers. They are yours."

The Micmac set down his musket. *"Pesagwestoo.* I shoot crookedly, and strike your hat instead of your heart. I am glad I am a poor shot, *Wenooch!''*

The two other Micmacs lowered their fusils and came forward. As the leading man retold the story their faces showed no trace of emotion. But Gallant saw the fingers gripping the fusils tighten until they were almost colourless.

The tall warrior turned back. "We have lost our aged ones, our parents. And one of my daughters, their sister. *Eoonasea!* It is crazy!" He shook his head.

Then the black eyes were on Gallant's again. "In the language of a *Wenooch* I am called The Wolf."

"And I am Gallant, and this is Béssac."

"Ha! Your tongue can twist those names. Mine cannot. You are *Wenooch.''* The Wolf looked at Béssac for a long moment. "And he is *Nabe'skw!''*

Gallant turned to Béssac. "You've a new name, mon vieux. He's christened you The Bear."

"And how did you kill the *Inglunkawa?''*

"Kedankeigwemkawa'', said Gallant, after a moment's thought over the right words. "We ambushed them."

The Wolf nodded. "And did they die by your hands?"

Gallant held up three fingers. "And one by Béssa . . . er, *Nabe'skw.''*

"Good. I am content. In time I shall mourn properly. But not now." He turned to the two younger men, who it became clear were known as Lynx and Weasel.

"We were hunting for three suns, and we have game. A fat buck. We will all share it tonight." He looked at the wigwam entrance. "I would see my daughter."

"I'll see to that fire", said Béssac.

Gallant led the Wolf into the wigwam, where the gloom made it difficult to see. The marine dug out his flint striker

86

and within a few minutes had a strip of birch crackling in his hands like a small torch.

The Wolf squatted beside his daughter's bed, and rested his hand on her forehead. After a long moment he looked across at Gallant.

"*Nedagobawe.* I am a shy man, and cannot speak always my thoughts. But I must thank you, *Wenooch.* She lives." He looked back at the girl's face. "Is it the flux? *Maldawik-chamkawa?*"

Gallant shook his head. "*Mogwaa.* No, Wolf. It's something else. A sickness carried by vermin, somehow. Or so I have learned."

The Wolf made a sweeping gesture with one hand. "It is the same throughout all *Megomaage,* all the land of the Micmac. My people sicken and die of this fever, this evil spirit."

Gallant felt the girl's forehead once more. "So many as that?"

"*Aa!* The burials fill the woods. I have never seen such death, *Wenooch;* not since before I slew my bear and became a man!"

Outside the wigwam Béssac's fire was beginning to roar, and several feet away the two Indian brothers had slung up the deer by thongs through its hamstrings and were skilfully butchering it.

The Wolf rose. "*Aagei!* I am ready for food and drink." His dark eyes flashed at Gallant. "You have none of the water which burns with you?"

"Brandy?" Gallant felt his neck tingle. He knew the uncontrollable appetite the Micmac sometimes developed for alcohol, and the chaos and savage drunkenness it produced. "No, Wolf. We carry none."

"Good! *Mijooajejooeanek!* In the days of my childhood my father drank the *Wenooch* brandy and became like a crazy bear. He killed my uncle and almost my brother." The Wolf shook his head slowly. "If you carry any, *Wenooch*, see that my sons do not see it."

Gallant stood up. "There is none", he said quietly.

There was a grunt from one of the two young men, who had brought meat from the deer and were spitting it to roast above the fire. To one side Béssac was squatting warrior-fashion on his haunches and gnawing at an enormous chunk of dripping, half-charred venison.

"God, capitaine!" he said through mouthfuls. "You should taste this! What beautiful meat!"

The Lynx was silently holding out a portion to Gallant on the end of a knife. Gallant took it and sat down beside Béssac. The meat was warm and tender, its tang unmistakable and unforgettable. Gallant felt a ravenous hunger overcome him and he tore at the meat with relish.

"What happened in there?" said Béssac, after a moment.

"Not a great deal. I suspect Wolf is a clan chief, or perhaps a warrior chief. An important man." Gallant tore off another succulent mouthful. "He says a lot of the Micmac are dying of the same fever."

"What about the girl?"

Gallant sucked greasy fingers. "Got to get some spruce-bud tea into her. And I'll boil some of this meat to get a broth."

"Kesenookwei! It hurts! It hurts! Father!"

Gallant sprang up, startled, as the Wolf did the same on the far side of the fire. It was the girl, crying out.

In an instant the two men were within the wigwam, on either side of the small, blanket-wrapped form. The girl looked at them in turn with lustrous, dark-lashed eyes, filled now with a flicker of pain.

"Ntoos! Daughter! You live!" said the Wolf.

The girl looked at him in joy, a smile trembling on her lips. "Oh, Father. You are here! My head . . . hurts so!"

The girl's head tossed, and Gallant knew she was being racked by the fearful headaches the fever brought. But if the fever stayed down, they would pass.

"You will be all right; the pain will go", said Gallant quietly. "I'll make medicine that will help."

He rose and ducked out the doorway. He moved back to the fire and squatted down, beginning to cut small chunks of meat into the little brass pot.

The Wolf was suddenly beside him, huge in the flickering firelight. *"Wenooch!"* he rumbled.

Gallant looked at him. "Oui?"

"Wigumadeek", said the Wolf. "For what you have done, we are friends, you and I. I value my daughter above life itself."

"She is beautiful", Gallant smiled.

"It is more than that, *Wenooch.*" The Wolf sank down on his haunches and stared at the flames. To one side Béssac and the Wolf's two sons sat, still busy with the venison.

The Wolf's words came slowly, now. "It is in your eyes that you seek something, *Wenooch*. You and the Bear, there, who greases his jowls with the meat like a man. You are in danger here as much as we, now that this island and the walled village of the *Wenooch* king are in the hands of the pink-faced men of Boston." He fixed a piercing gaze on Gallant. "What is it you seek, my friend?"

Gallant picked up a water gourd Béssac had filled and poured it into the little brass pot, with the meat. Then he hung the pot on a chain which dangled from the green sapling tripod which sat over the fire.

"The king of France, Wolf, and the king of another nation are giving themselves and each other great gifts of gold; gifts that include an image of the Blessed Virgin herself. Worth enough gold to fill a hundred canoes", he said. "I am sent to find such things that belong to my King, and return them to him."

"And why do you travel this trail? Toward the walled village, where the *Bostonkawaach* will surely kill you?"

Gallant chewed on a piece of venison. "Within the walled village is another *Wenooch*. One who stayed when the English came. He knows, I hope, what may have happened to my King's gold."

"And you will seek him out?"

"Yes."

"Even if you may die?"

Gallant paused. "Yes. It is my duty, Wolf."

The Wolf looked back into the fire, silent for a long moment as the flickering of the flames made small pinpoints of light dance in his black eyes.

"Hark, *Wenooch! Neenawe!* It is I, Wolf, who speaks. Wolf, who slew his bear in his twelfth summer, and has lost no struggle with man or beast to this day. I say to you, *Wenooch,* that you have earned the friendship of the Wolf by the gift of that which he cherishes most, the life of his daughter. Then hear, *Wenooch,* that I and my sons shall see you and the Bear to your goal, to the walled village and the wigwam of the other *Wenooch* you seek!"

"The heart of the Wolf is great", said Gallant, after a moment.

The Wolf grunted. "*Aa!* We will wait until the Flower is

once more well. I shall bury the implements my mother and father must take with them to the Spirit World. And I shall mourn.'' He spat into the fire. ''Then we will march together for the walled village.'' He ripped an enormous gobbet of meat from the smoking roast that hung over one side of the fire and bit into it with gusto.

''Weboodeek! Now we eat! Together!'' he said. ''For strength to fight!''

''Starboard your helm'', said Lieutenant Anthony Robinson. ''Steer sou'west by south. And for God's sake watch the foretops'l leech!''

''Sou' west by south, zur'', said *Salamander's* helmsman, and sweated over his work.

The vessel was a league to the eastward of the precipitous Île Royale coast, all taut on a driving starboard reach across the howling westerly that swooped down off the mountainous highlands of the great northern arm of the island. Under topsails and reefed courses, *Salamander* was making tremendous way as she knifed and roared over the deep-blue swells, the hissing spume flung white in the brilliant sun to either side of her slicing cutwater. But the excellent progress of his ship did little to lift the black cloud of anger and exasperation which had lain over Robinson since his departure from Louisbourg several days ago.

He squinted into the late afternoon sun at the dark and forbidding shore, and spat incautiously into the wind. His mind was recalling again the orders that had come to him in the anchorage at Louisbourg; orders that bade him break off the search of his initial mission and cruise *Salamander* to the northernmost cape of the rugged island in search of a rumoured squadron of pirates.

''Pirates, for God's sake!'' he had snarled to Thomas Morgan.

And now *Salamander* pressed on in her lonely patrol, but Robinson had vowed that his track would bear the mark of his original purpose as well as a scout for real or imagined pirates. In any event, if he completed this patrol within several days, he might then be able to work south to Sable and start the sweep he . . . .

"Deck, there!" The foretop lookout's voice rang down, shattering Robinson's chain of thought.

"Deck, aye!" he replied, through cupped hands.

"A ship, sir! Same tack as ours, but close inshore! Bearin' about six points off the starboard bow, sir!"

Robinson had been carrying a long leatherbound telescope under his arm. He snapped it open and peered inshore.

At first all he could make out was the dark evergreen mass of the shadowed shore, with a line of white surf along the shore edge.

"Sighting, sir?" said Morgan, at his elbow suddenly. The first lieutenant had heard the lookout from his cabin.

"Not sure, Tom. Ship inshore is all I know so far. Come on", he said, making for the weather rail. "We'll look at it from the maintop!"

Several minutes later the two officers were clinging to a precarious perch in *Salamander's* main crosstrees.

Robinson opened out the long telescope and squinted through it. "Could be anything, Tom. A New England fisherman, or a lumber scow off course out of Newfoundla . . .!" He stopped, gaping through the glass.

"What is it, sir?"

"That ship, Tom! I know that ship! It's a Frenchman. A small frigate, what they call a 'corvette'. Look for yourself."

Morgan squinted through the glass. "Rakish rig. Bourbon ensign, all right. Blue and tan hull paint. And moving well in the bargain!" He handed back the glass. "She looks as fast as us on this reach."

Robinson was glued to the glass again. "It is the same bloody ship, Tom!"

"Which one, sir? You keep mentioning . . .?"

Robinson looked hard and meaningfully at Morgan. "And who might we have been a-chasing of, as the colonists say, these past few months?"

Morgan gaped. "The Frenchman? After the gold hoard?"

Robinson nodded, his lips a tight line. "By God, I'd stake my life on it, Tom. That's her. I know that ship, all right; just the same as she looked in the Med!" He smiled humourlessly.

Morgan swung down with him over the futtock shrouds and down the shaking ratlines. "Beat to Quarters, sir?" he puffed, as they regained the quarterdeck.

Robinson leaned on the rail and looked inshore at the white

smudge of the corvette's sails against the green mass of the land. "No, Tom. We're going to shadow him for the present. Even if he's seen us, he'll have to tip his hand somehow, somewhere."

Robinson pursed his lips thoughtfully.

"And when he does", he said, almost to himself, "we'll go in and spring the trap!"

FIVE

In spite of himself Paul Gallant could not resist the sharp intake of breath as he stepped out from the tree line on a hill well to the northwest of Louisbourg. There lay the harbour, with the lighthouse on its northern arm and the rooftops and the twin spires of the town itself on the broad point of land of the southern arm, snug behind its walls. The morning fog was rolling like a grey comber back out to sea from the fortress, and the slate roofs and grey stone were gleaming like gunmetal in the morning sun.

"Careful, capitaine. Some hawk-eyed rosbif'll see you", muttered Béssac, crouching behind him in the shadow of a gnarled pine.

Gallant nodded and squatted down on his haunches, pulling a few twigs out of the buttonholes of his mud-spattered gaiters. He let himself delight slowly in a long view of the town, the pale and stretching walls, and the backdrop of the twinkling blue sea.

"Quite a sight, hein?" he said quietly.

For almost an hour Gallant used his glass to study the scene before him, slowly and methodically. He noted the activity around the harbour shores, the mix of shipping at anchor, the lighters and ship's boats plying into the jetties. Finally he was swinging his gaze to the town itself and the long, imposing line of the landward fortifications.

In the embrasures of the King's Bastion he could see the dark snouts of guns. And then in the next moment he caught the quick spark and twinkle of sunlight on a sentry's bayonet. Then on another, and another.

"Christ", he breathed. "The wall's alive with 'em!"

"Eh? What, capitaine?" said Béssac, rousing.

Gallant lowered his glass and got to his feet, staring down at the town. "The walls are under incredibly heavy guard, Béssac! Sentries every forty paces or so. From the Dauphin Gate, there, on the left. And on the King's and Queen's Bastions!"

"So?"

Gallant looked at him, his mind racing. "So it means they're expecting something, old friend. Or have they had a mutiny . . .?" He pursed his lips in thought.

"We'd better swim in", he said, unexpectedly.

Béssac's expression was incredulous. "Sweet Mary, protect me. He means it!"

"It's the only way, Béssac."

Béssac leaned on his musket and stared morosely down at the town. "How far?" he said, finally.

"That's the spirit!" Gallant laughed. He pointed a little eastward along the harbour. "There's the Royal Battery, hein? Right at harbour's edge. I think if we wait till nightfall we can work down from here to the shore, off its right-hand tower there. Tide's not heavy, and we can wade in the shallows on the sand flats. Follow them right round to under the Dauphin Gate."

"Then what?"

Gallant smiled. "That's the problem. There's a guard house just to the inside of the gate. Always manned. And there's usually a sentry out beyond the gate past the lift bridge. So if some rosbif hasn't put a ball into us at that point we've got to swim for it. Out into the harbour and round the angle of the Dauphin into the quayside face proper."

"I can see it all now", muttered Béssac. "What's that like?"

"Sheer face of planks over stone. Covered in slime and weed. No hand holds."

Béssac sagged visibly. "Mon Dieu, capitaine! And at night? And the water'll be like ice?"

Gallant looked back at the fortress. "We'll be aiming for something, though, my friend."

"And that is . . .?"

"The Apron Battery. Remember? The little battery that juts out like a tongue, maybe a score of pieds into the harbour right there? We used to have bronze three- and six-pounders in the embrasures. Christ knows what the English've put there."

Béssac had the look of a doomed man on his face. "Don't tell me the rest. We're meant to swim in under the embrasures and haul ourselves up and in."

Gallant silenced him with a sudden gesture, and pointed wordlessly off down the long stump-strewn slope.

Béssac squinted. Then he saw what Gallant was pointing at. The distant figures of men moving uphill toward them.

"Come on", whispered Gallant.

In a crouch the two men moved quickly back into the shadows of the tree line and slid in behind the dark branches of a massive pine.

"Do you think they saw us?" muttered Béssac.

Gallant shook his head. "No." He peered out through the pine boughs. "They're coming right this way, however. Looks like five, perhaps six men. Woodcutters. Axes and billhooks over their shoulders."

"Then . . .", began Béssac.

"Exactement. Back to the Wolf's camp until we come back tonight for our little dip." The marine slipped off into the gloom of the great trees.

An hour later the two men were descending into a secluded and cool glade that held, in a small clearing, several rough bark shelters and a smoky cookfire. And in front of the shelters the Wolf and his sons were stepping out to greet them with warmth.

"*Wenooch* returns!" boomed the Wolf. "You saw the walled village?"

Gallant nodded, setting down the butt of his musket. He was breathing heavily.

"*Aa*. It is as I remembered it", he said.

The Wolf smiled. "Except that now the *Inglunkawa* live in your lodges."

The Lynx extended a cup of water to Gallant. The marine drained it and handed it back with a nod of thanks.

"They do", he said, wiping his mouth with the back of his hand. "But that is of no consequence, Wolf. *Nabe'skw* and I will march back, at nightfall, and enter the town."

The Wolf and his sons exchanged sharp glances. As they did so Gallant caught a movement out of the corner of his eye, and turned.

"Mother of God, girl, what are you doing?" he burst out.

The Micmac girl had appeared from behind one of the rough trail shelters. She was bent almost double under the weight of an enormous load of firewood, held on her back by a broad woven tumpline across her forehead. As Gallant watched, aghast, the girl dumped the bundle beside the smoking fire and straightened, grinning in white-toothed pleasure at his expression.

"Sacristi, Wolf, she shouldn't be doing squaw work! Not this early! The fever . . .!"

The Wolf held up one hand in calm protest. "The girl is well, *Wenooch*. Did she not keep up on the march, these last two days? Did she not refuse the litter even on the first day we broke camp, but ride in it on the shoulders of you and *Nabe'skw* only because you demanded it?"

Gallant stared back at the girl, who was looking impishly back at him and then at her father. He had to admit that there was nothing of the invalid about her as she stood, a pink blush aglow under her tan cheeks, her eyes asparkle and full of amusement.

Béssac, who had taken his turn with a refilled drinking cup, shook his head at Gallant.

"Forget it, capitaine", he said. "She's just damned tough. Like all these sauvages."

"*Nabe'skw* is right, *Wenooch*", said the Wolf in an even voice, "even though he does not know I understand enough of your snake-tongue speech to know what he said!"

But then he smiled, teeth even and white in the strong face. "She is well. You should be glad your medicine worked, *Aaa?*"

Gallant sighed and leaned his musket against the small shelter that was his. "All right. Your daughter is your business."

96

The Wolf nodded. "Good! Now why do you and *Nabe'skw* not eat and rest? Then tell us what you plan to do."

Gallant and Béssac threw off their other gear and were grateful for the thick and tangy strips of venison that the girl brought to them in birchbark bowls; strips of rich meat over which she had scattered nuts and tiny, nugget-like strawberries. And with them she brought both men's tin cups, brimming with cool brook water.

Béssac grinned amiably at the girl as he took his food from her. "A feast, by God! And served by a cherub."

In Micmac fashion the girl was mute as she served the two men, who had hunkered down on the pine-needle carpet in the shadows to one side of the glade, upwind of the smoke drift from the fire. But as she knelt beside Gallant her eyes flashed briefly up at his, and she leaned forward just enough in her motions so that the soft curve of her breasts touched the marine's arm.

Gallant's eyes sought hers. "Thank you, *Wosowech*", he said quietly.

The girl's mouth moved into the slightest of smiles. In a beautiful and graceful motion she rose off her knees and padded away, the leather of her moccasins whispering on the pine needles.

The day wore on, and in the quiet and sundappled seclusion of the glade the men whiled away the hours working on tools or weapons, or dozing in the shadows of the rough lean-tos, ignoring the midges that hummed in clouds in the air round their faces when the wind sent the fire smoke another way.

Presently the Wolf settled into a crosslegged posture beside Gallant, who was honing the gleaming blade of his long sheath knife on a piece of hard leather.

The Micmac grunted. *"Ankaptaan!* It is time you told me, my friend, what it is you intend to do."

Gallant nodded. "All right." He used the knife to clear a bare patch of dirt before him, and he drew quickly with the point a sketch of Louisbourg harbour and the town behind its walls.

"My plan is this, Wolf. Tonight, at midnight, you will lead *Nabe'skw* and I back along that trail we followed today."

"That will be simple enough."

"Perhaps so. But at the harbour edge . . . here, where the two-walled place stands . . . *Nabe'skw* and I will wade along

97

the sea edge round to here, and swim to here, where there is a way into the walled village.''

The Wolf stared at the sketch. ''You do not lack for courage, *Wenooch*, if you would do this. But what will you do within the walls?''

Gallant smiled and sheathed the knife. ''That is my worry. I will hunt the man I told you of.''

The Wolf grunted. ''But you must then leave.''

''Yes. My ship will be waiting, back along the coast. Near where we first came upon your camp.''

''And how is it I and my sons will help, *Wenooch?*''

Gallant pointed to the little map. ''Be there in the tree line, Wolf. Watch all the gateways. Wait there for us for the next two days, day and night, and have our weapons and packs ready for us. And lead us away quickly!''

''Then you wish us there as of tomorrow's light?''

Gallant nodded.

''*Aa.* It is done. But after the two days . . .?''

Gallant's grin was sardonic. ''Go about your business, Wolf. It will mean we are prisoners, or are dead, neither of which you can do anything about.'' He shrugged. ''Get yourselves clear of the *Inglunkawa* and pray for the day when the *Wenooch* king once more rules that place.''

The Wolf was silent for a moment. ''I wish you anything but death, *Wenooch. Kespunekatae!* My legs tire easily now, and I am not the man I once was.'' He looked at Gallant. ''And my daughter, *Wenooch*. You have seen the way she looks at you?''

Gallant rubbed his brow and looked into the lengthening shadows the afternoon sun cast in the glade.

''I have been honourable with your daughter, Wolf . . . .''

''I know that.''

''And I am on a mission that may cause my death . . . .''

''I know that too.''

Gallant looked at the dark, patrician face. ''Then you must know for her sake that I must not 'see' how she looks at me.''

The Wolf's black eyes looked away. ''Such things as the fate of lovers, or would-be lovers, I leave in the hands of *Kesoo'lkw*. Whether you live or die is His whim.''

''Amen'', breathed Gallant.

''But know this, *Wenooch*. I would split the skull of almost any man who sought her, for she is worth more than ten ordinary men. But if she wishes your seed within her, and seeks to sleep by your cookfire, it is well with me.''

98

Gallant was unable to think of a reply, so unexpected had the Wolf's declaration been.

A bluejay screeched overhead, and at the sound the Wolf uncoiled effortlessly to his feet.

"Enough talk of women and love!" He strode off toward the edge of the glade. *"Najitkisume!* I'm going to bathe. Sweat in the hut of hot stones and then a plunge in the stream!" He stopped and looked back. "Come too, *Wenooch!"*

"Do you sleep?" said a small, soft voice.

Gallant sat up, startled, on the soft mossy bed where he had lain and looked at the wigwam's opening. A small figure was there, wrapped in furs and silhouetted against the last dying flickers of the cookfire. From the other shelters Gallant could hear the snores of the other men, and beyond them the cricket songs and the low hoot of an owl.

"No, *Wosowech*", he said, and felt a slight tingle run up his spine. He fumbled in the darkness for his breeches and wrestled them on. In the next minute he had moved to sit beside the girl, his eyes watching the firelight play over her face and the fur robe she had drawn close around her. She still wore a little pointed blue cap, and the flames were reflected in tiny mirror images in the beadwork round its edges.

Gallant looked from the girl up at the steady, unwinking splendour of the stars, bright between the looming dark shapes of the trees. He scarcely felt her head rest gently against his chest, and looked down in surprise to find she had drawn the robes closer about her and was snuggling against him like a child.

"I've . . . been watching to see the stars of the Great Bear move but one-quarter the way round the sky. Then I must wake the others."

"And then you will leave", said the girl, quietly.

"Yes."

"And will you die, hunting the *Wenooch* king's gold in the walled village?" she said in sudden directness.

Gallant looked down at the ebony river of hair that flowed from under the little cap nestled against his chest, and felt a strange bittersweetness rise in his chest.

"Perhaps, *Wosowech.* I pray not", he said, after a moment.

"I pray as well. I have prayed to *Kesoo'lkw* at every dawn to keep you . . . keep you well."

Gallant was silent for an instant. "You have?"

99

The girl nodded. "And now that I am close to you like this, I . . . I imagine you are *'nchenumoon,* my husband, and that there is no war and no *Wenooch* gold to take you away."

Gallant sat motionless, the realization of what the girl was saying slowly coming home to him.

"What is it you are thinking, *nigumaach?"* said the girl, turning to look up into his face. She had used the endearment of a woman for her chosen man, and new shivers moved up Gallant's spine.

"I . . . I think you pay me a great compliment, *Wosowech"*, he said. "I had no idea . . . ."

The girl snorted. *"Aagei!* I pay you no compliment, *Wenooch!* When a woman wants a man, she tells him!"

Gallant smiled at the fire in her eyes. "You are truly daughter of the Wolf", he said.

The girl looked back at the fire.

"Who is she?" she said.

"Who?" said Gallant, taken aback.

"The woman whose heart owns yours. The one I see in your eyes."

Gallant could not reply for a moment. "She is far from here, *Wosowech"*, he said quietly, after a moment. "In France".

"I must have her name."

"It is of no matter."

"Her name, *Wenooch!"*

Gallant stared into the fire, feeling the stir of long-repressed emotion within in.

"Abigail", he whispered finally. "Abigail Collier."

The girl was silent for a spell. Then she whispered, "Does she call you *kesalkoose?* Beloved?"

Gallant's voice was toneless. "At times."

"She was a fool to let you go."

"It was none of her—!"

The girl tossed her head. "It is in your eyes, your yearning for her. You can hide nothing in those eyes, *Wenooch."*

Gallant looked again at the long, shimmering hair, and how it fell in smooth midnight waves over the furs about her.

"And I can feel your eyes on me now, *kesalkoose!"*

The girl turned to face him, lifting on to her knees, the spark of the dying fire mirrored in her eyes. With a slight motion she shrugged the fur robe off her shoulders. It slipped, held for a moment on her breasts, and then settled in folds round her wide-set knees.

Gallant felt heat suddenly in his cheeks. The girl was naked.

She saw his eyes move uncontrollably down her, moving over the round, pink-nippled breasts and over the smooth muscles of her stomach, the small hollow of her navel. She smiled and arched her back as she knelt, stretching the tawny body in an exquisite motion of animal beauty.

"And is she this beautiful, your Abigail?" came her excited whisper.

It was as if a wall of repression and endurance had suddenly burst within Gallant; a wall he had built stone by stone. But now, without warning, the wall shattered under the smoking allure of the Micmac girl, and he felt a wave of need and heartache flood into his veins.

With a low growl in his throat he swept up the girl and lifted her in to the mossy softness of his bed. The blood drummed in his temples as he flung off his shirt and breeches.

The girl's arms were reaching up for him, her whisper soft and urgent in the darkness.

"Come, my *Wenooch!* Be a man, and fill me with joy! *Mowwuhsugawedaase!*"

Ah, Abigail! rang a silent cry through Gallant's heart. And then his arms closed in a steely embrace round the excited girl.

His Britannic Majesty's Ship *Salamander* rose and then hissed down into the flank of a black swell as she pushed through the predawn gloom off the Cape Breton coast. A thin band of pink light along the eastern horizon marked the divide between the low cloud scudding overhead and the inky, white-cap-flecked surface of the sea. Against this light the ship moved like a spectre.

Below in his cabin, the light of a single bulkhead candle flickering in its sconce over his desk, Lieutenant Anthony Robinson glanced again at the chart spread before him over his desk and then looked up to meet the attentive eyes of Thomas Morgan.

"We'll know now in moments, Tom. This last board should have brought us back to within half a league of the shore." Robinson jabbed a finger at the chart. "If he's there we know we have him!"

Morgan nodded. But the *Salamander's* first lieutenant sounded a good deal less assured than his commander when he replied. "Quite, sir. Provided the lay of that longshore current was as we thought it would be. Nonetheless, I . . ." he hesitated.

"What?"

"Damned if I know, sir", said Morgan, with tight lips. "Just a feeling. Premonition, if you like."

"You're worried about putting in after that corvette?"

"No. Yes. We may have her trapped well enough, sir. I'm not sure we'll get her."

"How so?" said Robinson, clamping on his hat and moving to the cabin door. He had learned to listen to Morgan whenever he voiced these feelings. Below the Celtic intuitiveness of the man there lurked a first-class seaman's mind.

Morgan buttoned closed his long seacoat.

"That coast bothers me, for one, sir", he said. "That Spaniard's Bay divides into two arms that go well inland. She's likely gone into a stoat hole hard up in one, if she's there at all, and going in to get her means getting close on a shore that, by God, is still hostile. We'll have no sea room. And to fight under those kind of terms, well . . . ." The Welshman did not finish.

Robinson paused at the door. "Your damned third eye's served us well in the past, Tom. But it's not worth tuppence of worry until we know if the bugger's in there, is it?"

Morgan stood with a troubled look on his face for a moment, and then followed Robinson along the passageway and up the companion to the upper deck.

Robinson's voice barked out as he ordered the reefs shook out of the topsails and the setting of the courses. As *Salamander* lifted to the increased spread of canvas, Morgan was musing that worrisomeness had been part of their days for some time now. *Salamander* had hovered far astern and off-shore of the French corvette, often hull-down to seaward, watching with infinite patience as the Frenchman had run on reduced sail slowly down the coast, always close inshore, sometimes inexplicably anchoring for several hours before moving on again, steadily reaching down the shore across the strong and steady westerlies. It had been as if the corvette had been waiting for something to occur, rather than seeking a specific goal.

At noon a day earlier a dancing, spray-rinsed little British cutter had caught *Salamander* on a long seaward tack and passed a dispatch bag before plunging on northward to find the cruisers off Newfoundland. The orders in the bag had not brightened Morgan's outlook when in the privacy of Robinson's cabin the latter had revealed their contents.

Command at Louisbourg had now become confused with the return of Vice-Admiral Isaac Townsend's squadron, and the peculiar arrangement of the governorship; Commodore Knowles was listed as governor, but for some purpose he was permitted to command at sea at the same time. That a naval panic of sorts was in force had been made evident in the orders with later dates of Admiral Martin, commanding the Western Squadron off France. The latter had failed to prevent the sailing of the enormous fleet of the duc d'Anville, which it was believed was making for Cape Breton and New England in a sweeping attack. The size of the fleet was such that it might easily brush aside Knowles and Townsend.

And in Louisbourg itself there was genuine and well-founded fear. Little had been done to repair the breaches in the walls, and Knowles had no more than a half-dozen guns mounted to landward. The garrison of four regiments, Fuller's, Warburton's, Shirley's and Pepperrell's, were recruited in the last two instances from New Englanders, who were proving almost impossible to recruit and worse to discipline.

Morgan pursed his lips and looked at the emerging dawn light. Eight to nine hundred men had perished in that grim garrison over the winter.

It was ironic. History seemed set to repeat itself within a year. But now, a weak and ill-prepared British garrison in Louisbourg awaited the assault of a powerful fleet. Providence would see if the results of this attack would follow those of 1745, although even more unsettling was the news that a six-thousand-man force of Canadian militia was marching on the fortress overland from Québec.

Morgan pulled his seacoat closer round him against the chill wind. But the most baffling problem remained the last intelligence from Townsend, which had reiterated to Robinson that the loss of several merchantmen along the Nova Scotian coast and at least one smaller warship was incontrovertably the work of—and here Morgan's eyebrows rose again as he recalled it—not only a single vessel, but possibly a small squadron of vessels engaged in piracy!

There was another chilling thought. *Salamander* was engaged in the hunt for a fabulous hoard of bullion, a hunt the details of which were known nowhere outside the Admiralty

Board Room. Had there been some ghastly breach of confidence and secrecy somewhere? Were the Brethren of the Coast being drawn to *Salamander's* and the French corvette's prey, like jackals to a lion's kill? It did not bear thinking on. *Salamander* could fight a good fight for her size, but against a number of ships handily sailed by ruthless corsairs . . . .

A pretty mess, thought Morgan. An enormous French fleet at sea. An army marching in from Canada. The Royal Navy stretched as usual to the bloody limit. The Louisbourg garrison rum-sodden and mutinous behind ill-prepared defences. And a band of cutthroats in the void between these two forces, plucking at the scraps the great struggle had thrown aside, and would throw aside again. A band of cutthroats perhaps waiting for *Salamander* to complete her task, and then pounce on her.

"God damn", said Morgan to himself, and spat with distaste over the lee rail. He turned and climbed the short ladder to *Salamander's* quarterdeck, making his way aft to the wheel.

From where he had been standing along the weather rail Robinson moved to join Morgan. He squinted at the compass card, looked aloft, and turned to the helmsman. "Watch your helm, there! Lay off a spoke or two the minute you see those luffs start to lift!"

"Beggin' yer pardon, zur", said the spreadlegged man, "Oi can't rightly make out the sails in this light."

"Then feel it, man!" said Robinson testily. "Let her tell you with the hull, when she lifts from her heel!"

"Zur", said the helmsman.

Robinson shook his head as he turned back to Morgan. "Bloody hands have to be watched like a hawk", he muttered.

Morgan grinned at his commander and pulled a broad brass watch from his coat pocket. In a few minutes he would need to make his rounds of the ship.

"The Vice-Admiral seems remarkably concerned with this question of increased piracy, sir. And particularly with the notion of a squadron of them about."

Robinson reached beneath his broad cloak to hitch up his breeches. "To be frank, Tom, he has some grounds to be."

"I can see why. Particularly our mission . . . ."

"Precisely. Piracy is always a nuisance. You know that as well as I. But sometimes it can take King's ships away from the King's business at just the wrong bloody time. That's the worry on Townsend's mind, and why he's set us to cruise for 'em as well as hunt our Frenchman there." He cleared his throat and spat manfully over the rail. "Damn me, it was barely a score of years ago that one bloody Brother of the Coast led the Navy a chase!"

"Not Long Ben Avery?"

Robinson grinned. "No. Although that whoreson had a rough enough career. No, this was a countryman of yours, Tom. Bartholomew Roberts. Took about four hundred ships in his career, if you'd believe, before he met his end. And a King's ship had to do it. Got the bugger off the Guinea coast."

"Who got him?"

"Chaloner Ogle, in the old *Swallow*. And it cost the devil of a sum in sterling and men, from what I heard of the tale. Last thing we'd like to have to do with a Froggy armada set to fall on our ears." He lowered his voice. "And if the buccaneers knew what we were after . . .?"

"That's come to my mind already, sir."

"Um." Robinson paced back along the weather side of the quarterdeck to squint up at the mizzen topsail, and then moved back to Morgan.

"Peculiar thing of it all, Tom, is that one hardly ever heard of the bastards cruising in these latitudes. They usually like warmer seas under their keels, and reefs and keys to duck about in."

Morgan nodded. "Most used to fancy New Providence, or am I wrong?"

"Dead right. Tortuga, the Bahamas, Green Key, The Cat . . . all of 'em. First buccaneer in there worth his salt was a rogue named Jennings, and the place's been aswarm with them since."

He scratched his chin. "We're past the really serious days of Atlantic piracy, Tom. Or so we've thought. For about thirty years there, say up to 1720, they were as thick as flies on the Main and off the Americas. The way I've heard it, it wasn't until Their Lordships established the West Indies squadron that anything could be done about 'em."

"Why was that?"

Robinson snorted. "Hell, Tom, there were just too many! In Queen Anne's War damn near everyone had privateers by the bagful at sea: us, the French, the Spanish, the Dutch—the lot. Probably outnumbered the poor bloody merchantmen at any one time. And when peace came, most of 'em just hauled down their colours and ran up the Black Jack. And went a-hunting." He pursed his lips. "And there was a hitch to anyone trying to run 'em down, too."

"Oh?"

"Aye. The bastards, half of 'em, were in league with the 'better sort' of people all up and down the Thirteen Colonies! Governors, assemblymen, damn near all those nose-in-the-air Williamsburg planters, were all on the take from 'em. The pirates bought safe anchorages and freedom to take aboard stores that way. Christ, as I hear it, they were welcomed in like conquering heroes, from Charleston to Boston!"

Morgan shook his head. "Didn't the Admiralty Prize Courts step in? Couldn't they bar the pirates from putting in? Surely . . . ."

Robinson laughed. "Tom, the Admiralty appointed commissioners for each colony as far back as forty years ago to deal with piracy, and the colonists out here just laughed at 'em. They weren't about to cut off a flow of gold and plunder for Whitehall's sake." He shook his head. "No. It took a Royal Navy squadron on station over here to put an end to the worst of it. Then, of course, the damned Yankees were all contrite and righteously opposed to piracy!"

He paused, and a thoughtful look crossed his features. "That might, by God, be a worry in the back of Townsend's mind, eh? Take a large invasion army of Yankees and set 'em to take and plunder a French port. Then add a clutch of pirates, maybe even a squadron of the bastards back in strength because of the damned war. Christ, if *I* were him I might be seeing shady connections in it all."

"Confusing, as you say, sir. There are enough unanswered questions about all this that I . . . well . . . ."

Robinson tapped the rail gently. "You've still got your premonition?"

Morgan smiled. "It may be of no account. But I do, yes."

"Well, Christ grant that you're wrong, Tom."

Robinson stood braced to windward of the wheel. Morgan had gone below to do his rounds of the ship, and from forward the ship's bell rang out, clear and sweet, in two strokes of two. Robinson looked over his shoulder, off *Salamander's* stern past the great ensign staff where the ensign snapped and whipped, past the stern lantern toward the eastern horizon, where a flattened orb was lifting blood-red above the gunmetal sea, the promise of a clear and brilliant day.

Now we'll see her, he thought. She'll be anchored well in, and this time we take her!

"Mr. Stoddard!" he roared. "Duck up the forecourse clewlines! I can't see a damned thing of that coast!"

There was a squeal of blocks forward, and the lower corners of the great quadrilateral of the foresail curled upward in rhythmic pulls, lifting the canvas until, by crouching, Robinson could see clearly the land on *Salamander's* bows.

Spot on, he thought to himself with some satisfaction.

Salamander's bows bore just to one side of the broad opening mouth of Spaniard's Bay, as Robinson had planned they would when he lay out the ship's course the evening before. He had no wish to anchor overtly anywhere off the coast, let alone within the broad bay they had seen the Frenchman enter. Determined to finish the chase now, he had planned for a rapid entry deep into the double-armed bay and as equally rapid a capture of the corvette, whether by gun action or boat parties, although he wanted to use his guns.

From the left side of the broad bay mouth a thin line of white surf snaked out into the darker water. There was a narrow spit of land, a few ledges of rock marked on Robinson's chart of the coast, and that likely was it. Doubtless that meant *Salamander's* distance off was closing rapidly. Robinson would have to alter course to move into the centre of the broad mouth of Spaniard's Bay, and skirt that sandspit. God knew what depth *Salamander* would have under her keel in there.

Morgan reappeared up the starboard waist ladder, a thoughtful look on his face.

"All well?"

The Welshman nodded. "Well enough, sir. Few too many rats about. Time to smoke her clean shortly, I should think."

"We're well into the line of the bay's headlands, Tom. We'll need to bear off more to the middle ground." Robinson was pointing forward.

"Aye, aye." Morgan was already moving to the waistdeck rail even as he spoke. "Mr. Stoddard! We shall wear ship, if you please! Sheets and braces!"

He turned back to Robinson. "Course, sir?"

Robinson peered at the swaying card. "West sou'west."

With an easy motion *Salamander* fell off her tack until she was broad on a reach, and the southerly wind was hard abeam. Now the trim warship was working into the bay deep enough so that from where Robinson and Morgan stood on the rolling quarterdeck the point of land that marked the division of the great bay into southerly and westerly arms was bearing dead ahead, and now but a half-league off.

"Wind's backing, sir", said Morgan.

"Aye. God, Tom, look at that damned coast!" said Robinson. "Trees, trees, nothing but trees!"

"Have to cut your way into it, all right." Morgan was looking over the side. "Sir, there may be ledges that the chart hasn't marked. Perhaps . . . ."

"Damned stupid of me. Of course. Leadsman to the chains, Tom." He looked at the rising sun, now casting a broad orange path across the sea to the ship. *Salamander* was beginning to feel the sheltering of the bay, and the swells were lessening as she moved in.

"Mr. Stoddard! The wind's backing!" called Robinson. "See to your sheets and braces!" He lowered his voice as he turned back to Morgan.

"Call the watch below, as well", he said. "Expect we'll likely clear for action the moment we get that damned sighting I want . . . ."

"Deck, there! Deck!" came the foretop lookout's cry.

"Speak of the devil", said Robinson, through his teeth. He cupped his hands. "Deck aye!"

The lookout's voice rang down, faint above the hum of the wind in *Salamander's* rigging. "Ship, sir! Well inshore, to larboard!"

"The south arm!" Robinson whispered, eyes kindling. He raised his voice again. "Under sail or at anchor?"

"Canvas is furled, sir! Like as if she's dropped 'er killick! She's hard in against th' shore, sir!"

Morgan was opening a broad-barrelled leatherbound telescope he had fetched from below at the lookout's first call, and handed it to Robinson. The lieutenant threw off his cloak and raised the long glass shoreward.

It took only a moment to locate. "By God. There she is, Tom. All stopped and furled, and anchored or even moored, by the look of her! Not even her colours showing." He handed the glass to Morgan. "Have a look."

Morgan hefted up the telescope, which was fully a yard in length.

"She's damned well into the upper reach, sir. Narrow channel, there, if any. What does the chart show of it?"

"Bloody little. Winds in, turns as it narrows. Has a river emptying into it at the head. Is she that far in?"

Morgan handed back the glass. "I fear so. By the way the shore angles down it looks as if she's well in past manoeuvering room, sir."

Robinson bit his lip. What in damnation had the corvette done overnight? The twin arms of the bay had undulations enough to have allowed her to anchor almost out of sight from seaward, without hauling up into the bottleneck she apparently was in. What kind of game was the ship playing?

"Right, then. We'll go in as far as we can. Try for gun range. If we have to we can use sweeps, a kedge or even the damned boats. If we can fetch her out of there a prize, well and good." He narrowed his eyes. "Otherwise we'll have to burn or sink her there."

"Why not anchor out in the roads and send in the boats, sir? Where, after all, can she go?"

Robinson considered for a moment. "Perhaps. I want gun action, I'm afraid. Keep the leadsman's chant clear and loud. We'll see how far we can or should get in there."

He pushed the telescope shut and handed it back to the Welshman. "Clear for action, if you please, Tom. And then beat to Quarters."

As the British vessel glided into the calmer waters of the bay it would have appeared to an observer a silent picture of function and beauty, passing in quiet splendour; all grey arcs of canvas, lacy network of rigging, and the sleek and ducklike hull. And there would have been no outward evidence at first of the burst of activity that Robinson's last order had produced.

Salamander's decks rang with the hum of activity and work, and above it Robinson raised his voice, calling forward to where Morgan stood just aft the foremast timber-bits.

"Bar shot, if you please, Mr. Morgan! Or chain shot, if we have it!"

"Aye, aye, sir!"

Ten minutes later a silence of sorts had returned to the ship, but now it was a watchful one, with all attention turned to the next command that might issue from the pacing figure on the quarterdeck. The ship had become a weapon, and his was the finger on the trigger.

Morgan regained the quarterdeck, buckling on a hanger and waistbelt. He handed Robinson a similar one.

"You'll be needing this."

Robinson grinned. "Aye, Tom. I'd forgotten. Thank you." He buckled the sword on quickly. "Our state?"

"Cleared for action, sir. Guns loaded and run out, most with bar shot. The people are at Quarters."

The lieutenant nodded. He glanced off over the bows at the nearing shores of the southerly arm of the bay. The French vessel's small hull shape was clearly visible now, a blue and mustard flash against the dark green forest wall.

Robinson cleared his throat. "Larboard a point. Another. Steer sou'west by south. Mr. Stoddard! Sheets and braces, if you please!"

Salamander forged on into the narrowing bay, and at Robinson's side Morgan had the heavy telescope out again, and was squinting forward through it.

The Welshman spoke slowly, reciting what crossed his circular little field of vision. "Hawser off her bows . . . line astern as well . . . moored, then . . . God, bloody well inshore, mark you . . . gunports closed . . . all furled and stopped." He snapped shut the telescope. "That's odd", he said.

"Um?" said Robinson.

"The Frenchman. There's not a man moving on her, on deck or aloft. Not one. And she's battened down tight as a Plymouth dowager. With one exception."

"Which is?"

Morgan pushed his hat forward over his eyes and leaned on the rail, his eyes narrowed thoughtfully. "Got her damage net rigged. Now, why in Christ's name would she do that?"

Robinson scratched his chin. "Damaged gear aloft?"

"No. Can't think why the fellow's left it rigged." Morgan's face was pensive. "I don't like the looks of this one bit."

Robinson's smile was quick. "I know. Your damned premonitions." He looked inshore. "The bay's narrowing fast. Leadsman's been chanting at six fathoms, and it'll go less in a minute."

He pointed at the corvette. "She's too far in for safety, we agree. Very well, I propose the following. And see if this settles your wary mind, eh?" he said, grinning at his friend. "We'll clew up fast enough to lose way no closer than, shall we say, two cables off her. That's good range for a good long gunshot. Anchor, but stay with the cable up and down while I send over a strong well-armed boat party. That's if a round or two from the fo 'c 'sle guns do nothing. What could be more cautious, and still get the bugger?"

Twenty minutes later *Salamander's* sails were clewed up to their yards and she rode to a single anchor cable, hove short, in the now greatly narrowed arm, both dark and wooded shores scarcely more than a good musket shot away. Ahead, so far in under the loom of the great trees that it seemed impossible she was not hard aground, the silent and still shape of the corvette lay to her mooring, the white, tapering rolls of her furled sails on their yards stark against the green backdrop. The wind had died, and now only cat's-paw breezes sent dark ruffles over the otherwise still surface of the arm.

On *Salamander's* quarterdeck Robinson looked for a last time at the eerily quiet shore, that lacked even the call of a bird. Virtually every man in *Salamander* was doing the same thing, by instinct lowering their voices to hushed whispers. The silence was unnerving.

Enough of this, by God! thought Robinson.

"Mr. Morgan! Fire as you please!" he bellowed.

Forward on the fo'c'sle Morgan's sword gleamed in the sun and the voice of one of the ship's two bowchaser gun captains barked in command. A pink spurt of flame huffed up from the vent of the nine-pound gun, and it fired with a ringing bang in the next half-second, the report echoing and re-echoing round the shore of the arm. A gout of heavy smoke punched out and spread over the ship's bows toward the water. Through it Robinson saw the usual patter of wadding fragments sprinkle across the water, and then with an audible slap and hiss the round shot punched into the water scant inches from the French corvette's side, a towering plume of water jetting up as high as the foretop yard, to collapse in a rain of spray.

From the tops of the close-packed trees on the starboard shore an enormous flock of crows rose into the air, their raucous and protesting caws filling the air, and wheeled in a flapping black cloud inland.

Robinson watched the corvette with hawk eyes as the smoke dispersed. There was not a flicker of movement.

"Again, Mr. Morgan, if you please!"

The gun thumped again, and on this occasion a bursting halo of fragments leaped from the midships rail of the corvette, splashing into the water alongside. The braces and lifts of the French ship quivered visibly at the impact. But no other movement was forthcoming.

"God damn me! Not a move!" said Robinson. He nodded after a moment's pause. "Lay aft, Mr. Morgan! I'll have the boat's crew away! Marines and ten others, under arms!"

Several minutes later *Salamander's* longboat was riding under the battens at the ship's side, and the first of the marines was clambering down into it.

Morgan rejoined Robinson on the quarterdeck. "I'll be taking the party over, sir?"

"Be damned, Tom. D'ye think I've no interest in seeing what the devil is going on? We'll both go!" His voice raised to a bellow. "Mr. Stoddard! Mr. Morgan and I will go in the boat! You'll cover us with the chasers! Mr. Hawkins will be the officer in command and I expect you to see that naught goes amiss, sir!"

He slid his slim hanger from his scabbard and tested the ply of the blade.

"All right, Tom", he said briskly, "let's see what game Johnny Crapaud over there is playing!"

The boat pulled away from *Salamander's* side across the calm water of the arm, the marines clustered along the centreline of the thwarts holding the muskets of the seamen who manned the oars.

Robinson turned in his seat. Behind them *Salamander* rode to her cable, the line of run-out gun muzzles and her clewed up canvas giving her a smart and deadly look. He looked now at either shore, where deep shadows beneath the trees were even more evident from this angle. And there was still no sound, still no movement from the corvette or shore, save those sounds made by his own men. He shivered.

Beside him in the sternsheets Morgan cleared his throat and pointed at the corvette with his chin. The French vessel was looming ahead rapidly.

"Starboard side, bos'n", said the Welshman quietly. "Dead under the battens. And we need not rush in so fast."

The rhythm of the oars slowed. The boat glided in under the high curve of the French ship's counter, and Robinson could feel his heart pounding in his chest. Perhaps the ship was empty, left for some odd reason, and it would merely be a matter of putting a prize crew into her. No shooting, no casualties. He looked up at the gallery windows, now directly overhead. If someone leaned out of those windows with a full-packed musketoon, however . . . .

"Way enough! Boat your oars!" Allan's voice was a sand-paper whisper.

Rapidly the seamen took a single long last stroke and then heaved the long, dripping oars inboard, to thump them down across the thwarts in the middle of the boat, forcing the already cramped marines to sit on wet wood or crouch in a squat beside the thwarts.

Then in the next instant the boat bumped and scraped along the corvette's splintery wale, and ahead the bowman was reaching with his hook for the foremast chain plates, just forward of the chesstree. They were there.

Heart racing, Robinson rose, eyes still riveted on the rail above. God, what a trap they could be moving into! But, then, what an easy prize as well.

"Right. Follow me!" he whispered hoarsely. "Mr. Morgan, take your people for'rard if the waist is clear. My people will move aft with me!"

He sprang for the battens, wrestling for a moment with the cumbersome hanger, and finally scaling up the side with the little sword clutched pirate-fashion in his teeth. He swung over the rail and dropped to the deck in a ready crouch, eyes wide, ready. He looked quickly round. The deck was empty.

Now, behind him, the men of the boarding party led by Morgan were pouring over the rail and fanning out behind the two officers, muskets held at the ready, their eyes watchful.

"Where the bleedin' 'ell is they?" muttered the sergeant of marines, in the silence, fingers twitching on the shaft of his halberd.

Robinson nodded to Morgan, licking his lips. "All right. Take your lads for'rard, Tom! I'll move aft!" He threw a quick glance over his shoulder back at the reassuring shape of *Salamander*, suddenly very far away.

Robinson hefted his hanger. "We'll get below and see if they've left any . . . ."

"Aaaiieeee! Now, me buckos! At 'em!"

The banshee shriek rang out from the maintop of the corvette, and Robinson looked up to see a dull-painted canvas cover thrown back and a wild, bearded face below a bandana thrust out over the top. The man suddenly pushed forward a huge, bell-mouthed musketoon that roared out with a belch of flame and a thunderous report at the knot of men standing below.

There was an impact beside Robinson, and a seaman screamed and clawed at his face, which had suddenly disintegrated into a red pulp, and collapsed writhing to the deck. Even as the report of the musketoon was still echoing in the air a marine threw up his musket and fired, and with a gurgling cry the bearded man in the top jerked forward over the edge and fell with a sickening crunch to the deck.

"Cover!" roared Robinson. "Fore and aft! Off this open deck! Quickly, lads, or . . . !"

The hatches of the corvette were flung back and a savage-looking mob of wildly-clad men spilled out, weapons gleaming in their hands, and almost immediately they sent a thunderous roar of musket and musketoon fire point-blank into *Salamander's* men, the sputter of pistols amongst it.

There were screams loud in Robinson's ears, and curses of frustration. Several of the British seamen fell kicking in agony.

A blind rage rose in Robinson, and he gathered himself for a rush, only to be suddenly pinned by the heavy body of a man which slumped across his feet.

"The net! The net!" Robinson heard Morgan's wild cry ring in his ears.

Robinson kicked away the dead marine and looked up through the swirling smoke, ears ringing with the tumult. He had a momentary glimpse of the broad mesh pattern of tarred rope rushing at his face before the great net crushed down, its weight driving him to the deck with a painful jar in both knees.

A dreadful sense of what had happened screamed in his brain and with savage force he fought to rise. All around him he could see and feel *Salamander's* men struggling and cursing, the screams of wounded ringing out here and there as, with horrible glee, the defenders of the corvette danced round the struggling mass of men under the net, firing into the tangled heaps or thrusting their cutlasses in. Then there was a bark from somewhere aft in the ship, and the mob fell back, leaving the British seamen wrestling with the impossible weight of the net, their footing missed on the blood-slick deck beneath them.

But then, in the next instant, the air was rent with the thunderclap of a ship's broadside, and Robinson fought to his feet, clutching at the net binding his head and shoulders, and staring out over the corvette rail, aghast.

"Oh, my God!" he breathed.

A rippling wave of cannon smoke billowed seemingly out of the very trees in the shoreline off which *Salamander* rode, a billow joined by licking tongues of flame and gouts of smoke from the opposite shore. Bracketed in the cannonade, the ship vanished in a forest of leaping geysers, and then with an audible crack *Salamander's* main topgallant mast shattered at the trestle trees and toppled forward in horrid slow motion.

114

"Dear Christ!" Robinson heard Morgan's groan from somewhere under the net nearby. He, too, could see.

The trees along the water edge from where the gunnery had come were moving, unbelievably, incredibly, moving. Like great doors, two enormous floating booms of rafted log clusters, atop which full-size trees were braced and lashed, were starting to swing open. Anchored at one end, they were being pulled open by teams of longboats, manned by straining figures of oarsmen tiny beside the huge booms. The green masses of floating trees were moving aside as if they were scenery flats in an elaborate stage production.

Then Robinson gasped, as the hidden side of the booms came into view. To *Salamander's* starboard side the swinging boom slowly revealed the looming dark hulk of a powerful-looking warship, with ease a thirty-two gun frigate or larger. The hull had English lines, but in place of the reassuring tan, black and white hull paint the vessel had been masked in an ominous black wash that made it look huge against the shore, its equally black masts and yards blending against the spires of the evergreens. From its ensign staff a broad black banner emblazoned with some form of white symbol lolled, and even as Robinson stared, his hands clutched in helpless fury in the pressing weight of the net, the black ship's side exploded in another furious broadside at *Salamander*. Now detonations sounded again from the opposite shore, and Robinson could see that the swinging boom on that side had revealed two smaller ships, more the size of the hapless *Salamander*. They, too, were black-hulled, their gunports licking flame as they blasted round after round out at Robinson's ship. *Salamander* was hidden now in leaping geysers, and the foretop and main course yards canted at crazy angles.

Morgan's voice rose again. "D'ye hear me, sir? She's struck! *Salamander's* struck!"

Robinson stared at his ship in agony. Her hull still bracketed by leaping shot splashes, her masts and yards quivering from impact after impact from the point-blank broadsiding, the little ship was taking a terrible pounding. Robinson imagined what a hell her decks would be. He sank down beneath the net. A bitter darkness clouded his heart.

There was the sound of heels on the wooden deck, and in front of Robinson, where he sat bent under the net, a pair of gleaming black boots had stopped. With infinite difficulty

Robinson strained against the weight of the rope and looked up.

"Well, sir. Be you capting o' this mob?" said the figure.

Robinson stared for a moment. He was looking at a tall, nightmarish shape. A man well over six feet, clad in red, with wild, matted hair and a black beard. The man stood with his boots spread wide, hands on hips, an animal amusement at the pain of the quarry showing in the burning eyes.

"Well, ain't ye no tongue?" said the creature. "Be you capting?" He reached out with one toe and prodded Robinson in the ribs roughly.

"None of your damned business, you bastard", muttered Robinson.

In the next instant he gasped in pain as the glossy boot drove into his ribs, and he folded on the deck under the net, clutching his side. Stars spun in front of his eyes.

The glossy boots squeaked as the man squatted.

"You be polite-like to Ben Spooner, sir, and ye'll not have to have me boots in yer ribs", said the man in a smooth low tone. "But if ye choose not to act the gen'l'man, why then by rights I'll take me boots to ye. Or cut out yer tongue, if ye choose not to use it."

Robinson gasped for breath. "You're no damned Frenchman! Who the blazes . . .?"

The man calling himself Spooner stared at him and then cackled. "Frog? Me? Why, bless me, sir, I'm a good Englishman same's as you, aye?" He rose to his feet and called out to the hovering mob.

"D'ye hear, lads? The King's man thinks we're Frenchies! Lord knows how he might come to think that!"

There was a burst of hoots and raucous laughter from the mob, in which Spooner joined. And then he was squatting in front of Robinson again, the cold muzzle of one of his pistols pressed through the mesh into Robinson's neck.

"Now, you tells me who you be, quick-like", he said in a cold and menacing tone, "or me pistol 'ere cuts a hole big as me thumb in yer jugular. And then me lads stick their carvers into all those nicely trussed up lads o' yours. *Now who be ye?*" The pistol ground into Robinson's neck.

"His Britannic Majesty's Ship *Salamander*. I am Lieutenant Anthony Robinson, in command of her. In search of French vessels such as this, with whom we are at war!" Robinson spat. "And what sort of damned Englishman are you if you have to ask that?"

The beard split in a serpent's smile. "Oh, I be English born, sir, and English bred, but we take no allegiance to good King Ge-arge, bless 'im, nor no other king, Froggy or otherwise. That yonder is my ship, the *Pearl*, sir, and ye'll not find a better ship among the Brethren!"

Robinson turned cold. Of course. "Pirates!"

Spooner's face sobered. "Aye. Pirates it be. And glad to have a King's ship for the pickin's, if ye'll pardon the liberty, sir."

Robinson pursed his lips. "Where is the French crew of this ship? What have you done with them?"

"Why, they be in irons, says I. Ben Spooner's clamped them in irons, and right below these decks, sir. They weren't a struggle neither to fox, just like you and your lads, here." Spooner smiled. "We'll enjoy pressing that smart little ship o' yours into our squadron, sir, 'tis certain we will. And this little Frenchie here as well."

Robinson's blood chilled. "And what will you do with us? And the Frenchmen?"

Spooner's eyes glittered like a snake's.

"Why, sir, we knows, don't we, what happens to one o' us poor Brethren when a King's ship catches us, eh? It be not a proper fate for a poor Christian lad, be it, and the King's men all squared away to do justice and not receivin' o' a bit o' the charity of Providence."

"You can't mean you'll . . .!"

Spooner smiled. "Oh, yes, sir. I can mean it very well."

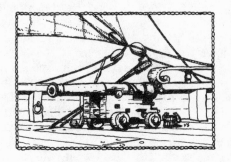

SIX

The night wind off the sea was bitter and penetrating, carrying with it the drifting wetness of the fog. There was no moon now, four hours after midnight, and had there been no cloak of fog the night would have been inky black enough. But with it the two men who stood shivering in the enveloping sodden shroud might well have been at the bottom of a mine pit.

"Sacristi, capitaine!" said Béssac, his teeth chattering. "This is going to b-be terrible! How in God's name do you expect us to s-strip down and . . . !"

At his elbow Paul Gallant's voice hissed a warning, and Béssac felt the marine's strong hand grip his arm.

"Quiet, Béssac! For God's sake remember we're just barely a pistol shot away from the West Tower! And the Bostonnais are sure to have sentries up there!"

"Hah! That's what you say. How in hell you think you know where you are is more than I can fathom!"

Gallant's grip was like a steel claw. "Trust me, damn it! The Wolf brought us out smack above the barachois. We followed a path down I knew as a boy."

The two men were standing on the narrow and uneven slope of a stony beach, and a few feet from their toes the gentle swells of the harbour water lapped at the rocks. They were a short distance to the fortress side of the harbour shore from the hulking masonry of the Royal Battery.

Neither Gallant nor Béssac carried his heavy musket. Instead Béssac's belt held the heavy dragoon pistol, and Gallant carried nothing but his long sheath knife. Each man carried a large squarish birchbark basket. The products of *Wosowech's* hands, they were bound with sinew and tarred watertight. Gallant changed his grip on his.

"Nothing moving", he said. "We can start working along the shore."

"How far?"

"Far as we can. I don't relish the swim any more than you. But we might have a long one."

"Why?"

Gallant's voice was quiet and matter-of-fact. "I've miscalculated a hair. Tide's in. There'll be no sand flats along to the barachois, just short rocky beach."

Their dampened shoes noiseless on the uneven rocks, the two men began making the ankle-twisting trek along the edge of harbour shore, following the stony beach as it curved toward the barachois at the end of the harbour, and then angled out as one side of the great promontory on which the fortress stood. It was treacherous footing, and within twenty minutes of their start Béssac was once again feeling a trickle of sweat between his shoulder blades.

Suddenly Gallant stopped and crouched, and before he could stop himself Béssac almost sprawled headlong over his commander's back.

The mate crunched to his knees. "What in the name of . . .!" he began, in a hoarse whisper.

Gallant's hiss cut him short. "Quiet, Béssac! Get down!"

Gallant's whisper was right at Béssac's ear. "A patrol sentry!" he said, barely speaking at all. "Heard him talk to another one. They must have some kind of perimeter watch set up. Wait a minute."

The two men lay motionless for what seemed an eternity, until finally the faint sounds faded entirely.

Gallant rose to his feet in a catlike silence. "Close enough!" he whispered. "The man's likely gone on his beat; he'll be back in a few minutes, I'll warrant!"

"Does that mean . . .?"

"The way's blocked?" Gallant was silent for an instant. "Likely. They must have some kind of advanced picket out here. To keep people out. Or in."

Béssac touched the butt of the pistol for reassurance. "What now, then?"

Unexpectedly Gallant dropped his basket and threw his hat into it. Now he was ripping off his coat.

"Come on, Béssac! Now! Strip down!"

A few minutes later both men were naked, the baskets holding their clothes and weapons. With an audible intake of air Gallant picked up his and stepped precariously out over the painfully hard stones toward the water. As the first wavelet washed icily over his feet his teeth chattered involuntarily.

Behind him Béssac swore luridly. For all that it was mid-summer the harbour water was glacial.

"Oh, C-Christ!" moaned the mate. With a sound like a wounded animal he suddenly sloshed forward several steps and then sprawled forward into the water. A moment later he broke the surface, his mouth twisted into a rictus as he gasped out a staggering obscenity. The water flashed white as he flailed out, grasping at his floating basket.

Gallant could not hold back the snigger that rose in his own throat, and then made himself topple forward. The water was so cold, so inconceivably cold that for a moment it felt as if he was being scalded from head to toe. He threshed out wildly for several seconds, all control momentarily gone.

"See what I meant?" gasped Béssac.

Gallant willed his knotted and flailing muscles back under control and clutched at his basket. He let the thing support his weight and kicked out with his feet, frog-fashion.

Beside him Béssac began a rhythmic threshing. He tried not to think what might be lurking in the black harbour depths below his naked vitals, and kicked strongly out. The two men made slow headway through the black wavelets, the fog still a dark mass all about them save for the faint loom of light that had shown off to the right, in the direction of the fortress.

Béssac's sudden, sharp curse startled Gallant. He threshed round in the water to see the mate's dim form loomed over by a dark, shadowy shape. A shadow against which Béssac's basket and then his own bumped and rubbed.

120

Gallant reached out, treading water with weakening strength. His fingers touched rough, overlapped boat planking, then scrabbled up to a splintery gunwale, where they found two thole pins. He clutched at them.

"A skiff! Sweet Mary!" he croaked.

Beside him Béssac grunted in disbelief until his own hands found the small boat's side.

"You . . . get in this side, Béssac!" Gallant puffed. "I'll get round to the other . . . keep from overturning it . . . ."

Sobbing with effort, now, Gallant thrashed around the boat's transom to the other side. The boat rocked and thumped as Béssac began to haul himself aboard. With enormous effort Gallant lifted and tumbled his basket over the gunwale, treading water furiously, and then hauled himself painfully in over the rough, hard wood.

He lay panting on the floorboards, half held up by a thwart. In the shadows of the bow Béssac lay wheezing, his white skin pale and ghostly in the gloom.

"That was a near thing, capitaine", said Béssac, after a moment. "A few more minutes in that water . . . ." He shivered and did not finish.

There was a returning strength in the mate's voice as he looked round the boat, feeling forward over the bows. "Capitaine, this thing's tied onto something. It's not adrift. The painter runs off forward and up somewhere."

Gallant, on the stern thwart, looked up. The bright patch of the fog was moving overhead now, and in a minute they might be able to see where they were.

"Can you see anything?" Gallant said, feeling round him under the thwarts of the boat.

"No. It's too dark. I . . . Mother of God!"

Béssac's shocked tone snapped Gallant's head up. And in the same instant he saw what the mate had seen.

"Sweet Savior. A ship!"

Béssac's face swung toward him, a pale spectre in the swirling fog tendrils.

"Damn me, capitaine, it's a man o' war! We're tied on to the lizard on her quarterboom!"

Gallant stared up. A huge dark hull had materialized out of the fog; a hulking wall, the quarter and high sweeping stern of a British line-of-battle ship. From the ensign staff, twenty-five feet above Gallant's head, an enormous British ensign lolled, lit faintly by the orange light of the ship's great stern latern.

Béssac darted his head around, scanning along the ship's rail forward into the fog. "The deck watch!" he hissed. "They'll have to see us!"

Gallant glanced at the skiff's midships thwart to reassure himself that the small craft's oars were there. He drew his sheath knife, reversed it, and poised it in the palm of his hand.

"Catch, Béssac!" he whispered. "And for God's sake don't drop it!"

"The painter?"

"Yes!" The knife flicked through the air and slapped into Béssac's outstretched palm.

Gallant licked his lips and watched the rail above in unbearable suspense as Béssac hunched out over the stem. The little craft rocked with the mate's effort as he sawed at the strong fibres.

Then he was slumping back, spitting in satisfaction. "We're free!" The knife flashed again in the air, into Gallant's waiting hand.

The marine sheathed the knife and glanced up again. The huge ship's side was receding slowly but perceptibly, as the small currents of the harbour took hold of the skiff. Slowly the ship fell astern.

Béssac leaned forward. "Capitaine, when that fog lifted for a moment I caught sight of more ships!

"You're sure of that?"

"Yes! But where did they come from? There wasn't a night-soil barge in here earlier today!"

"Damn me, Béssac. It's a squadron! Has to be. Likely the squadron the English have stationed here. They must've put in during the afternoon or evening."

He pointed to the oars. "You row, or shall I?"

Béssac grunted and clambered aft to the midships thwart, where he wrestled the oars into their tholes and sat, ready to pull.

"You mind telling me where?"

Gallant pulled his hat down over his eyes. "Back to those ships."

"What? You're crazy. We wouldn't get ten feet through 'em, capitaine, if this fog raises a hair!"

Gallant leaned forward. "Come on, old friend, use your head. If we strike out in any direction God alone knows where we'll end up! I don't have a glimmer where we are. We could end up smack out to sea through the channel!"

"So . . .?"

"So we get back in amongst that rosbif squadron, hein? They're probably anchored in the roads just off the quayside face. We row about like some kind of odd ship's duty boat till we see an English ship's boat pulling in. The rosbifs'll have a lot of hands ashore after the rum and women, and boats will be plying in to fetch them."

"And we follow one in?"

Béssac spat on his hands, shifted his grip on the looms, and took a deep stroke.

"One thing, capitaine. What if we're hailed?"

Gallant listened to the slap and gurgle of the water against the little boat, and the creak-clump of Béssac's oars.

"We bluff it. Or act drunk. I imagine you can do that."

The boats Gallant planned on proved difficult to locate, once the two men had moved back in among the anchored British hulls. The fog was now at masthead height, although the town could still not be seen. Hunched down on their thwarts, their hats pulled well down over their eyes, Gallant and Béssac pulled slowly about in a random pattern between the towering ships, ears tingling in anticipation of a hostile hail from one of the pacing deckwatchmen, and the bark of a musket or swivel that would mean the game was at an end.

Then Béssac was pointing over Gallant's shoulder.

"There", he said in a low voice. "Ship's boat. Six men and . . . looks like an officer in the sternsheets."

Gallant did not turn in his seat. "Heading in?"

"Must be. None of them are drunk."

The marine spat over the side. "Right. Follow them."

Almost leisurely Béssac held water with his oars and spun the little skiff until its bows bore on the English boat, which was pulling strongly past a forty-gun ship. The ship's deck was well-lit with lanterns.

One ship at least is in a watchful state, thought Gallant.

As it came into Gallant's view he saw that the English boat was going to pass close along the ship's starboard side, and likely would be hailed.

Damn. And so would they be, if they followed.

"Pull after him, Béssac. Quickly, before he's gone in the gloom! And for God's sake don't say anything in the next few minutes unless I ask you!"

Gallant peered ahead. Sure enough, the boat was close aboard the big vessel. And now there was movement high above on the forty-gunner's deck, and a lantern was raised high.

"Boat ahoy!" The hail from the ship carried strong and clear across the water. The answer from the boat came as clearly.

"Hinchinbrook!"

That's luck, thought Gallant. We're following a confounded ship's captain!

The stern gallery of the forty-gunner loomed above them now, tendrils of fog wisping eerily about it. The windows of the great cabin were rosy with candle glow. As the splash of Béssac's oars began to echo from the undercurve of the ship's counter Gallant heard murmurs from the weatherdeck, and saw a head beside a lantern peer over at them.

"Boat ahoy!" boomed a voice overhead.

Gallant forced his mind to recall the English voices he had become familiar with during an imprisonment at Port Mahon, in Minorca, long before. He shaped his lips around the English sounds.

"Aye, aye!" he growled. It signified the boat carried an officer, but not a ship's captain.

But the interrogation did not end there.

"What ship, eh?" the insolent voice from above was broad with dialect.

Gallant filled his lungs. "Mind your own damned business!" he barked, in the accents of a well-born Englishman.

There was a brief scuffle overhead, a slap, an oath, and then a different head appeared over the rail. A new voice rang down.

"Pay no mind to the likes o' him, yer honour. 'Ee don't know 'is manners."

Béssac stroked on, and the skiff bobbed along under the black hanging flukes of the ship's starboard main anchor.

After a few minutes Gallant let out his breath and swung round to look astern at the receding anchor lights.

"Thank the Virgin for that!" he breathed.

"Can you see anything of the shore?" said the mate, after a moment.

Gallant shook his head. "No. Just the boat lantern. Nothi . . . Wait! It's blowing away, Béssac! The fog! Look, you can see the whole quayside. And we're dead off the Frederick Gate!" Gallant was referring to the great arched gateway that stood guarding the entrance onto the jetties from the waterfront street of Louisbourg.

Béssac let the oars drag and turned round to gape. Like a curtain going up the fog had lifted to reveal the panorama of the harbour town. The roofs and grey stone of the buildings were masked by the dark, but across the water to the skiff rivulets of light suddenly danced from the brightly glowing windows and flung-open doorways of a score of buildings.

Over the water there came an alehouse clink and tumult, snatches of song ringing from flung-open doorways. Figures were visible silhouetted against the light, along the quayside and round the great gate, moving and staggering in the shadows.

"My Jesus, capitaine!" gasped Béssac. "The whole damned town is *drunk!* So much for your religious fanatics!"

Gallant laughed without mirth. "That's the Bostonnais, Béssac. The ones who aren't holier than God Himself live like the devil instead." He stared. "Look at them. We'll have no trouble slipping through that mob."

Béssac swivelled back. "You mean we . . .?"

Several minutes later the few seamen who lay in the floorboards of the many ship's boats that clustered at the principal jetty stirred. Their boats were jostled by the bumping, flailing arrival of another small skiff, crewed by two men in a queer mix of seaman's and woodsman's clothing. The boat guards cocked an inquisitive eye as the two men stumbled and groped their way across the rafted boats to the jetty.

The two men giggled and spat, and were humming little tunes as they finally fell more than stepped the few feet up to the jetty planking. Here they rose weavingly to their feet and stood propped against one another comically.

The older man weaved upright, and, propelled by the leaning weight of the younger, began to totter up the jetty toward the Frederick Gate. The boat guards relaxed and cursed the ill luck of the draw that kept them away from the rum. They turned away and soon forgot about two more drunken seamen.

Gallant's eyes flicked this way and that, keen as a hawk's under his hat as they reached the high wooden archway of the gate. The picket barricade gaped wide, and no sentry challenged the two men as they reeled through in their theatrical drunkenness.

"Christ, Béssac!" Gallant whispered. "Wide open, and not a man stopped us! By God, old Morpain'd have shot someone for that!"

There was a sudden flurry of violent action in the shadows of the gate off to the left, and two men's voices raised, snarling in English curses. In the next instant Béssac and Gallant side-stepped a pair of soldiers, hatless, their coats wide, who fought and fell with a thump on the quayside, their fingers locked in silent, ghastly struggle about each other's throat. The two men rolled over and over on the rough ground, each man as he came uppermost kicking and kneeing his opponent unmercifully.

"Allons, vite, Béssac!" Gallant seized the mate's arm and in the next instant was propelling him in a stumbling run across the open quayside to the corner of the first block of town buildings.

They slumped against the rough stone, below a swinging tavern sign. From a doorway a few feet along the building several soldiers, the brick-red breeches and coats lit by the lantern glow from within, stepped out, drawn by the fight's noise.

Gallant's voice hissed Béssac's ear. "The old Hôtel de la Marine! It's crawling with rosbif soldiers! Come on!"

Gallant leading, they dodged to the other side of the street and began running up it, following its slope up and away from the quay area. Béssac could see Gallant's gaiters flashing ahead of him and he followed them blindly up, watching as each split-second flash of light from the windows they passed outlined the marine's form. They pushed and twisted past bodies in the dark, bodies that turned and swore at them inventively. Once, Béssac had to stretch to step over the sprawled form of a moaning man, the air about him reeking with stale rum and vomit. The ruts in the street were muddy, and more than once both men slithered off balance and almost fell as they slapped along through the muck.

Béssac looked up. On either side the sharp peaks and gables of the one and two-story buildings were becoming outlined against the grey-black night. The sky was visibly lightening.

Gallant stopped in the next instant, and Béssac drew up panting at his shoulder.

"Dawn, soon", breathed the marine. "Got to get off the street before then."

There was a bark of orders ahead in the gloom, and Gallant could see a lantern, swinging fast and low as if carried by a running man.

"Town watch!" he said. "Back against the wall! The drunken act again!"

A moment later a small squad of soldiers, their bayonets

fixed and held at the ready, doubled past. As they swung by, squelching through the stinking offal in mid-street, they paid no notice to the two slumping shapes that lolled at the corner.

"Which way?"

Gallant looked quickly up and down the narrow streets, his voice low as more dark shapes appeared out of doorways nearby.

"Morin's cabane is on Rue de Scatarie. Number eighty-three, I think. That'd be at the end, well over to seaward."

Keeping to the more shadowy side of the street, the two men ran on, passing building after building, shuttered door after window as they worked back into the town from the quayside area. Now, as they ran, the streets were almost deserted, and the low houses and sheds dark and silent.

At one corner Gallant paused and stared round him in the gathering grey predawn light.

Béssac puffed up. "What's wrong?"

"Look at these houses, Béssac. It's uncanny."

"What?"

"No marks of war, hein? No shot holes, no burnings. As if the French were all off somewhere, to be back tomorrow. No real trace of the English."

Béssac spat in exasperation. "Damn it, capitaine, the rosbifs probably repaired the damage. But they'll do us a lot if we don't keep moving!"

Ten paces down the street Gallant came abreast of a narrow lane, dark with shadow. In that shadow there was a scuffle of movement, and then a voice barked out.

"At 'im, Zeke! Get 'is purse!"

A hulking form in a long seacoat and uncocked hat lunged out and collided with Gallant. The stench of rum and tobacco filled his nostrils, and powerful arms clenched round his neck. He felt a boot strike at his legs, looking for a hooking throw.

"Oh, so?" boomed Béssac, and before Gallant could react to the attack he felt the impact of the mate's weight against his body and that of his attacker. All three men slammed against a building wall, and suddenly the thug's vice-like grip was gone from Gallant's neck. There was a crunching sound as Béssac flung the man bodily off, hard against the wall on the opposite side of the street.

Gallant regained his balance and drew the sheath knife, hefting it lightly in his hand. Béssac moved in beside him, feet wide, ready.

The man against the wall spat and wiped his mouth with his sleeve.

"A couple o' real bucko lads, here, Billy. Come out' n' help me crash 'em both!" he snarled.

"Thieves, for God's sake!" muttered Gallant.

The shadow in the alley materialized into a broad, stocky figure with a wild thatch of hair, swinging a short and ugly-looking club. It joined the man at the wall.

"Cosh 'em, Billy!" said the long seacoat, and without warning he flung himself forward at Gallant.

This time the marine was ready. He spread his feet wide as the man rushed in, and then when the thug's grip was almost on his throat he ducked low and drove his shoulder hard forward into the man's belly. The man grunted with the impact, hurt, and pounded hamlike fists on Gallant's back. Gallant straightened with a jerk, and his head banged the Englishman's jaw shut with an audible pop.

"Fall, you bastard!" swore Gallant, and he drove his heavy shoe hard into the man's groin. With a horrid noise in his throat the man dropped to his knees and fell forward into the street muck, beginning to retch.

A snarl sounded at Gallant's left and he spun to see Béssac locked in a wrestler's grapple with the second man. The two rolled back and forth in the muddy ruts, growling like dogs. Then, suddenly, there was a pink flash between the bodies and the ear-splitting report of Béssac's dragoon pistol. Béssac's opponent shrieked in brief agony and then sprawled out in the mud, legs twitching.

Gallant grabbed the mate's arm. "Run, Béssac! This way!"

The mate needed no further prod. He leaped over the corpse and in the next instant was matching Gallant's wild sprint down the dark street. Shouts were sounding behind them now.

"Christ, they'll get us! Those damned footpads . . .!" Béssac stopped as Gallant unexpectedly ducked into a low doorway in the front of a long-walled small house.

"This is it!" cried the marine. "It's Morin's! In, and quickly!"

Gallant shouldered against the door, and it crashed open, a glow of firelight spilling from the room into the street. Gallant pulled the mate in by bodily force and slammed the door shut. They pressed to the wall on either side of the door, and with a start Gallant realized he still had his knife clenched in his fist, the knuckles now raw and bloody.

Their breath coming in great heaves, the two men listened as the sound of running feet and shouts rose outside the door, pounded past, and then gradually faded.

"Sweet Mary, I thank you!" breathed Béssac.

Gallant and Béssac turned their eyes to the room in which they stood. It was bare and simple, of whitewashed plaster long gone grey and stained, with a rough-sawn plank floor that was littered and dirty. The beamed ceiling was low and uneven and shadows played across it from a wide, pot-strewn fireplace in which a smoky fire in need of tending hissed and popped.

There was a ramshackle armoire to one side, and in the middle of the room a table stood, with two plain chairs. In one of them a slim, dark man lay with his head and arms on the table, apparently asleep. He was dressed like a gentleman, with carefully rolled and queued hair, and a broad-cuffed russet coat over breeches and waistcoat of the same colour. His white hose was silken, and the small, tapered-heel buckled shoes he wore had been lacquered in russet to match his clothes. An overturned wine glass lay beyond his outstretched, ring-laden fingers, the wine a long, running stain — like blood — across the table. At the noise of the two men's entry the man had stirred slightly. Now he was once again snoring.

Gallant wrinkled his nose, as the heavy air of the room hit him full force.

"Faugh!" said Béssac. "What a perfume!"

Gallant snorted. "Needs a bucket of burning sulphur, all right." He listened for an instant at the door. "I think we're all right."

Béssac nodded, eyes bright in the flicker of the fire. "All the same, I'm reloading this cannon." He fumbled in one pocket for a lead ball, which he clenched in his teeth as he pulled a small brass flask from his other pocket. With quick, expert movements he charged the pan and barrel of the heavy pistol, and then spat in the ball and rammed it home.

The pistol slid again into his belt, and Béssac slapped it with satisfaction. "All right, capitaine", he said. "Ready for anything."

There was a clump of movement overhead, and then feet paced across the ceiling and down a stairwell hidden round a third corner of the room.

The two men exchanged a quick glance. Gallant changed his grip on his long knife and padded across the floor noiselessly, to press against the wall just behind the stairwell corner.

Béssac crouched behind the slumped man in the chair and eased the great pistol from his belt.

The footsteps came to the bottom of the narrow stairs, light-sounding and hesitant. Then they stopped.

"Nicolas?" said a husky, woman's voice. "Nick? Come on, lovey, ain't you laid on the spirits enough for one ni . . . ."

Gallant sprang like a cat. He was behind the woman, one hand clamped like steel over her mouth, pulling her back into an arch against him. The other hand held the knife across her throat. The blade gleamed in the firelight.

"Not a sound, madame", hissed Gallant, in English. "Not a sound, or I'll bleed you like a lamb!"

The woman froze, her large, china-blue eyes wide with fright.

"I'll release you, now, if you'll be quiet. Scream, and I'll kill you. Do you follow?" said Gallant, in a chillingly cool matter-of-fact tone.

The woman nodded. Her head was a mass of tousled blond curls under a mobcap, and they shook as she moved.

Gallant released his grip and lowered the knife, and the woman cowered back against the nearest wall, her breath coming in pants. Her face was petulantly attractive, but heavy with white powder and grotesque clown-rouge on her cheeks. A small heart-shaped velvet patch of black was fixed at one corner of her mouth. She wore a flounced and caped boudoir gown of blue, and it was carelessly fastened at the bodice, so that both men could see virtually all of her round and powder-whitened breasts. Another black star patch rode in the deep valley between them.

"What d'ye want? Who in hell are ye? Footpads? Ye'll find nary a quid in 'ere! An' if it's a blanket 'ornpipe you be after, try somewhere else! None o'me girls is in!"

Béssac winced and threw a glance at Gallant, finding the expression on the marine's face he had expected. The woman's voice was coarse and grating, its uncouth accents destroying whatever animal and lustful attractiveness she might have had.

Gallant pointed the knife at the sleeping figure at the table. "Is that Nicolas Morin?"

The woman raised her chin, the fear in her eyes lessening a shade. "Belike. And what if 'tis?"

"We have business with him, madame."

"The likes o' what?"

130

"It is not your concern", said Gallant, evenly. "I ask you again. Is that Morin? You called him Nicolas."

The woman looked from one to the other. " 'E ain't owin' you no bad debts, eh? You . . . you ain't 'ere to stick 'im, 'cause he owes you? That ain't it?"

Gallant looked steadily at the woman. "I mean him no harm. Nor you." Under the steely gaze of the tall, dark marine the woman flushed and dropped her eyes, hands moving to close her bodice.

"You are not his wife?" said Gallant, unnecessarily. There was no menace in his tone, and the woman sensed it immediately. She left off attempting to close the gown.

'Im 'n' me? Nah! He's no sort for a husband for poor Nancy, 'ere! Look at 'im. A bloody Cap'n Queerlegs he is. Not the sort o' man a girl me'd take to wed. Puts on a gennulman's airs, all o' the time!"

"Can you rouse him?"

She snorted. "Dead out for th' night, he'd be. But I can try." She smoothed the gown over her hips.

"You're Frenchies, too, ain't you", she said. It was more of a statement than a question.

Gallant and Béssac exchanged a quick glance.

"Yes", said Gallant. "Madame, time is very short. I must talk with Morin, for his sake and ours. Yours, too, if he is something to you. Then we'll be gone, and trouble you no further."

The woman put her hands on her hips, a tough and business-like stance that seemed more in character. "All right", she said, briskly. "Only one way to do it. And he'll bruise me for it certain in th' morning, the darlin'."

She went into the back room of the cabin and reappeared after a moment clutching a large brass pot full of water.

"Wakey, wakey, love!" she said, and emptied the contents of the pot over Morin's head.

The effect was stunning. Morin shot up from the table in a jerking reflex action that sent the chair flying behind him. He was tall and lean, only a hand or so below six feet in height. He pawed at his face, lips snarling in incoherent curses.

"Nancy! God dam' you for an insolent rosbif whore! You'll pay for dis! Ah, Merde!"

Morin kicked aside the table, hooded eyes blazing, and rose to move at the cowering woman. Then he froze as he saw Béssac and Gallant, and the heavy gleaming pistol in the former's belt, the grim, hunted looks of both men. His eyes widened in momentary shock, and then narrowed again, guardedly suspicious.

"What is de meaning of dis? Who are you?" he hissed, drawing himself up to his full height. One hand stole toward his waistcoat, where Gallant could see a suspicious bulge.

"Please, m'sieu' ", said Gallant, in French. "I am Lieutenant Paul Gallant, commanding His Most Christian Majesty's corvette *Echo*. This is my Second, M'sieu' Béssac. You need not reach for that weapon." He stepped forward.

"You are Nicolas Morin?"

"And if I am?"

"You were and are an agent for His Excellency the Minister of Marine, and the duc d'Anville?"

"An absurdity."

". . . responsible for reports of interest to the King and the Minister having to do with ships, cargoes, seamen's loose tongues, and the like?"

"In a few moments, I shall call the Town Watch . . . ."

". . . and lately entrusted with the knowledge of what has happened to a certain vessel, a Spanish one, and her cargo of bullion, which included a figurine of some value, entitled the Señora?"

Morin's cheek twitched imperceptibly. He stared at Gallant and then lowered himself slowly into his chair.

"Who sent you?" he said.

"We are emissaries of the duc d'Anville, Morin. Sent to find you. And to learn what has happened to the bullion and the Señora."

"To do what?"

Gallant smiled. "And return it . . . them . . . to the King, of course."

"And how am I to believe you are who you say you are?" Morin said, at length.

"Merely my word."

"I see", said Morin, with a small smile. "Very well. I am Nicolas Morin. And I should remind you I am living at peace here, messieurs, as an honest clerk and entrepreneur."

"In a brothel?" said Béssac, half under his breath.

Morin's eyes flashed. "The circumstances of my life are not your . . .!"

Gallant raised a calming hand. "Please, m'sieu'! We are not here to compromise you. Once we can learn what we need we shall leave, as quickly as we came." He paused. "His Excellency made it quite clear the dangerous circumstances by which you . . . ah . . . continue to serve His Most Christian Majesty."

The basilisk features hardened. "You have no conception of the danger! But no matter." After a moment he said, "Very well. What is it you must know? Aside from the obvious questions, of course. You realize the danger you put this entire operation in by coming here?"

"I know, m'sieu'. I know. But please bear with me." Gallant tapped his knife blade on the table. "You knew of ship movements inbound to Louisbourg a few weeks before last year's siege, did you not?"

"I did. Those I had warning of, from agents in the Boston colonies, or farther down."

"And what of Spanish ships? The *Santa Maria de la Vela*, for instance?"

Morin paused in the tracing of a finger in the wine stain. Behind his motionless features Gallant caught no hint of the man's thoughts.

Then abruptly Morin leaned forward. "It is wrecked, Lieutenant", he said. "The *Santa Maria* is a wreck. In Baie Mohone, I have been informed. In any event that is where the stripped hull was beached."

"*Beached?*" Béssac and Gallant exchanged a meaningful glance.

"Just that. She was stripped elsewhere and then run ashore, to suggest a wreck. It is a customary ruse of people like the boucaniers, if they have no wish to be traced or suspected."

Pirates, thought Gallant. But then that had always been a possibility.

"What of her track toward Cape Breton?" he said.

Morin smiled. "I know a good deal concerning that."

"And that means precisely what?" Gallant found he was beginning to feel an annoyance at the man's smooth manner, and his neck was beginning to tingle.

"You will understand, Lieutenant, that what I am about to show you is something of the utmost secrecy?"

"Of course", said Gallant.

Morin rose and went to the brassbound chest. Fishing a small key from his waistcoat he opened its lock and rummaged inside as he crouched beside it. Finally he brought to the surface a large, leatherbound ledger.

"It is all here", he said, quietly. "All! Sailing orders, secret rendezvous of French vessels running English blockades, ruses, schemes, inbound convoy routings of the Compagnie des Indes ships. Kept since the Bostonnais took this place, and incorporating the movements of their shipping as far as I could learn! The motions and cargoes of every ship bound in or out of this fog-sodden hellhole!"

He put it down on the table and sat down. "And more. Information I had to pay hard coin, a great deal of it, for. Pirate activity, Lieutenant! Even privateers' hauls! And most important for you. . . ."

Gallant jerked up. "The burial or hiding places of illegal plunder, such as . . .!"

". . . such as the cargo of the *Santa Maria!*" finished Morin, with a smirk of satisfaction. "Of course! Information furnished to me at enormous risk. Information the collecting of which requires that I live discreetly" . . . and here he looked about the dingy room . . . "and under the disguise of a certain dissoluteness."

Gallant's lips were dry. "You know the value of that cargo, Morin? Its importance to the King?"

Morin spread his hands. "You're joking. But of course I do! How I've racked my brains to find a way to get this information to France! But now, with your fortuitous visit . . . ."

"Then you understand the urgency of my mission", said Gallant. "I must . . . ."

". . . find and recover it. Of course." Morin's eyes glistened. "I shall help all I can, of course. As is my duty."

Again the peculiar tingle touched Gallant's neck. He pressed on. "Your . . . account book. Does it give any details of the *Santa Maria* hoard's location?"

Morin shrugged. "Regrettably little. I have much more precise data on a hundred other burials and caches. But of her? All I could learn was that the bullion and the rest are still there, in Baie Mohone."

Gallant swore. "Damned little use that is. The place is infested with islands. We've just come from there!"

"There might be another source . . ." said Morin, after a moment.

"Yes?"

"A . . . contact of mine. An informant. Confidentially, a top man, I'm told, of one of the Yankee pirate vessels involved, and a man who knows where they hid it all. I was to meet him.''

Gallant bit a lip. "When?''

Morin pulled out a silver watch from his waistcoat and squinted at it in the flickering firelight. "Oddly enough, in a half-hour from now. In the King's properties, by the artillery shed. I'm paying him a ruinous sum on His Majesty's behalf.'' He spread the slim hands. "It's possible I could get him to reveal more. Even bring him here.''

Gallant nodded, after a quick glance at Béssac. "All right. Keep the appointment. And try and get him back here. We must learn what we can as soon as possible, Morin.''

"Please, Lieutenant. Am I not a servant of the King as well?'' Morin's smile broadened, and again Gallant felt the odd tingle at the back of his neck.

"Indeed. Béssac and I will stay out of sight here, then.''

"Good'', said Morin. "It should take but a few moments.'' He rose and locked away the ledger in the chest, and then scooped up the cloak and an elegantly cocked hat which had lain beneath it.

He paused at the door. "I should be back in two turns o' the glass, as you seamen say. In the interim'', he said smoothly, with a meaningful flick of his eyes toward the kitchen, "do enjoy Nancy's hospitality. She is quite an experienced hostess, you'll find!'' And in the next instant the door latched shut behind him as he stepped out into the grey dawn light.

After a moment Béssac spoke. "Christ, capitaine. Do you think that was wise? Letting him slip out like that? I don't trust his looks an inch!''

Gallant's lips were a tight line. "You're not alone there, mon vieux'', he whispered. "Quickly! See if you can spring that lock!''

In an instant Béssac was crouched in effort by the heavy chest. After a moment or two there was a loud 'click' and Gallant was grinning at him as he lifted the brass-studded lid. "There's no lock you can't put a little pressure to, capitaine!'' he whispered. "Not for an old wharf rat like me!''

"Quick! Give me the ledger!'' Gallant took it from Béssac's outstretched hands and scanned quickly round the room.

Then he saw it. A corner of the beams supporting the flooring of the floor above, lifted and warped a little by damp and settling. Stretching himself from atop the chair, Gallant wedged the ledger in until it was well out of sight.

"There!" he said, dropping noiselessly off the chair. "A card in our deck, should M'sieu' Morin have other games he wishes to play!"

"Sacristi, capitaine, don't you trust anyone? Not even gentlemen like Morin?" said Béssac.

Gallant merely grinned back. He moved to the door and opened it slightly, peering through the crack at the street. The dawn light was beginning to touch the rooftops of the buildings along the street as the fog lifted away. Gallant could see no one moving. He eased the door shut quietly.

"Check on what our well-endowed hostess is doing back there, mon vieux. There might be a rear door," he said.

Béssac was back in less than a minute.

"She's there. Muttering over the other fireplace back there. And there's no other door."

Gallant pursed his lips. "All right. You take a first watch at the door, here. First sign of Morin, or anything odd, give a yelp, hein? If we get a squad of rosbifs in here . . . ." He did not finish.

Béssac settled the pistol in his belt and took Gallant's place at the door. "I can imagine. A little different than slugging it out with footpads."

There was a scuff of feet behind them, and the woman reappeared, her face flushed from the heat of the fire.

She blew a wisp of hair away from her eyes. "There's naught but lobscouse, if ye've a mind t' that. An' ye can have a piggin or two of Nick's brandy."

Gallant nodded. "That'll do fine."

With a long look at him the woman went back into the kitchen, and there was a rattling of tin and pewter.

Gallant loosened the sheath knife. "I'm going upstairs for a quick look, Béssac. There might be another way out from there. And we might need it."

Béssac grinned. "Mind some leftover trollop doesn't get you."

With an answering grin on his face Gallant moved to the narrow stairs and padded up them silently to the second floor.

The cabane's simple roof frame of rough beams was close overhead as Gallant emerged from the stairwell. He had to duck his head as he glanced round, and he smiled in spite of himself. The small, low space had been roughly divided by plank partitioning into three smaller cubicles and one larger space, with the latter having the dubious benefit of a small and grit-smeared window. Gallant peered in a cubicle, and saw that it held nothing save a candle sconce, a stool, and a rough plank bed with a straw and ticking mattress. A single coarse blanket lay crumpled across it.

He ducked under another beam into the largest corner, that with the window. The light from it made a blue shaft through the shadows of the room. A braided, circular rug covered part of the splintery planking, and there was a sea chest to one side of a spool-posted bed.

And is this where she entertains? he thought.

He looked up into the shadows of the beams. No trap door exit there. He moved to the window, and found it was a one piece frame, nailed in place. Out through the bubbled and wavy glass he could see the grey shingle of the next roof along.

We could go through that in a pinch, thought Gallant. A trifle messy, but possible.

There was the sound of feet behind him on the stairs.

"Have a look at this window, Béssac. Think you could squeeze through that, if we kicked it out?"

The voice that answered was a good deal softer than the mate's, and Gallant spun in surprise to see the woman standing at the partition.

"I'd hate t' lose that windah, love. Nick's naught but a ruffler, but 'e bought that hisself, for me." She walked slowly in past Gallant to peer out the window, and as she passed her hip brushed against him.

"Oh, don't worry 'bout your friend, if that's what ye be thinkin'. 'E's a trencherman, eh, by the look of 'im, an' I gave 'im a portion that'll keep 'im at table for some minutes."

Gallant's neck tingled with danger. Béssac should not have left the watch at the door. He kept a calm voice as he replied, "Ah. Then I could use some, as well." He made to go.

"Wait!" The woman had moved to him and put out a hand, to stop him.

"Well?" Gallant's face was impassive, but alarm bells were beginning to sound in his head.

The woman laughed, and a kind of warmth seemed to light her face under the white masklike paint. "Coo, will ye look at me! Tryin' t' make conversation with a gennulman! Me! As if I ain't known 'alf enough men!" She gave a creditable impersonation of a demure young girl, smiling and biting her lower lip teasingly while lowering her eyes and then looking up suddenly through her eyelashes at the tall marine.

Gallant raised an eyebrow, his ear cocked for sounds from below. "Indeed", he said.

The woman pressed on, sitting on the bed and beginning to smooth the cover idly with her hand as she talked. The boudoir gown's bodice, if tied a few moments ago, was once again loosened. She caught the direction of his glance and leaned forward, slightly arching her back as she talked.

"Seein' the likes of gennulmen like you n' your friend makes a lady think about her life, if y'know what my meanin' is. How nice it is t' meet people o' quality, like."

Gallant was all too aware of his unshaven and grubby appearance, the mud-spattered breeches and gaiters.

"About that lobscouse, Madame. . . ."

"Nancy. Me name's Nancy, eh?"

The marine shook his head. "Relax and save your compliments, Nancy. And get downstairs. Now!" Gallant put his hand on the hilt of his knife.

"But yew don't understand, love! I got a business to run 'ere, an' the only sort o' man I be able to turn to 'as been the likes o' Nick!"

The woman swung up to kneel on the bed, heedless of the slipping robe, and put out her hand again on Gallant's arm. The china-blue eyes were wide and appealing. "Bein' near a man like yew . . . a lad who'd do proper for 'is Poll . . . it's what makes a girl thinkin', 'bout how nice it'd be t'ave just a little o' that . . . for a moment, mind . . . ."

Gallant pulled his arm away. "Damnation, woman, if you press me, you'll suffer for it! Now, in sweet Christ's name get off that bed and . . .!"

The woman rose off the bed and tugged hard at the remaining ties of the gown, and shrugged it off. Her body gleamed whitely in the half-light of the room, broad and full curved like that of a sturdy farm girl. She rose on tiptoe and twisted her body slightly, so that Gallant would see the silhouette of her large, upthrust breasts against the window light.

"For God's sake!" breathed Gallant.

"Come on, love!" she hissed, hands challengingly on hips, her chin lifted as she looked him boldly in the eye. "What kind o' man are ye? A baby? A geldin', eh? Come ride a good 'un!" She ran her hands down her body, her eyes hot. "Come on! Do me!"

Gallant's face flamed, and an unbidden response to her ready animal call stirred in his vitals. And then he was remembering the hooded eyes of Morin, and the crumpled blanket in the cubicle, and the smell, always the smell, crowding in, sickening him.

With a voice like steel he pointed to the door. "Cover yourself, Madam. Now. And get down and fix . . . ."

The floor shook with two sharp impacts beneath Gallant's feet, and he heard the door below open with a splintering crash. There was a rush of sudden shouts and snarls, and then in the next instant Béssac's big pistol boomed, a shriek of pain with the echo of the sound. There was another crash, and the sounds of desperate struggle.

"Béssac!" Gallant sprang for the stairs. But not before he saw the look of crowing triumph in the woman's eyes.

You clever, scheming bitch, he thought wildly.

Gallant bounded down the stairwell, knife ready in his right hand. He landed in a crouch at the foot of the stairs, only to freeze there.

"Make one move, mongsewer, an' it'll be yer last!"

The gleaming point of an English infantry bayonet was poised inches from his chest, its possessor a broad, flush-faced soldier in the red clothing and buff leather of the garrison soldiery.

Gallant looked around, wide-eyed, taking it all in in one sweep. The door, smashed at the hinges and hanging crazily open. The table, split and in pieces against the wall. Béssac's plate of stew, slopped on the dirty floor. Five other motionless English soldiers, long Brown Bess muskets in their hands, the bayonet points gleaming. Béssac, sitting in the middle of the floor beside the sprawled body of another soldier. The mate's temple was red with blood, and his hands were to his forehead.

And leaning against the doorway, his face beaming in a smirk of triumph, Morin.

Captain William Gandon Henry, commanding the duty battalion company of Fuller's Regiment, and at that moment the rather harassed Officer of the Guard for all of occupied Louisbourg, pushed his chair back from the low desk. The despicable state of discipline among the New England regiments and the general hubbub in the town caused by the rumours of French invasion fleets made the duty of Guard Officer difficult at best.

Today it was beginning on a particularly bad note.

He opened his mouth to speak, but then paused until the hobnailed crash of a company doubling past outside the door died away.

"Come, come, Lieutenant. If indeed that is what you are", he said finally. "Do you really think I can accept your explanations as genuine?"

He rose from the chair and moved to stand beside the desk, the buttons on his full coatskirts brushing its edge. The coat was brick red, with cuffs and other facings of faded yellow.

Henry folded his arms and sat on the edge of the desk, regarding Paul Gallant with the expression of a man who has a difficult and tedious workload ahead and does not really care to have a complication added to it.

Gallant was sitting with his hat in his hands in a small ladderback chair in the middle of the room. The room was lit by a glare of light from the tall window to one side, and Gallant recognized it on entering as the former bureau of Louisbourg's French governor. Now it held little but the desk of this hard-eyed Englishman, whose pale glance was boring into the marine in annoyed suspicion. A small fire sputtered in the blackened fireplace behind Henry, and at the door an impassive sentry, a man of Henry's own company, cradled his long musket.

Gallant sighed and looked away at the window.

"You have my story, Captain. I can add nothing more."

Henry pursed his lips. "I see", he said, after a moment's thoughtful study of his own glossy shoe-tips. "You are a French merchant captain, ashore here merely in the hopes of ascertaining if your former property has been confiscated or destroyed. Warehouses and the like."

"Yes."

"And your companion. Your 'mate'. The rustic with the unfortunate pistol. He is one of your employees."

"Yes."

Henry paused. "And you know nothing nor are involved in the efforts of a French fleet under M'sieur d'Anville to retake this place."

"No. Not a bit."

Henry returned to his chair.

"I believe you're lying, of course", he said.

"That is your privilege."

"Indeed." Henry smiled slightly. "Most certainly I think you are lying as to your profession."

"A life at sea, Captain, is all . . . ."

Henry did not let him finish. "Oh, come, Gallant! I'm not a fool! Need I detail it for you?" He flicked his eyes coolly down Gallant. "A naval infantry waistcoat, or I'm damned. An officer's gaiters. Military shoes. Military cocked hat. The shoes, I might add, with a remnant of a creditable job of heelballing. A queue a sergeant-major would approve of."

He smiled. "Need I go on?"

Gallant returned the smile. Henry was a competent professional soldier, if appearances were anything, and the marine could not help himself warming to a worthy enemy. "I cannot stop you from being misled by my odds and ends of clothing, Captain."

"Ah, but am I misled, Gallant? That is your name, by the way, is it not? As Morin claims?"

Gallant was silent.

"No matter", said Henry, with a shrug. "Morin told us all he knew, of course." A look of distaste came over his ruddy features. "What a loathsome creature he is. Do you want your fate to hang merely on the word of a creature like that?"

"I agree he is loathsome."

Henry leaned forward suddenly. "All the more reason, Gallant, to take this matter up between ourselves. For God's sake, you're a gentleman, or my father was a dog! Between us, tell me what you were about! You can then give your parole, have the freedom of the town, and be exchanged in as soon a time as I can arrange . . .!" Henry's expression had become that of an equal pleading to another.

Gallant recognized the compliment and smiled again. "You are an honourable man, Captain Henry. His Britannic Majesty is well served by you. But I have said all I may say. All that duty allows me to say."

Henry's shoulders sank perceptibly.

"You will not relent?"

"No, Captain."

"Then you give me no choice, sir. To my infinite sorrow."

Henry reached for paper and pen, and wrote a brief paragraph, which he signed with a flourish, sanded, and lay in front of him.

"Sergeant Jackman!" he roared.

The chamber door banged open, and the sergeant that had arrested Gallant stepped in and slapped his hand to the front cock of his hat in salute. "Sir!"

Henry indicated Gallant coldly. "This man and the other

141

are French spies, Sergeant. They are to be secured in irons in the archway cells at once. See that they get a meal. A good one."

"Sir."

Henry's eyes bored into Gallant's. "You will select six of your best musketmen from the Guard, Jackman, and at six o'clock tomorrow morning you will take the prisoners to the musketry ground before Black Rock."

Gallant heard Henry's last words echoing in his ears as if out of a vast cave.

"There you will shoot them. They are to be buried with courtesy, outside the Queen's Bastion." He looked away at the rain on the window. "That's all, Sergeant. Take this man out of here."

" 'Sir!' " barked Jackman. He clamped an iron hand on Gallant's shoulder. "Come along, yew!"

Gallant rose on wooden legs, feeling oddly empty of emotion. And then in the next moment the chamber door had banged shut, and the sergeant and his squad were marching Gallant along the uneven, rain-glistened pavé toward the archway and the cells. The terreplein was crowded with shuffling companies of soldiery, slopping through the muck and drizzle, the drill commands echoing off the walls and ramparts and mingling with the hiss of the rain. Gallant closed his eyes and felt the rain mist against his face, felt it seep down into his neck, felt it run down his cheeks in place of the tears he hoped would not spring there of their own accord.

The cells' door was swinging open, now, the shadows dark and looming. Béssac's face, white and concerned, was rising out of them. Then both men were roughly pushed into a sitting position on the sloping planks of the rack bed, and the cold grip of the leg irons was clinking shut round their ankles. And then in the next minute the squad was gone, the hobnail crunch swallowed by the rain's hiss.

For several moments neither man spoke. The grey light of the lowering sky, filtering into the cell through the lone barred window, threw shadows on Béssac's face, outlining the fatigue lines, the deep circles under his eyes. The mate was hunched up, hugging his knees, staring at the cold black iron rings that gripped his ankles, joined by a crossbar.

"Well?" said Béssac, after a moment.

Gallant stirred. His tongue felt as if it were made of wood.

"I told them we were merchantmen. In to check out old warehouses."

"I can imagine what they thought of that", grunted Béssac.

Gallant smiled. "Of course. Morin had told them everything he knew, anyway. Damned little, but they believed him. They're contemptuous of him."

"Who wouldn't be! The damned opportunist . . . ."

Gallant opened his eyes and stared up at the low, heavy beams of the ceiling. Béssac had to know the rest.

"They accused us of spying, Béssac. And not being in uniform."

Béssac was silent and watchful, thinking for a moment. Then he said, "Go on."

Gallant's look was steady. "We're to be shot, mon vieux. Tomorrow, just after first light."

Béssac looked at him for a long moment, his features like stone in the grey light.

"You're not joking, are you", he said finally.

Gallant shook his head. "No. Not this time."

Béssac dropped his head, a short laugh on his lips. "Well, damn me", he said softly. "All those years. Sailing to hell and back. Moorish knives, English cannon, storms that'd rip your hair off. I got through it all."

He smiled ruefully. "Now I get it from a damned firing squad. And not even afloat."

A gust of wind pattered rain in short bursts against the window.

"I'm sorry, Béssac. If I hadn't dreamed up this scheme of coming into the town . . . ."

". . . You'd have figured out some other business just as damned well dangerous!" Béssac laughed, and there was a spark of his old bravado in it.

Gallant nodded. "All right. Sacristi, old friend, I'd have risked our lives any other way but this if I'd had a choice."

Béssac shrugged. "I know it." He looked down at the irons. "You did your best. You've always done your best."

He looked Gallant in the eye. "And I've never followed a better man!" he said in a hoarse whisper.

Gallant looked away, touched.

There was a crash at the door as the heavy bolt slammed back, and with a burst of light and wetness from the archway the door banged open. A tall English sentry, his hat dripping water, stepped in with keys jangling.

" 'Eads up, Froggies. Yew got visitors.'' he said, and then stepped aside as two rain-sodden figures stepped in through the door.

Gallant's eyes went hard as flint. The bulkier figure was hidden in a great seacloak. But the other, eyes glittering under the dripping tricorne brim, was unmistakably Nicolas Morin.

The cell door banged shut, and the four men looked at each other.

Gallant met Morin's gaze. "What is it you want, Morin?'' he said, through his teeth. "If you're here to enjoy us panicking over our impending doom . . . .''

Morin raised protesting hands. "Sweet Virgin, what a thought!'' he said mildly. "A few questions are all that are on our minds, Lieutenant. M'sieu' Salter, here, and I hope you will have no objections to replying.''

"To serve what, Morin?'' said Gallant. "We're to die in any event.''

Beside Morin, the man called Salter bared yellow teeth.

"That depends, now'', he said in English. "It might keep a load o' musket shot out of yer guts. An' then it might not.''

Morin smiled at the expression on Gallant's face. "Don't look so surprised, Gallant. He doesn't really speak French. But he understands very well indeed. And as he has such a violent nature I'd be careful what I say . . . .''

Gallant fixed a cold stare on Salter, and pursed his lips. "And who in hell would you be to offer escape from a firing squad?''

"A good deal, you fool'', said Morin, evenly. "He's their Chief of Commissariat. And a messmate to Knowles and Townsend both, the governor and the squadron commander!''

"Very well'', said Gallant in English. "Just what is it you wanted to know?''

Ned Salter grinned. "That'd be more like it.'' He sat down on the edge of the rack. Rummaging under the cloak he drew out a large tobacco plug and tore off a gobbet with his teeth, beginning to chew methodically. After a moment he spat a brown arc into a corner, glanced at Morin as if for approval, and squinted at Gallant.

"You were huntin' the *Santa Maria*, eh?'' he said, abruptly.

Gallant nodded. There was no point in trying to deny it. "Yes.''

"But where's your ship, then?''

"At sea. Dropped us and put out.''

"But with orders to pick ye up agin, 'long the coast.''

"Did I say that?"

Salter spat with gusto and grinned again. "No matter. We knew what you was at when you ran down Mongsewer Morin, here." His eyes gleamed.

" 'Sides, I knows yer ship. A corvette, ye calls her, an' lively, too, in the bargain. And ain't she called *Echo?*"

Béssac stirred into life at the mention of the name. "You won't get her, you rosbif bastard! You may have us, but at least . . . ."

Salter spat into the corner, and wiped his chin. His cheek bulged with the wad. "But we have, mate. If that's what you're sayin'. We've taken her, proper. A slick an' tidy capture it were, too."

Gallant stared at him. "You're lying."

"Not a bit", said Salter. "You was t'meet her off Spaniard's Bay, you were. And it were there we let her run afoul of us, ye might say."

Salter was watching the flicker of emotions on Gallant's face. "Let me clear the deck o' facts fer yew a trifle, mate. You sailed in pursuit of a Spanisher, a big buggerin' merchantman loaded to the gunnels with loot n' bullion."

And on his next words Gallant knew Salter was not attempting a lie.

"Aye, bullion, an' the sweetest, prettiest little lady of a statue you'd ever clap eyes to, one o' them Madonners the greasers be always castin' up. An' this 'un was of pure gold, in the bargain!"

Gallant kept his face impassive. "Interesting. I was to find out the fate of the bullion and the figurine. It appears I have."

Morin laughed dryly. "Oh, you've not heard half the tale, Lieutenant. Not half. Go on, Salter."

Salter shifted the plug to the other cheek. "And now, for all that, you and your winger there, 'll take a musket ball in yer vitals. Pity, ain't it?" His grin was mocking.

Gallant felt his jaw muscles tighten. "Get him on with it, Morin. Or else leave us alone!"

Salter spat into a different corner. "Oh, but I wants you t' hear the tale afore we asks some questions. Why, I'd not sleep knowin' I sent ye to yer Maker not knowin' how well you was foxed!"

Gallant tried to keep an offhand tone in his voice. "Then perhaps you should tell us. What of the figurine? And the bullion?"

The New Englander grinned. "Why, we took her, Gallant.

The *Santa Maria''*, he said. "Scarcely a league off Cape Sable, too. Me 'n' my lads."

"Lads? You mean . . . the Royal Navy isn't . . . ?"

Salter exchanged a look with Morin. "Hell, there's more 'n' a handful of us, b'God, and hidden where the bloodybacks or some damned King's officer won't find 'em!"

A piece of a vast puzzle fell suddenly into place in Gallant's head, and he stared at Morin and Salter in unmasked amazement and startled comprehension.

"Mother of Christ! You're not really a Bostonnais King's officer! And you, Morin, you've been . . . hell, you're pirates!"

Salter smiled.

"The Yankees and the English don't know a damn thing about all this, do they! At least not the ones here!" Gallant went on. "You learned of the *Santa Maria* through Morin and that journal! He's been directing your every move! You took her and gutted her, ran her up on Tancouque, and then took off the bullion for yourself!"

Salter shifted the plug again, his grin widening.

"And so when we came in and attacked *Magnet* . . . ."

"You rendered us a fine service, Gallant", said Morin.

"Aye", said Salter. "That bucko Rand was getting a little too close for comfort."

Gallant stared. "Too close? You mean, all the time . . .?"

Salter grinned. "We was moored by, tendin' to other business, like. The loot ain't on Tancook, as we calls it. But it ain't far away, in lots o' tidy nooks 'n' crannies. Y'see, we've known these waters for well over ten years. And we've had a chance to set up some right smart hideyholes that no one'd ever sniff out, Gallant." He noticed a fly crawling on the stained and grubby planking of the cell floor and struck it with a well-aimed brown stream of juice. "Over the years we've had a little business goin', y' might say. Us Brethren o' the Coast, under helpful direction from a businessman o' the likes o' Mongsewer Morin, here. Why, strike me, you lay for one o' them big Compagnies des Indes barges that used to stand in here and you'd have enough booty for a year's high livin' in Portobello, where it ain't never cold! An' it be easy to do, when you knows the ship's track . . . ."

The man was warming to his boastful tale. As he rambled on, Gallant sat aghast. What Salter and Morin were revealing, in the odd vanity of criminals, was an organized and carefully run scheme that saw the ruthless pirate covens of the Carib-

146

bean, under the direction of an inside man, Nicolas Morin, carry out a grand plan that regularly picked off choice vessels from the stream of ships that had put into Cape Breton each year. Masked by the swarm of 'legitimate' privateers Louisbourg itself had kept at sea during the long wars with the British, Morin and his vicious associates had carefully milked the wealth of the seaborne Indies trade touching the town, as Morin in the admirauté office carefully noted movements and lading bills of ship after ship. And in some remote spot, perhaps Baie Mohone itself, far from their known warm water haunts, they had hidden the amassed plunder.

"An interesting tale", said Gallant. "But you still haven't said what you want from us."

Salter scratched his chin. "Put 'er this way. The comin' of His Britannic Majesty's rule here gave us a plus, so t' speak, for I was able to get in on the thing back in Boston Town and come in this place legal-like. But it ain't turnin' a profit for the effort, like as it should. Nowadays there's naught but the rum trade clearin' this port. So we've a mind to strike our colours."

He grinned. "So we're weighin' anchor, so t' speak. Liftin' our wages o' the last years, from all the hideyholes, and layin' course for the Main, where no King's ship'll find our haunts. And there we'll see each of us gets his lawful share, and retires, like the press gang lads say, to a snug farm where he can enjoy his bottle and fondle his lass!"

Gallant could not resist a small smile. "And the 'wages' include the Madonna and the bullion, I'd suspect."

"Aye", snorted Salter. "But that's sharkbait, Gallant. We've a hundred times as much!"

Gallant and Béssac exchanged a quick look.

"So your statue . . . you calls it the Senyurra or some other damned greaser name, ay? . . . she'll be melted down for good coin, you may lay to it." He leaned closer to Gallant, and the tobacco stench on his breath was foul and sickening.

"But we took yer little corvette, all right. And a blunderin' King's ship that was followin' in her wake, so to speak."

Gallant was silent.

"My old messmate Ben Spooner's been in the offing fer a day or two. So he was a-waitin' for anything, includin' yer little gunboat. Easy to set a trap, particularly after we caught one o' those unfortunate lads you put ashore. Spooner's lads were a-foragin' when they caught him . . . ."

A flash of the bloodied Micmac camp passed before Gal-

lant's eyes. "Yes. I found a Micmac camp they'd 'visited'.
Your 'lads' like killing women and old people, Salter?"

Salter sneered. "Now ain't that a pity. And a pity it was,
too, that we had t' slow roast your man over a fire, on a grill,
nicely, before he'd tell you'd be back to be picked up by your
ship. He didn't scream too much afore he died."

Béssac kicked at his leg irons, a cold fury in his eyes as he
sensed the meaning of Salter's words. "You bastard!" he
swore.

"And so old Ben, why, he just put in there with the old
Pearl and her consorts, and, nice as you please, your little
corvette landed right in his lap." He snickered. "And a
damned fool King's man who was followin'!"

"Go on", said Gallant, grimly.

"Well, now, there's not much more to tell, eh? I'll be addin'
yer ship and t'other to our little squadron. That'll take a day
or two t'get 'em set up and ready for sea agin. I'll hoist the
Black Jack on 'em, and then we'll leave this God-cursed coast
with what's ours, and resettle in a gentler clime, like!" Salter
leaned forward. "And that brings us to the main problem,
after all o' this."

Gallant raised an eyebrow. "Which is?"

Morin moved closer, his stare like the sharp edge of a knife.

"We play no more games, Gallant. My journal. Surely you
remember? Wherein I list ship movements, locations, and certain other information", he said, in a tone of quiet menace.
"I should like it back."

Gallant smiled. "Lost it, have you? Need it to dig up your
damned booty?"

Morin's eyes glittered dangerously. "Don't toy with your
life, Gallant! Where is it? Tell me, and go free! *Where is it?*"

Gallant could not resist a snort. "Why should I tell you, if
I knew? And don't pull that knife, Salter. I don't give a damn
what you do to me!"

Salter had paused in midstep forward, hand on his knife
hilt. The sound of the passing sentry's hobnails in the archway
outside echoed briefly, and when they passed Salter moved
in again, his lip curling.

"Listen, ye great fool!" he said. "So ye care nothin' fer
a nicked nose? Well, just you remember some o' Cap'n
Henry's lobsterbacks'll be puttin' hot lead into you, come
mornin'!" He bared his teeth, the gaps between them strongly

148

evident. "I could prevent that! Just tell us where you put the damned journal!"

Gallant took a deep breath and glanced at Béssac. What he saw in the mate's eyes made him go on.

"It's gone."

"What? What do you mean?"

"I burned it. In your fireplace, Morin."

"Y-you *what?*" Morin goggled, the icy calm surface cracking. He lurched forward, skin suddenly pallid. "You . . . you *burned* it? The work! The years! The . . . you . . .!" He stood, rocking on the balls of his feet, staring, his lips working and his fist clenching. With a strangled sound he lunged forward and struck Gallant's face, openhanded, with all his strength.

Eyes smarting from the blow, Gallant twisted his mouth into a mocking sneer.

"How brave of you, Morin! A woman's blow! And on a chained man!"

With a flash of his ratlike teeth Morin flung back his cape and whipped his slim hanger from its scabbard. He poised for the killing thrust, only to be stopped abruptly by Salter's outstretched arm.

"No! The sentry'll hear, certain!" Salter hissed. His own blue eyes blazed at Gallant, and for a silent, terrible moment his own hand gripped his sword hilt with whitening knuckles. Then he snarled and spat on the floor.

"Leave it, Morin!" he said, his voice hoarse with anger. "The booty we have'll still make ye a rich man! To hell with yer journal!"

Morin struggled against his grip. "He's lying! Lying! He's got it hidden! I'll cut him till he tells . . . .!"

"No! We've work to do! Spooner'll have the *Pearl* off Minadou by midnight, and the other two'll not be a day or two astern!"

"My work . . . my journal . . . lost! All lost!" Eyes wild, a white foam gathering at the corners of his mouth, Morin broke away and staggered to the door. He flung it open, letting in a swirl of wind and rain, and plunged out past the startled sentry.

As Salter swung his cloak closed and stepped to the threshold he looked back at Gallant.

"You've hidden it somewheres, ain't ye, ye crafty bugger?" he said, in a chilling tone. "I'd find out, if I had t' burn yer eyes out!'' He spat again on the floor. "By God, I hope they get you in the guts! And leave you. You'll take days to die. Days!''

The heavy door crashed shut, and the two men were gone, the howl and rattle of the wind and rain obliterating the sound of their hurrying feet on the drawbridge toward the inner town.

After a moment Gallant looked over at Béssac, who was resting his head against his knees, his face shadowed.

"So. They took *Echo* as well'', said Gallant, tonelessly.

"I heard. That was a damned brave thing, capitaine. To say what you did.''

"I . . . wonder what has happened. To Akiwoya and the others?''

Béssac sniffed. "I'll bet it was a whoreson of a fight.''

Gallant awoke with a start. It was pitch black in the cell, and he shook his head, unsure for a moment where he was.

"Awake at last'', said Béssac "damned good thing. I thought you's still be snoring when they carried us out to . . . ah . . . .'' He did not finish.

Gallant was about to speak when a sound beyond the heavy door stopped him. Over the hiss and patter of the wind and rain it sounded, clear and chilling. The crunch of hobnailed leather, approaching.

"Oh, Christ'', murmured Béssac. "Here we go.''

"Courage, mon vieux'', said Gallant, quietly.

The boots were suddenly loud, now, ringing on the pavé under the archway. And then, to a barked command, they came to a ringing halt. A key rattled loudly in the lock. Then the door was kicked back, streaked and wet with rain, the glow of the archway lanterns spilling across the gritty planking.

A tall English sergeant, hat and watchcloak dripping, stepped heavily into the cell. Behind him, in the archway, Gallant could see two sodden and miserable musketmen, the heavy Brown Besses secured under their arms to shelter the lock.

"Right, then, mongsewers'', said the sergeant, in a cold voice. "Time for a wee walk in th' rain.'' He grinned mirthlessly as he leaned his long halberd against the wall and unlocked the irons of both men. "Come along lively, now!''

Gallant stood up, the cramped muscles in his legs protesting.

Numbly he crammed his hat down over his eyes and, Béssac behind him, stepped out into the chill of the archway. The wind was pitiless, and he shivered in spite of himself.

The little party clumped off over the drawbridge, the rain needling in hard against them now, and trudged toward the murk of the town. The footing was treacherous, and more than once both prisoners and guards slipped and cursed in the mud.

Before long they were passing through the defile of the Queen's Gate, out over the dry ditch, out through the counterscarp and the long slope of the glacis, out into the darkness and along the murky, exposed track that led toward Black Rock. Now the wind, unhindered, tore at them and made them catch their breath and bend into its force. The rain stung in their faces, and to their left, frighteningly close, the sea-edge roared and thundered.

Gallant stumbled, and the sergeant's halberd thumped painfully against his back.

"Move along!" A fair trot yet! Mo. . . ."

The sergeant's voice choked off, ended by another sound. A single blow, hard and leathery. Now there was a single, stifled shriek of agony from beside him now, shut off almost before it escaped the victim's lips. And now another blow, the sickening crunch of a tomahawk.

"Christ! What . . .?" Gallant swore. The musketman on his left was down, a dark figure hunched over him. And to his right the other man had vanished.

"Capitaine!" came Béssac's startled cry from behind.

Then, suddenly, a figure loomed in the night, huge and frightening before Gallant. A figure that sent a chill of recognition through the marine.

"Wolf!" Gallant burst out. "How in the name of . . .?"

"*Neenawe*! It is indeed I, *Wenooch*!"

Gallant stared as on either side of the Wolf the figures of his two sons, their caped blankets whipping round them, materialized. And more dark shapes were around, on all sides.

And now from behind the Wolf came another figure: smaller, lighter, but swift and lithe. A figure that ran to Gallant to crush against his chest and throw slim, strong arms around him.

"Ah, *Wenooch*!" she cried, a sob catching in her throat. "*Ootetawm*! I am here, dearest!"

Gallant's face was inundated by the perfume of her wet, free-streaming hair. Her lips moved on his, and then dropped to kiss his hands. Almost of their own accord his arms closed around her, oblivious to the sodden wetness of her blanket and the buckskin and trade cloth beneath.

"*Wosowech!*" he murmured. "Sweet Jesus!"

The Wolf loomed over them, huge in the night, pulling the girl back.

"Later, children! This is not the safety of our lodges by the fire! We must run!"

Gallant looked quickly round to find one of the musketmen. He bent over the body, flipping it on its back. The man was broad and heavyset, and wore the facings of Warburton's regiment. His tricorne lay several feet away, and in the middle of his forehead a great tomahawk cleft oozed red and gaping.

Ignoring the dead, staring eyes Gallant hefted him up and slipped off the broad shoulderbelt of the cartridge box. Then he tugged the man's bayonet and tomahawk out of his waistbelt, tossing the tomahawk recklessly to Béssac as he came up.

"Grab it, mon vieux!" Gallant cried. "Something to swing at the rosbifs with! See if you can get the other musket!" Quickly, he scooped up the heavy Tower musket and fixed the bayonet. A quick look at the pan showed that it was primed.

A rare chance that you'll fire tonight! he thought.

The Wolf was at Gallant's shoulder, and the girl slipped in on his other side, her hand seeking his.

"Now, *Wenooch!*" said the Wolf, his eyes burning coals in a rain-streaked face. "We must run for the forest line! There is not time to waste!"

From behind, Béssac spat, hefting his axe and musket. "Ready, capitaine!"

Gallant nodded to the Wolf. He felt *Wosowech's* hand tighten in his. "Go, Wolf! We'll follow!"

The Wolf drew his blanket over his head and, hunched against the force of the wind and the rain, he sprinted off the cart track into the night, moccasins slapping in the ooze and muck of the great marsh that stretched toward the trees and safety. One after the other, the little party struck out after him, with Béssac bowling along after the Wolf's sons and the other warriors, hand holding down his sealskin cap. Gallant slung his musket over his shoulder, tightened his grip on the girl's hand, and followed.

The couple struggled through the marsh, their eyes smarting with the stinging, wind-driven rain, their feet slipping and splashing as they stumbled on after Béssac's dim shape. On the Wolf ran, leading them across the broad and trackless marshland toward the invisible shelter of the forest wall.

Then suddenly ahead the Wolf and his sons were crouching, tomahawks out. Béssac was turning, his warning shout loud above the wind.

"Soldiers! Soldiers! The picquet line!"

Out of nowhere they materialized, white gaiters aglow and ghostly, what light there was faintly touching the cold steel of their bayonets. Nine, perhaps ten of them, rain-sodden, grim faces in shadow, in a ragged line across their path.

Gallant's stomach balled into a knot. He thrust the girl down. "Stay here!" he barked.

He whipped the musket off his shoulder and sprinted forward, his blood roaring in his ears. Two struggling masses loomed before him: Béssac, in a wild wrestle with a tall, bellowing soldier, another already sprawled in grotesque stillness at his feet; the Wolf, springing up from the still-twitching body of his man, knife running with dark blood.

A blur passed across Gallant's vision, and before him one of the Wolf's sons went sprawling, stunned by the butt of an English musket. A second man thrust in, bayonet levelled, for the kill. He was swearing, a stream of gutter filth pouring from his lips in a steady snarl.

"Here, rosbif!" roared Gallant. "To me!"

Bayonet levelled, he lunged at the man. He felt the bayonet ring against steel, then slide down the man's musket, felt it thrust home, the impact stomach-churning as the blade drove into the man's belly through the thick red coat. The Englishman choked, dropping his weapon and clutching at Gallant's with both hands.

Sickened, Gallant jerked the blade out, and the man fell away. In the next instant a second man was rushing at the marine, and before he could think, blind fighting instinct had twisted Gallant away from the musket butt that whistled through the space where his head had been.

The man was still twisted round from the momentum of his swing, exposing his side. With every ounce of strength Gallant set his feet and drove the butt of his reversed musket into the opening, hearing the redcoat grunt as the wind burst from his lungs. As he turned back Gallant stepped in and lifted his knee into the gasping man's groin. The soldier folded as if by a giant hand, and with another punching downstroke of the butt Gallant smashed him to the ground.

"No! No! Behind you! Look out! Look out!"

The girl's cry, wild with alarm, rang in Gallant's ears, and he spun on his heel.

But this time he was too late. He had a glimpse of red cloth, buff belting and a savage, twisted face behind the butt plate of the Englishman's musket drove like a horse's kick into his stomach. Incredible pain shot through him, and the wind left his lungs in a cough. He reeled back, bent double, stars spinning before his eyes, and fell awkwardly to his side, a groan caught in his throat.

The Englishman spat and stepped in, quick and deadly. He raised his musket for the killing thrust.

"Say yer beads, ye damned Papist!"

Down came the thrust.

The girl's voice screamed, loud in Gallant's ear. "No!"

There was a blur of movement before Gallant's eyes, and as if in a dream he heard the soldier grunt with the effort, heard the blow strike home with a sickening sound. But he felt nothing.

Then he saw her, kneeling, the blanket falling from her shoulders, the long black hair streaming down in the rain, down over the slim buckskin-covered shoulders, down the curve of her back to the crimson steel point that jutted out, cruel and terrible. He heard her choked, little-girl wail.

"Oh, God. Oh, dear God!" Gallant cried.

Another figure blurred past in swift movement. The figure of Béssac, who sent the soldier with the bayonet flying with a sweeping blow of one broad fist.

Gallant was on his knees, reaching for her, the rain pelting in renewed intensity across them, the splashes leaping in the mire of the earth. And she was falling, her muscles slacking, her head lolling back as she collapsed into his outstretched arms with a terrible languor.

"*Wosowech!* Dear Christ!" Gallant was heedless of the muck, the rain dripping from his face, holding her in his arms, feeling her arms reach up, feeling for him, to find his sleeves and grip at them, then moving to his chest. Her face was upturned, the rain unceasing across its paleness, her eyes open and looking for his, a brightness burning in them.

Gallant stared in horror at the red stain that was spreading in her robe, the dark trickle that had begun to run from the corner of her mouth.

"Ah, girl! Why? Why?" he cried, over the wind's shriek.

Her voice came, low and clear, through a heartbreaking

smile. "*Kesalkoose* . . . beloved. Better that . . . I should die . . . and not you . . ."

Gallant tore at her clothing, frantic now, the tears beginning to well up in his eyes. He thrust his hand to the horrid wound, trying to stop the warm, sticky flood with pressure.

"Die? You're not going to die! You hear? You're not going to die!"

She shook her head, the rain running over her cheeks, her forehead, over her lips parted again in the smile. "My . . . brave *Wenooch!* You . . . never cease to fight . . . Ah! *Kesenook-wei!* It hurts!" She arched, shuddering in his arms.

Gallant looked wildly round, at the staring, horrified faces of Béssac, of the Wolf and his sons.

"Help me!" he cried. "A bandage! In the name of Jesus, something to stop the blood . . .!"

Her small hand had come up to his lips.

"Too late, my heart. I . . . it is near. Do not fear for me. I know . . . how to die. *Nedowena!*"

Gallant was rocking her now, like a child, his face in her hair, the tears tumbling burning and salty from his eyes, his throat no longer able to hold back the sobs that, one by one, tore out with such pain that they might have been ripped from his soul.

"You will remember . . . that I loved you . . . when first my eyes saw you, *Wenooch*. For all . . . that you are. And when . . . you take again your Abigail . . . you will not forget me . . . ."

Gallant could not answer. Eyes shut against the tears, against the unceasing rain, he crushed her against him.

SEVEN

The shadows of early morning were recoiling from the forest floor as the sun climbed higher into the clear azure sky. The great trees were still and unmoving, the only flicker of motion amongst them being the circling forms of hawks, and now and then a flight of puffins or a solitary gull. There had been rain during the night, and the beaded droplets on branch tips reflected like miniature prisms the green, sundrenched face of the forest.

They also reflected in tiny images the figures of two men, bent with purpose, who strode swiftly along beneath the trees, pushing toward the sea that lay silvered and twinkling in the distance.

At a mossy fallen log, a broad giant felled by a long-ago storm, the leading man stopped and unslung his musket and pack. He squatted with Indian grace against the moss surface, turning his face to the sun. The other man, older, padded into the sunny glade and slumped down beside his companion.

"Sacristi, capitaine", puffed the older man, "we must be almost there, hein? We have to be!"

The younger man sat motionless, his face to the sun still, a harsh set to the jaw muscles that the sunlight did nothing to dispel.

"A league, more, Béssac", he said quietly. "No more. You've done well to keep this pace."

The mate snorted. "Not much choice, have I? Lose you and I'm stranded in this mosquito-ridden hellhole!" He appropriately slapped at his neck, but with a keen eye still fixed on his companion.

"Capitaine, you've hardly said a word these two days. Hell, I can hardly get a grunt out of you." He paused. "It's still her, is it? You're still thinking about the Micmac girl?"

Gallant bowed his head. After a moment he nodded.

"Capitaine, there was nothing you could have done for her. The Wolf said as much. If you keep brooding about this, nothing will work. And then, by the Virgin, she will have taken that rosbif bayonet in her belly for nothing!"

Gallant's head snapped up, dark eyes ablaze. "Sacristi, Béssac, sometimes you go too far! Watch your tongue, or . . .!" The marine broke off, staring for a moment into the compassionate gaze of his friend.

"I'm sorry. I . . . you didn't deserve that", said Gallant, with some difficulty. "It's just too damned hard to see any real sense in it just yet. Give me time, hein?"

Béssac nodded, wordless. Inwardly, the gruff mate was adding another page to his book of experience, which for him had always equated women with trouble.

"But you're right", said the marine, presently. "I'll scupper us brooding like this."

Béssac spat, relieved. "Bien oui. Get your mind off her. Off it. Tell me what the situation is again. Sweet Mary, I forget in ten minutes!" said Béssac.

Gallant could not resist a small smile, touched by the mate's bearish efforts at consolation.

"Alors", he said. "Salter said he thought it would take two, maybe three days to make *Echo* and the British vessel sea ready. And then he said that the biggest buccaneer vessel . . . the *Pearl*, hein? . . . was sailing right then and would be off Minadou. So that means that, ahead there", and here Gallant pointed toward the forest wall, "if we reach Spaniard's Bay in two or three hours we should find *Echo* and the other one aswarm with brigands while they ride at anchor. That's if they haven't already sailed.''

Béssac looked glum. "Fine. And we just wave our muskets and yell at the buggers to turn over our ships!''

Gallant grinned. "Could be. But some kind of chance to really stop them sailing might turn up. As long as we can just get to her first, I'll feel a lot . . . .''

Gallant froze. Béssac had made an urgent warning motion with one hand, and had risen to a crouch, carefully drawing up his musket to the ready position. The mate was peering intently into the heavy evergreen groves off to their left.

Then Gallant heard it as well. Footfalls, slow and cautious, across the forest floor. And from more than one man.

"Five men. Maybe six!'' whispered Béssac.

Gallant nodded. He picked up his musket and hunched in low and close beside the log, raising his head only enough to scan the trees.

He tensed himself to fire. I'll take one of you rosbif bastards with me, he thought. Just step out of those trees so I can get a clear aim . . . .

"Capitaine! Capitaine! Don't shoot, for the love of Jesus.''

Gallant started, staring at the trees. The voice had been French, and familiar.

"What in hell . . . ?'' he began.

Three men, then four, then five emerged abruptly out of the shadows. Men in seamen's clothes with slung blanket rolls and heavy French muskets.

"Capitaine! It's us, off *Echo!*'' said the leading man.

Gallant stood up, easing the hammer of his own musket down, as he recognized the faces of the men he had let go ashore when he and Béssac had begun their own trek.

"Well, damn me!'' he murmured. "The last people I had expected to see were you lot!''

The leading man grinned, hefting up his musket. "You told us, hein? Fail to return these and we'd be hung? Hell, we're here to turn 'em in, m'sieu'!''

And in the next moment the men had clustered round Gallant, eyes bright, laughing, and Béssac had bounded over and was engaging in back-slapping embraces while he bellowed, "Thibault, you cur! How in God's name did you stay out of harm's way? And you, Abbelly! They could've smelt you coming!''

Gallant looked round the faces. "There were two others.

What happened to them? Where are they?''

The leading hand, Abbelly, tightened his lips and shook his head. "Won't be here, capitaine."

"Why not?"

"When we went ashore, me n' the lads, we swore an oath. Be back at a point . . . inland, there, about two leagues, on the Miré . . . and then we'd work back to meet the ship together. Arsenault quit right off. Said he was getting himself back to Cobequid and to hell with the ship and . . . and you, capitaine."

Gallant nodded. "All right. I expected some of that. But what about the last man?" Gallant felt, with a cold chill, that he already knew the answer to that question.

"Rousseau was taken by some English. He was with Saint-Juste, here . . . ."

"Oui, capitaine", said another man, doffing his tuque. "We were going to have a quick look at his uncle's fishing station over by Baleine before trying to get north to Niganiche. They caught us in the bush. I got off a shot and then ran. I think he got one and then they took him. I . . . I couldn't do anything else but go on alone."

Gallant pursed his lips. "I know. Rousseau was killed by the English, I'm fairly certain. Or at least, by the pirates."

The men stared at each other. "Pirates? On this coast?"

Béssac spat. "We've been dealing with two bunches of rosbifs, lads. The Bostonnais, who are human beings under all the damned Protestant caterwauling . . . most of the time . . . and a gang of cutthroat buccaneers, who've been stealing and plundering both sides in these waters for years!"

"You may as well know", put in Gallant, "that *Echo* is in their hands." He stilled the outburst of curses and questions with a raised hand. "She put into Spaniard's Bay, all right. But from what we learned inside Louisbourg there was an ambuscade, and she and an English vessel that was shadowing her were both taken. And as far as we know she's still at anchor there, being repaired and readied for sea. Or so we hope."

The men's faces were grim. "And M'sieu' Akiwoya? And the others?" said one.

"Christ knows", said Gallant. "But the pirates aren't a gentle lot. We've seen that."

There was silence for a moment as the men digested this dark news. Then Abbelly stepped forward.

"Capitaine, I think the lads would agree with me that we'd like to know if there's something that could be done, or something you've got planned. If *Echo's* still at anchor there, m'sieu'. There's not many of us, but if you and M'sieu Béssac have a scheme of any kind, we'd be ready . . . ."

Gallant lifted his chin. "To try and take her back?"

There was a growl of agreement, and the men turned all eyes on Gallant.

"Very well", he said, in tantalizing slowness. "I believe we are about a league from the shore of the bay. I have a feeling the ship'll still be there. And I think we really ought to see about going and getting her back, hein?"

The voices rose again. "Oui, m'sieu'! Bugger the rosbifs!"

"Then listen!" said Gallant, over the voices. "We've got to push on immediately. Single file. Muskets primed and loaded, set at half-cock. Fix your gear so nothing rattles or clinks. M'sieu' Béssac will show you how. And from here on in no one says a word, unless I or Béssac speaks first. Understood?"

It was not until evening's light was lighting the crowns of the forest and casting long purple shadows below them that Gallant and his men slid and stumbled down the rock and leaf-strewn slope of the last hill, at the foot of which Gallant knew they would step out of the tree cover and onto the shore of Spaniard's Bay. The dew had risen, now, and in the moist gloom of the forest pathway each man's breath was visible, the chill belying the earlier midday heat.

Ahead, Gallant suddenly saw a blue-water glimmer through the trees. He raised a hand to halt the party, and then motioned the men in around him.

"Bon!" he whispered. "We hold here while we scout out things. Abbelly, post a man to the rear and one to either side. You and the other man stay here to cover Béssac and myself in case we have to come pelting back in a hurry. He and I will scout ahead. And remember: if we are attacked and split, take your own direction to safety and rendezvous back where we first met, in two days. Ready, Béssac?"

The mate nodded. The men rose off their knees and moved quietly off to their posts. Gallant checked the priming of his musket, and then, with Béssac at his heels, he crept carefully forward toward the inviting glimmer of water, silver-grey in the growing dusk now.

Several minutes later Gallant was kneeling in a tangle of ground pine.

At his side Béssac swore softly. Visible through a roughly circular opening in the mass of trees that fringed the bay shore was the broad, wind-flecked surface of the southern arm. And anchored no more than a cable-length out, another vessel of comparable size tied close aboard alongside, *Echo* rode, graceful and sleek. At the sight of her familiar blue and tan hull Gallant felt a pang of recognition.

"Christ, she's beautiful!" breathed Béssac beside him. "By God, I never thought I'd see her again!" Then the mate clucked his tongue noisily. "Look at the boats tied on to her! And those men on deck and aloft. There's work going on, hein? And look; it's the same with the other ship!" He swore softly. "And look at the damned black rag at her ensign staff! That pirate filth . . .!" He did not finish.

Gallant was only half aware of what the mate was saying. Slowly and methodically, ignoring the pounding in his own chest, the marine scanned the scene before him, trying to observe every aspect of it that would help him decide what he would do. He had determined the moment he saw *Echo* again that he would be satisfied with nothing less than taking the ship back, whatever the cost.

The corvette and the other ship were moored, he could see now, their bows pointing to the harbour mouth and the open sea beyond. Ranged alongside *Echo* were several ship's boats, including the corvette's own longboat and jolly boat, and a rope-slung staging over the side forward of the mainmast channel indicated hull work had been going on. Even now, the marine could see a man leaning out over the starboard foremast chains, slathering the deadeye lashings and irons with tar, by the look of it. Both ships' canvas was tightly furled, and only *Echo's* main course yard was canted out of true. The squeal of a block reached his ears, and a distant hauler's chant, and he saw half a dozen men on *Echo's* deck using the yard to derrick a cask in a strop over to the deck of the other vessel, led on by the voluble commands of a behatted figure partway up *Echo's* main shrouds.

Béssac was whispering in his ear. "I count thirty. Maybe thirty-five with that bunch on the foredeck. And there could be at least ten more below decks." He clucked his tongue. "Christ save us. That's not good odds for seven of us."

Gallant flicked a glance at the mate. "If we tried an armed boarding, certainly." He smiled. "Surprise can lessen odds like that, mon ami. Or have you forgotten?"

"Eh? What have you in mind, capitaine?"

"In a moment. Fix in your mind her distance out from the shore. How they're lying. Where the lines are. Then let's get back to the others."

Béssac squinted at the ships for a moment. "Bon", he grunted. "I have it."

"Right. Let's go. And for God's sake keep down!"

In a low crouch, Gallant and the mate crept back into the concealing shadows. Within a few minutes they were back to the others, and the squad of *Echo's* men squatted round them, listening intently to Gallant's low, careful voice.

"Is she there, capitaine?" said Abbelly.

"Bien sûr. She's there, all right. Moored in the stream with an English vessel rafted on the larboard side. And both of 'em are crawling with buccaneers."

Gallant looked round their faces for a moment. Then he drew his bayonet and, clearing away the layer of leaves, he used its point to make a quick sketch of the harbour and the two ships in the dirt. Finished, he sat back on his heels and used the bayonet as a pointer.

"Here is the bay, hein? We are right . . . here. And here are the ships. Out about a cable, no more. We look out at her starboard side, and the English ship is moored outboard. It's thick trees right down to water's edge, here." At this point he marked in an X on the shoreline. "It was hard to say, but the tide looked to be at flood, the way the boats were lying at the booms."

He looked up abruptly. "Who here can swim? And well, in the bargain?"

"Christ. Not again!" moaned Béssac. But he, along with three others and Gallant, held up his hand.

Gallant nodded. "Bon. You, Robert, and you, Lauzon. Since you can't swim, we'll give you a hot task instead of a chilling one."

"Capitaine?" said one of the two.

"Here's the plan", said Gallant, briskly. He felt a rising thrill of anticipation within his stomach. "With as many bully boys as they have working in her now, we'd be shot like fish in a barrel if we tried to swim out to her in daylight. But come nightfall, they're going to secure all that rigging and deck work and go below to their mess. That means drinking and fighting and Christ knows what else. No doubt they'd leave an anchor watch, at least one or two men on deck in each vessel. But they're going to be feeling snug as beetles in old wood here, or I miss my guess."

162

"So we swim out after dark, and . . .", began Béssac.

"Gently, old friend. I haven't finished yet." He poked the bayonet at the sketch. "Even if we were to get up over the rail to the decks without getting a ball in our guts for our trouble, we've still the problem of keeping almost fifty men below hatches. And with what?" He looked round. "Five men? Two on one ship and three on the other?"

Abbelly stirred. "But, m'sieu'? What if you diverted their attention? Get 'em off the ship, or distracted somehow?"

Gallant grinned. "Exactly, Abbelly. Exactly. And that is what you two", he said, pointing to Robert and Lauzon, "will do for us!"

Excited now, the men moved in closer around Gallant's sketch as Gallant revealed the remainder of the plan. At a given moment, Robert and Lauzon were to move to a point well along the shore and light a large fire. Taking several extra muskets, they were to whoop and yell, discharging the muskets at random. Hopefully the disturbance of the buccaneers' presumably safe hideaway would bring the pirates on deck, and even perhaps send away a boat to investigate. That would give the best chance for action Gallant and his little party could hope for.

Gallant, Béssac and the other three swimmers would carry knives and tomahawks, and swim out to the far side of the ships. There, they would act as the situation allowed, whether it meant cutting the ships' cables, or scrambling aboard somehow. It was a perilous scheme with little guarantee of success, but even before Gallant finished speaking each man knew it would be that kind of daring, trust-to-luck stroke which alone would give any chance of recovering the ship.

Gallant thought for a moment. "It'll be at least four hours until we can try it. And it'll take at least an hour for us to collect the wood for you two firebrands to caper around." He looked up into the darkening evening sky. "Get some rest, all of you. But not cookfires. Abbelly, we'll post two sentries, hein? One looking inland, back up that slope there, and one toward the water. I'll do the first watch on the latter. The rest of you get into your blankets and get some sleep."

He paused. "Any questions?"

Not a man spoke.

"Bon. Get bedded down."

Gallant looked out through the trees toward where a glimmer of distant water showed. Likely you're going to need all the rest you can get, he added silently to himself.

163

Excitement proved too great a deterrent to more than brief catnaps, however, and even before daylight had faded completely the men were up and moving, quietly collecting the firewood. By the time the sky was alive with stars they had piled a pyre as high as a man's head about a quarter-mile down the shore, in an opening that could easily be seen from the two ships. Prowling along the water edge, Gallant had chosen the spot, gambling that the pirates' confidence would not lead them to post watchful lookouts. So far, it appeared he had been right.

Now, a pale yellow moon had risen, its light bathing the ships, the shore, and the forest floor where the men crouched.

Gallant carefully checked each man in turn. With the exception of Lauzon and Robert, who were burdened with several extra slung muskets each, each man had stripped to his breeches, and was armed with either a knife or tomahawk. Two men had slung their weapons with thongs round their necks, while the remainder had merely thrust them into their waistbands, and stood, hands on hips, awaiting Gallant's next orders.

The marine nodded at Lauzon and Robert. "Got your flint strikers? Good. Off you go. And remember, you set your fire and begin the musketry in ten minutes. No more, no less!"

With a grunt the two men were off, the moonlight gleaming bluish-silver from the musket barrels as they wove away through the trees.

Gallant turned back to the others, feeling for the long sheath knife in his waistband.

"All right. Allons-y!"

In tense silence the men followed Gallant down through the inky shadows toward the shore, picking their barefooted way over the tangled branches and ankle-twisting rocks beneath the leaf cover. Behind him Gallant could hear only the men's heavy breathing, and it startled him that the sound was almost drowned out by the sudden thundering of his own heart.

For what seemed an eternity he was ducking and weaving down through the prickly evergreen boughs which scraped and stung, needle-sharp, against his skin. Then, without warning, his feet were standing on the wavelet-lapped rocks of the water's edge, and before him, their hulls lit in ghostly relief by the moonlight, the two ships rode.

Silently his men closed in behind him. A few muttered quietly as they saw *Echo,* and he heard one knife snick in and out of its scabbard, a chilling sound.

"Bon. Listen, now!" Gallant whispered. "Béssac, you and Abbelly will swim together. Make for the hawser of the other vessel, outboard of *Echo*. You other two lads follow me. We'll head under *Echo's* counter and get round to the other ship's stern!"

Béssac was shivering visibly. "A-and when we get there, capitaine?"

"You wait, hein? Hang on the hawser. Tread water. But keep low until Lauzon and Robert begin their show! If the decks look empty or if the swines go off in a boat . . . hell, anything that lowers the odds . . . try and get up aboard her! If they ignore the diversion, swim aft to us and we'll see about cutting the cables. They ought to run aground, farther down, on the ebb. That's in a half-hour!"

He glanced quickly round the dark faces. "Questions? Then into the water, quickly! And no damned splashing!"

Gallant lurched in over the slimy rocks of the bottom. But this time, the water was sunwarmed, and there was none of the paralytic chill of Louisbourg harbour.

One by one the men stepped gingerly in over the rocks, eased down into the water, and began stroking out after Gallant and Béssac. Within a few minutes the little group was well out into open water, moving strongly toward the ships.

Gallant felt a quiver of fear as he kicked along. The moon was almost too bright. And were they swimming down a silver path of light to anyone watching on the deck ahead, five heads easily visible to eyes that might be taking careful aim with musket or pistol?

Then, abruptly, the wall of *Echo's* side was towering over them, the slap-lap of the waves under her counter loud in their ears. Still, there was no light, no sign of movement along the rail.

Gallant tread water, his heart pounding. The others gathered round him, puffing and breathing heavily. The excitement was adding to the strain of the swim already.

"Right!" Gallant whispered. "Split up! And wait for the fire ashore, for God's sake!"

Béssac and Abbelly moved off along *Echo's* hull. Gallant waited for a moment, eyes on the rail overhead, and then kicked on again, under the corvette's deep overhanging counter. It was in the concave shadow of the hull there, and the slap and splash of the three men's movements were echoed back along with his breathing frighteningly loud from the planking.

Sweet Mother of Christ, they have to hear that! he thought.

Then he was past *Echo's* rudder, the barnacle-encrusted trailboard brushing his shoulder painfully, and he was moving on, seeing for the first time the other ship. It was hard to tell in the dark of *Echo's* shadow and from water level, but it seemed to be virtually the same size as the corvette, a vessel the English likely would have called a sloop.

Thibeault, one of the two men swimming with him, breasted up alongside Gallant. "Look, capitaine!" he whispered. "She's a rosbif barge, all right. You can see her name, there, under the stern. *Sala. . . Salamander!*"

Gallant grunted. "Christ, hope there's no one with a keen ear in her! Where's Sainte-Juste?"

The second man kicked out of *Echo's* shadow. "Here, capitaine!" he whispered. "I had to rest there, under her counter. I heard something from inside the hull, m'sieu'! Voices, I'm sure of it!"

Gallant's neck bristled. "What?"

"In *Echo*, m'sieu'! Right aft. And I swear it was French!"

"French?"

"Oui, capitaine!" puffed Sainte-Juste. "It . . . one sounded like M'sieu' Akiwoya!"

Gallant's heart leaped, and he spat out an inadvertent mouthful of water. "Good man! If that's so, then there's still somebody alive!" He swung round in the water. "The business ashore should be starting soon. Where in hell is the aft mooring line?"

Thibeault threshed off. "Over here, capitaine. In the shadow. Runs down off her stern gallery. *Echo's* is over there, from her gallery. Damn poor seamanship, tying 'em on there, m'sieu'! One good squall line or swell, and . . . ."

Gallant and Sainte-Juste joined him, and the three men clustered round the great, slimy rope that slanted out of the water thirty feet off *Salamander's* stern. The three men hung on the line with relief, letting their legs dangle down into the dark depths.

Gallant looked back up at the sterns and rigging of the ships, watching for some kind of movement, and at his side Thibeault suddenly snorted in surprise.

"Capitaine!" said the man. "The boats!"

"Eh?"

"The boats, m'sieu'! There's only two. No others, tied to either ship! They're gone!"

Gallant stared, a spasm in his stomach. Thibeault was right. The cluster of ship's boats Gallant and Béssac had seen in the afternoon was gone. And somehow, like a fool, he had missed perceiving this on the swim out.

"What in the name of God . . .?" he began, under his breath.

There was a dull boom in their ears in the next instant, the sound of a distant musket. Then another, and a third in quick succession. A blood-curdling shriek and an answering drunken whoop carried over the water.

Sainte-Juste spat and grinned, shaking sodden strands of hair out of his eyes. "They've started their show! I'd know Lauzon's bellow anywhere!"

Gallant nodded, mind racing. What on earth had happened to the boats? And what did that have to do with the lifelessness of the ships? The forty men they had seen? It made very little sense, but Gallant found himself hoping Lauzon and Robert would be fleet of foot into the forest if they needed to be; the fire might draw more than Gallant and they had bargained for.

"Look, capitaine. Aloft. They've got a real fire going, hein? You can see it reflected on the yards!"

Then the man froze, and with him Gallant and Thibeault. A voice had rung out, an English voice, raised in a hail from the deck of *Salamander*. Gallant heard bare feet slap on planking.

". 'Hoy, Tom!" the voice cried. "All's well?"

There was an answering hail from somewhere in *Echo*, as if from a voice appearing up a hatchway.

"What th' devil's underway yonder?" called the first voice. "Be they injuns?"

There was a derisive snort. "Not likely!" came the reply from *Echo*, clearer now. "I'd mark that some o' the lads had enough o' workin' on th' Yankee pink, an' jumped the boom to have a party on th' far shore, belike."

Gallant's ears strained. Yankee pink? Boom? There was another burst of distant musketry at that moment, and more whoops. Lauzon and Robert were giving a virtuoso performance by the sound of it. But what the devil were the two buccaneers talking about?

"Well, that may be the lay of it", said the voice on *Salamander's* deck. "All quiet, there?"

"Aye", said the man in *Echo*. "Zack's well into the rum,

like the damned dog he be, and Billy's a-whittlin' his cane again, on th' gundeck.''

Three in *Echo,* thought Gallant.

"How be yer passengers?" said *Echo's* voice.

The man in *Salamander* guffawed. "Not a word from my King's men. I heard your Frenchies take to mutterin' a time ago, but I guessed you'd shut 'em up. Hell, Tom, we should've gone on that little skylark! Listen to that!''

King's men! thought Gallant. So the English vessel's crew, or part of it, was prisoner as well. Could there be just one watchman in *Salamander?* Watching a full crew penned below decks? In seemed incredible.

There was a soft rippling and splash in the shadows of *Echo's* hull, and then two shaggy heads appeared, pushing toward the three men on the cable.

Béssac was puffing heavily as he clutched at the hawser, and Gallant was making to put an arm about him when the mate shook his head.

"Never mind . . . capitaine! Just . . . a bit winded.'' He blew out his cheeks and shook his head. "We . . . waited, like you said, all right. **Saw the fire.** Only . . . nothing happened!''

"There's good reason'', said Gallant. "There's no boats! And by the look of it only a few of the cutthroats left aboard. Three in *Echo,* one in this one.''

"Well, by Saint Peter's . . .!'' gaped Béssac. "Where are they?''

Gallant listened to the distant shouts and popping musketry. "I don't know. But we've got to find out soon. The lads ashore won't be able to keep that up much longer.''

He gestured with his thumb at the hawser. "Listen carefully, now. Béssac, you, Abbelly and I will have to climb this line! Thibeault, swim forward! You and Sainte-Juste climb the line at her bows. Slip over the stem and get into the shadows on deck, then work aft!'' His mouth became a tight line. "First man to get to the watchkeeper takes him down quick and hard! Follow?''

The men nodded, their breathing quickening in excitement.

"Good. Move out, then, and not a sound. When we take the first man gather at the rail facing *Echo!*''

Thibeault and Sainte-Juste swam strongly off.

Beside Gallant, Béssac ran his fingers through his hair and spat to one side. "You're going to kill me yet, capitaine'', he muttered.

Gallant bared his teeth in a quick grin, and pulled out his knife. Before he clenched it between his teeth he winked at the grizzled mate.

"Sacristi, Béssac. You don't want to live forever, do you? Come on!"

Reaching up, Gallant swung under the canting line, kicking his legs up to grip it, monkey fashion. The line was slippery with slime, and trembled in his grip. He reached upward with both arms and, hanging like a gibbon on a branch, pulled himself out of the water.

Gallant canted his head back, the stern gallery of the English vessel looming upside down, still an impossible distance away. With his teeth gritted on the cold steel of the blade, his breath hissing around it, he monkeyed up higher and higher.

Halfway there. Gallant felt suspended crazily in space, conscious only of the slivery, knobbled feel of the great rope in his hands and between his legs, and the building ache in his shoulders. Vaguely he heard more distant shouts and musket blasts, more idle conversation between the closer voice in *Salamander* and the farther one in *Echo*.

Sweet Mary's bosom, how much farther? he thought wildly. Was he ten feet above the water? A hundred? He climbed on.

Then suddenly he was there, the carved rail and gilt-edged windows of *Salamander's* gallery hanging before his face. Carefully, heart thundering, he reached out, twisting for a grip, his fingers grappling like hooks for a hold on the slick, painted wood. With a knot of fear in his throat he suddenly launched himself, twisting in midair, to land clinging like a bat against the gallery, toes digging into its lower edge, the dark windows of the ship's great cabin scant inches from his face.

His skin crawled. Was there someone sleeping there, an arm's length away? Or a keen eye levelling a pistol in the dark at his forehead?

He shook his head and scrambled atop the gallery rail, then reached for the transom rail overhead. His fingers locked on a grip and he heaved himself up, toes on a precarious hold atop the window frame carving. It would take only a small effort to heave himself up and over, past the great stern lantern and the ensign staff, to the quarterdeck itself. He was there!

Then Béssac was thumping up beside him, grunting with effort, hands scrabbling over Gallant's to seize the lip of the transom rail. The mate's breath was coming in gasps.

"Mother of God!" he puffed.

In the next minute, Abbelly, a nimble topman, had swung

up beside Béssac and the marine in comparative ease.

All three men pulled themselves by sheer arm strength to the rail and peered over. In an instant they took in the moonlit panorama of the sloping deck, the coiled lines, the glints of light off brass fittings, the bell in its gallows forward, the lashed wheel moving gently against the lines holding it.

And the single bulky figure down in the ship's waist, gazing at the flickering distant pyre of Lauzon and Robert's fire.

"Look! It's Thibeault!" whispered Abbelly.

Gallant strained to see, aware of nothing at first. Then he saw them. Two shadowy figures, vaulting over the outboard cathead and the rail, then vanishing into the shadows of the foremast foot's fiferail.

Gallant slung a leg over the rail and rolled over, dropping to a crouch on the deck. The moonlight that washed over him seemed as bright as blazing sunlight. He took the knife from his mouth and crept forward, into the shadows of the larboard mizzenmast shrouds. Crouched low, Béssac and Abbelly moved noiselessly at his heels.

The marine threw a quick glance across at *Echo*. A glow shone out her midships hatchway, but there was no movement on her decks. They must be all below again, he thought.

A quick movement back aboard *Salamander* caught his eye, and as he watched he saw Thibeault move in short, silent rushes down into the ship's waist. Finally, he was crouched at the mainmast foot, barely a few feet from the lounging watchkeeper.

Now, Thibeault, now! Gallant's mind screamed.

Thibeault sprang. The knife gleamed in the moonlight, once, twice, and then both men were falling back, locked, to the deck. There was a brief, threshing struggle, and then Thibeault was rising in a crouch over his kill, jerking out the knife.

"Capitaine!" came his hiss. "He's finished!"

"Bon!" said Gallant. He rose to his feet, and with Béssac and Abbelly a few paces behind him he leaped down the waistdeck ladder and moved quickly to Thibeault, his feet whispering across the cool planking. Sainte-Juste had appeared now out of the shadow of the foremast, eyes white in his darkened face.

The men stood in a little tense ring, staring down at the dead pirate. He was heavyset, with striped canvas trousers and a grubby kilt below a checked shirt and short watchcoat. His head was bound with a bandana, and a small gold ring gleamed in his nose. His thick and ugly features were stretched in a

170

hideous grimace above the black, glistening gash that crossed his throat from ear to ear.

"Quickly and quietly done, Thibeault", said Gallant, grimly.

Thibeault bent over and wiped his knife on the corpse's breeches. "Practice, capitaine. Just practice."

Gallant eyed the man for a moment, a chill touching his spine. Then he snapped round to scan *Echo's* deck. A faint swell was moving in from the sea, and the two hulls creaked and groaned as they moved against one another.

"Work's just begun, lads!" he whispered. "Move across to *Echo*, now. And watch that damned leap, hein? That tumblehome makes it a good eight feet!"

Then he was up on the rail, and with a surge of his legs, in mid-air, the wind loud in his ears. He banged down against *Echo's* side, one foot on a batten, cursing at the pain that lanced through his bruised knees. Then he grabbed at the corvette's rail, vaulted up and dropped lightly to her deck.

Echo! he exulted silently. Mine again!

One by one the others dropped down beside him, knives and tomahawks ready as they crouched. Surely the noise of their landing would bring the three below up in seconds.

Gallant strained to listen, mouth open. There was the ring of a tin cup banged down on a mess table from below in *Echo*, and a voice carried up through the gratings.

"Tom! Few o' the lads must be back! I heard 'em comin' aboard!"

"Right. I'll up n' see what's the do", said a second voice.

Gallant glanced round at his little group. "Not a move!" he found himself saying. "This one's mine!"

There was a sudden loud clump of heels below him, and then a broad back in a leather jerkin was heaving up the hatchway ladder, below a ragged cocked hat that bore a bright flash on its crown.

Gallant stared. It was a strip of fine, manyhued Micmac quillwork, that only women's fingers could do.

At the sight of the decoration the image of the slashed Micmac girl, spread-eagled in her own blood rose before his eyes. A bubble of rage boiled out of nowhere into his chest.

The man had reached the top of the ladder and was stepping over the hatchway lip to the deck, swivelling to look for the returning boats. With a growl in his throat Gallant leaped.

As the man's eyes goggled and then bulged horribly, Gallant drove his knife with every ounce of strength up into the man's

171

chest below his rib cage. The pirate bucked, a shriek muffled behind Gallant's grip. Gallant sprawled his weight over the man, pinning him down as he threshed. Then the man was lolling back, suddenly slack.

Gallant rose to his knees and jerked out the bloody blade, wiping it on the man's shirt. Already his ears were listening for some movement below. Two down, and two to go.

Béssac squatted beside him. "Christ, capitaine! That was quick! Pity the bugger, eh?"

Gallant stared coldly at him, the rage still strong within him. "No, Béssac. Not at all. Not at all!"

"The next one's coming", Gallant whispered. "Thibeault, he's yours. We'll try for the last man alive. All of you, lie low!"

Thibeault crouched like a cat at the hatchway.

The second man padded in bare feet up the hatch. "What th' deuce be you up to, mate? It sounded fair like . . . ."

He got no further, as Thibeault's steely arm closed like a vise around his neck, arching him over the hatchway lip. The knife sank down once, twice. With a ghastly bubbling moan the man slipped out of Thibeault's grasp and tumbled with a crash down the ladder to the deck below.

Gallant spat. Damn! The third man would be warned!

"Come on! After him!" he barked.

With a bound Gallant was at the hatchway, and he leaped heedlessly down it, to thump down beside the dead man at the ladder's foot. Squinting against the glare of the glim that hung swinging under the deckhead, Gallant glimpsed a wizened, terror-stricken face backing into the shadows of the long gun-deck.

Even in the poor light Gallant could see he was old and wizened. Likely a craftsman kept on for his skills, Gallant thought. The old man's face was twisted in fear.

Béssac stepped in past the marine. The sight of the mate's broad, half-naked figure and frighteningly blackened face sent the old man cowering further in.

"Out, gran'père! Quickly!" Béssac's paw clamped on the man's frail shoulder and propelled him forward in a pathetic sprawl at Gallant's feet.

Gallant dropped to his heels, his eyes cold, the blade of his knife thrust against the man's wrinkled throat.

"Quickly, old man. Where are the rest of your kind? Eh? Speak, or I'll . . .!" The knife pressed in.

"Christ, don't! I . . . I'll tell 'ee, no fear, cap'n! They be refittin' the pink! Yonder shore, behind the boom!''

"What boom? What the devil are you talking about?''

"Floatin' logs, cap'n! Covered with trees, like, t' hide a snug cove! We . . . they took a Yankee pink a day ago! She be damaged a bit, see, so we be a-fixin' 'er to sail with us! Nothin' more, cap'n!''

Béssac's eye caught Gallant's. "That's it, capitaine! Explains where the boats have gone!''

Gallant nodded. "Maybe. I'm still not sure what in hell he's talking about.'' He jerked a thumb toward the ladder. "Get back on deck, Béssac, and quick. See if you can see any of this, and see what's happening with Lauzon and Robert.''

The mate sprang up the ladder, and the other Acadiens clustered round Gallant as he turned back to the old man.

"I won't ask what you've done to the poor wretches in that pink's crew. But what about my crew, hein? In this ship?''

"Please, cap'n! They . . . they be safe! Safe, I says!''

"Where?''

"Right aboard, cap'n, in th'orlop n' the cable tier! Some in yer hold, too. But they be well as babes and . . . .''

Gallant listened no further. "Thibeault! Abbelly! Get down there and free 'em! Break open the damned bulkheads if you have to!''

The marine turned back to the old man. "By God, you'd better be right, old man. They'd better be well!''

"They be, cap'n! Christ knows! An' the King's men, too, in their ship! We ain't hurt 'em a pinch, cap'n! Treated 'em fair, like as Christians ought. You can lay t' what old Bill says!''

"Capitaine! On deck! Quickly! Quickly!'' Béssac's voice was booming from the weatherdeck, taut with alarm.

Gallant sprang to his feet. With a flash of his fist he put a carefully-aimed blow on the point of the old man's chin that slumped him back beside the ladder foot.

Béssac was in *Echo's* bows, standing astride the bowsprit foot, his legs braced against its double timber-bitt. He was pointing ashore. Far off to starboard Lauzon's and Robert's fire still roared . . . God knows how they kept it going . . . with intermittent musket blasts still ringing across the harbour. But Béssac's attention was toward the distant larboard shore.

Gallant arrived at his side, sheathing his knife.

"What is it?''

"Look at that, capitaine!'' Béssac breathed. "I don't believe it!''

Gallant stared. With the moonlight strong now on the dark far shore, visibility was good. And Gallant was watching what appeared to be a long section of shoreline itself, trees and all, slowly opening like a door to the pull of a boat's oars. A door that revealed a lantern-hung small vessel lying in a hidden cove, her yards canted and her topmasts sent down as if undergoing repair.

And the light also revealed the clutch of half-dozen ship's boats, their sweep blades flashing dully in the moonglow, pulling out round the gate boat and striking out for the starboard shore and the fire. Lanterns gleamed in their bows, and even at this distance it was clear that each boat was crowded with men.

"Sweet Mother of God!" said Béssac. "There must be fifty men in those boats!"

From below there was a muffled crash, then the bang and thump of wood smashed and thrown aside, and then voices. Voices in French, raised in surprise, in hails, in hoots of joy and jubilation. And as they rang out Abbelly was bounding up the after companionway, face aglow with delight.

"Found 'em, capitaine! Safe n' sound, all of 'em! Hungry as hellhounds and sick to death of the smell of the bilges, but safe! M'sieu' Akiwoya, too!"

"Thank God!" burst out Gallant.

He spun to look at the line of boats, beginning to string itself out on the blue-dappled harbour surface. He had his crew again. And now, by God, he was not going to have Lauzon and Robert pay the price for that!

He looked down. The two nine-pounder bowchasers were still in place, tackles set up, gun tools still lying in their racks where *Echo's* crew had left them when the pirates had struck. The larboard gun's field of fire was hopelessly masked by the projecting bulk of *Salamander's* bowsprit.

But the starboard gun . . . .

"Béssac!" Gallant barked. "Get below. See if Akiwoya is in shape to report to me. As long as he can stand I want him and his best crew . . . likely that's Soucy's . . . up here on this gun! And send Abbelly to break into the magazine! There's no time to find out where the other bloody key is!"

Béssac stared at the distant line of boats, which would soon bear ahead of *Echo's* bows. "They're going for poor Lauzon and Robert, all right! And you mean you're going to . . .?"

Gallant grinned at him. "Yes, Béssac, yes! But only if you move!"

174

It was scant minutes before the huge black form of the African gunner loomed up on deck. Gallant fought back sudden wetness in his eyes as he gruffly embraced Akiwoya. Like the half-dozen other men who had stumbled on deck with him, the gunner reeked of bilge stench and looked gaunt and worn in the moonlight. But the eyes of all of them were alive with joy.

"Peste, capitaine, I'd thought you'd forgotten us!"

Gallant snorted. "Forget you? Hah! Thank God those swine did you no harm."

Akiwoya shook his head. "They would have, and damned soon enough, capitaine! Christ, what I wouldn't give for a hot fish stew!"

"Thibeault!" Gallant called, as he glimpsed the man in the waist. "Get below and see if the swine left anything in the bread casks! And if there's brandy left, broach a good one! It'll be a tasse all round!"

The man beamed. "À vos ordres, capitaine!" With three or four other men at his heels he leaped down the midships hatchway.

Gallant hoped the buccaneers had indeed been stocking for a major passage. *Echo's* half-hundred men were likely ravenous to a man, and Gallant felt he would have to get something into their bellies before they started dropping at their posts. And in the fighting he sensed was coming that would be sheer disaster.

Gallant gripped the rock-hard muscles of Akiwoya's shoulder. "Look yonder, Akiwoya. Larboard bow, but fine. See those boats?"

"Sacristi, yes! But who. . .?"

"Most of the pirates are in 'em. They were working on that little vessel close aboard the shoreline there. But now they're heading over in force to see what that fire's about. And two of our lads are tending that blaze. It was meant as a diversion to help us get aboard." He spat over the rail. "Can you . . .?"

Akiwoya's face split in a sudden grin, teeth white in his ebony features. "Say no more, capitaine!" He slapped the barrel of the starboard gun. "This chaser'll do it. But the magazine! The bastards got the key from me!"

"I figured as much. Abbelly's breaking into it." Then, as Akiwoya nodded, his mind already calculating ranges, Gallant tightened his grip on the man for emphasis. "You've got to hit them as hard as possible, man. We've no chance to get *Echo* out of here unless we put them on their ear for a bit.

And I don't want to lose Lauzon and Robert. You follow?''

The African punched one fist into the other. "Never you mind, capitaine. I need to repay those bastards for the little surprise they pulled on me!'' He spun to the gunners, who were tearing at heavy chunks of bread Thibeault had arrived with.

"Riopelle! Where's Soucy? Good! Stand by the starboard chaser, lads! Arpin and Riopelle, you'll do the monkeying! I want cartridge from the magazine, and I want it quickly!''

The two men, their cheeks bulging comically with the bread, leaped for the forward companionway. Akiwoya turned back in time to take the half-loaf Thibeault pressed into his hands.

Thibeault grinned at Gallant, hefting the breadbag that he carried. "The ship's stocked to the deckheads, m'sieu'! All fresh! They were heading somewhere, all right!''

Gallant nodded as he tore at a piece of the bread. It was sweet and soft, a far cry from the claylike biscuit that usually passed for ship's 'bread'.

He turned to Akiwoya. "How soon can you fire?'' he said, through a full mouth.

"Depends on how fast the cartridge . . . Christ, here they come now! Good men!'' Akiwoya flung aside the bread and sprang to the gun, hunger forgotten. "Bon, mes braves!'' he barked. "Take up the fall of the trail tackle! Let's get her run back! Riopelle! Out tompion!''

Béssac appeared suddenly, to thrust a leather flagon into Gallant's hand. Gallant put it to his lips and felt strong, exquisite brandy pour down his throat.

"Christ's Bowels!'' he swore, gasping. "Where did you . . .?''

Béssac grinned. "In your cabin, capitaine. Good, hein? Those bastards like to live well!''

Gallant swigged at the brandy, moving quickly to the rail. Akiwoya and his quick crew were already running the little nine-pounder out, the trucks and block sheaves squealing as they hauled. Ahead, the uneven cluster of boats was just beginning to move clear, almost dead on *Echo's* bows. It was no long shot for a good and well-lain nine-pounder. But in this tricky moonlight . . . .

"Trail right!'' Akiwoya barked. "Heave . . . heave . . .handsomely, now . . . Halt!'' He stood up, and nodded to Soucy, who immediately struck fire deftly in his tinder box and lit the match of a portfire.

"We can fire when they bear, capitaine", the African said. "That lead boat will ready for it in a minute!"

Gallant nodded, his mind thinking rapidly, calculating the chances the gunner had of hitting every boat. They were slim. And what if the unscathed boats turned and made for *Echo* at the first round?

Behind him, *Echo's* deck was filling with moving men as her released crew poured up, grinning with relief and joy as the cool night air struck their faces. Word of the drama unfolding spread through them and they crowded to the rail.

Gallant cursed. "By God, have you dullards forgotten everything? Béssac! Get the hands to stations for making sail, and axes ready at the moorings! Garneau! Stop staring at me like a schoolgirl and get those marines of yours hunting for arms below! The pirates must have kept our weapons, or added their own! I want a sharpshooting party here on deck in a clock's tick!"

Gallant's words struck like a lightning bolt through the knots of men. With Béssac's own snarls at their heels, they galvanized into a rush of movement that had the decks trembling to the thump of their running feet.

Béssac reappeared at the foot of the waistdeck ladder again. "Capitaine? Did you say making sail?"

Gallant grinned at him. "Béssac, if we can set those bloodsuckers on their ear long enough to get out of here, I'm going to do it! And haven't you noticed? The tide's turned fair!"

Béssac whooped, only to pause at Gallant's quick gesture.

"Get a fast crew into one of those two boats alongside, Béssac. Get 'em ashore to get our clothes and gear, and pick up Lauzon and Robert. Quickly, now!"

Gallant sprang to Akiwoya's side, behind the little gun and its tensed, waiting crew. He squinted down the barrel out through the gunport. The lead boat was no more than fifteen degrees away from being in the gun's line of fire.

"Good", said Gallant, briskly. "Fire as you see fit. But I want every damn boat, if you can do it!"

Akiwoya nodded and spat on his hands. "We'll see what happens, m'sieu'!"

Gallant stepped back from the gun, and Akiwoya took a last quick look round the crew. He motioned to Soucy, who blew the match head into a bright pink ember and then flicked a ready look back at him.

"Steady . . . steady . . ." murmured the African, crouching now well back of the gun, eyes following the hull shape of the first boat crossing the line of fire of the gun. "Steady . . . ."

Then he bobbed his head. "Fire!" he barked.

The portfire arced down, and a pink lancet of flame jetted up from the gun's vent. A brilliant flash followed in the next split second, and the gun's sharp report was ringing in Gallant's ears.

The marine had closed his eyes as Akiwoya had given the order to fire, and now he opened eyes unblinded by the flash to be blinded all the same by a gout of thick, acrid smoke that swept back over *Echo's* rail, engulfing him. Then it was gone, and as Gallant leaped for the rail he saw, out on the harbour surface, a candle-thin geyser leap up almost atop the leading boat. And then Gallant saw sweeps lifting and cartwheeling in the air, and the hull of the boat was canting suddenly at an odd angle. Shouts and screams carried to his ear across the water. Then the boat was gone.

"Got him, by God!" Béssac was exulting from *Echo's* waist. "Right at the waterline."

The second round slammed out, and as Gallant's eyes flicked open he saw a towering geyser, ivory in the moonlight, lift up beside a second boat. A near miss.

"Damn! Keep firing, Akiwoya. I want them all!"

The marine looked aft, searching for Béssac's bulk. "Béssac? That boat's crew?"

"Away, capitaine!" came the answering roar. The mate was leaning out over the foot of the starboard main shrouds, watching the maintopmen scramble aloft to their yard.

Gallant glanced inshore and saw the boat, already well in against the trees, the oar blades flashing like blue steel.

Akiwoya's gun banged again, and as the cloud swirled over the rail and rolled back to envelop Gallant before drifting away to starboard he heard the gunner curse in satisfaction.

"Holà! Got that bastard, Soucy! Blew the stem clean away!" His voice raised in a shout. "Capitaine?"

"I heard. Good shooting. The others?"

Akiwoya pointed. "They've turned back. Pulling for their little ship. I can't fire, capitaine. They've moved out of my arc of fire, behind the rosbif's bows, here."

Gallant looked aloft, sensing air on his cheek and against his naked chest. There was a light wind, and growing, and it was quarterly, to larboard. Light, but enough to move *Echo* seaward. They could drop canvas, axe away the stern mooring, break out the anchors and be under way in minutes! But Béssac's boat was still inshore, and as he peered inland now he could see no sign of it.

Béssac's voice rang forward from the quarterdeck. "Capitaine! They've gone alongside the pink in the cove, all right. Sacristi, I'd bet they're going to try and use her guns on us!"

Béssac was right. The last of the pirate boatloads was stroking hard for the little ship in the cove, behind its floating log gate. The boats already clustered against her were being leapt from by men swarming up the pink's battens. Oaths and orders were ringing clearly across the water, followed moments later by an unmistakable sound; the squeal of wood against wood.

"Gun trucks, by God!" Gallant breathed.

That was ominous. As *Echo* and *Salamander* lay, they faced the pink almost bows on. But the little vessel, for all that it might boast but a five-gun broadside, was moored flank on. It still might mean a killing hail of shot.

Gallant spun on his heel. "Béssac, see that we're ready for sea, hein? I'll want headsails and topsails, and thirty tough lads on the capstan at a moment's notice!" He glanced forward. "Akiwoya! I'll have your gun crews on the larboard gundeck battery, the eighteens only! Load and run out, and wait for gun action on that vessel in the cove!"

Akiwoya stared. "But, m'sieu'! How . . .?"

"You'll see soon enough!" Gallant spied three of *Echo's* marines appearing up *Echo's* after companionway, followed by Garneau, the sergeant.

"Garneau! Have you some arms?"

Then he saw that the marines were slipping into cartridge box straps, and were hefting muskets.

"Oui, capitaine!" came Garneau's reply. "We found the arms and pouches right where they'd tossed 'em!"

"Bayonets as well?"

Garneau's teeth flashed in the darkness. "Oui, capitaine!"

Gallant grunted in satisfaction. "Good. Follow me aboard *Salamander*. Béssac, the ship is yours!"

"Capitaine, what the hell . . .?" the mate began.

"Questions later, Béssac!" the marine shot back, as he swung up on *Echo's* rail. "You just be ready to ride that breeze out of here!"

Gallant leaped back across the dark gulf between the two hulls, Garneau and his marines clumping precariously after. Gallant strode quickly to the midships grating of the English vessel, which was very much a pair to *Echo* in size and function. And *Salamander*, too, bore the unmistakable marks of a vessel readied for sea.

"The English prisoners", said Gallant. "Did anyone bother to look in her for them, Garneau, as far as you know?"

The sergeant shrugged. "Sacristi, capitaine, all we've done since you broke us out is scramble around *Echo*! Not unless a seaman came aboard after 'em."

Their talk paused abruptly as Akiwoya's gun banged out again. Had the gunner found another target still within his arc of fire? But there was no time to ponder that. The sound of the report echoed sharply from the shoreline forest mass.

"They've got to be somewhere in her", said Gallant, "and perhaps right under our feet. Follow me down the companion. If they're not on the gundeck, get down to the orlop and the cable tier. And for God's sake don't skewer someone on those damned bayonets! At least not yet!"

Garneau grinned. "No fear, capitaine! Come on, mes braves!"

Gallant slipped over the edge of the hatchway lip and padded down the ladder, the glow of a single lantern at its foot silhouetting him. It had slipped his mind that he was still naked save for breeches, and with his face still streaked with black he looked to Garneau and the marines for all the world like a savage Turkish corsair rather than a King's officer.

He landed lightly at the foot of the ladder, glancing around quickly. Then he started as he heard the rustle of movement and gasps of surprise. His senses were telling him that a great many pairs of eyes were on him, and as his own eyes picked out more and more details he realized with an abrupt shock that there were men lying in groups but a few feet from him, up to a half-dozen in each space between the guns. Men in seamen's clothing, with heavy lines knotted round their ankles passed through the tackle rings on the guns. Men who stared at him in round-eyed amazement.

Boots clumped on the ladder, and Garneau's marines swung down behind Gallant, their bayonets bright in the lantern light. As Garneau himself swung down Akiwoya's gun barked out yet again, and a wave of stirring and murmuring rose all around Gallant.

" 'nother round! An' look at these lads! Frogs, or I'm damned! The Frogs've got us, boys!"

The voices rose in chatter and volume until a clear, cutting voice of authority rang out in the shadows to Gallant's left, in the corner behind the ladder.

180

"Silence, damn you! Not a man is to move or speak, without direct order!"

Garneau's bayonet levelled at his side, Gallant peered into the shadows to see two tall men in the disordered but recognizable dress of gentlemen struggling to their feet, a little unsteady due to the tight bonds about their ankles and wrists.

Gallant flicked for an instant through his memory of English. "You are the ship's officers?" he said, after a pause.

"What the . . .!" the nearer man burst out. "My stars, Tom, in English!" He looked back at Gallant. The Englishman was tall, slim rather than powerful, but with a look of command to his features despite the beard shadow and disarray. He was looking with some recoil at Gallant. "And who the devil might you be?"

For the first time in many moments Gallant was suddenly aware of his appearance, and he smiled lightly.

"I'm not a pirate, if you're thinking that, m'sieu'. These are my marines. We have taken the ships. Both of them."

There was another babble of voices until silenced by the tall officer's glare. The second man, darker of visage, spoke.

"What? Then you're the French crew? You freed yourselves?"

"In a manner of speaking. My name is Gallant. I command her. My apologies for my less than appropriate dress, m'sieu'."

The tall man stared, his eyes travelling over Gallant. "You . . . *command* her?"

"There is little time to explain, m'sieu'. Several of my men and I escaped the trap which took her. And yourselves. I presume you were pursuing us, n'est-ce pas?"

The tall man unexpectedly grinned, giving him an oddly youthful look. A light of recognition dawned in his eyes.

"Indeed we were. Then you must be . . ."

"Lieutenant Paul François Adhémar Gallant, His Most Christian Majesty's Naval Infantry, at your service. In spite of the breeches and blackface."

The Englishman was grinning again. "I knew it!" He inclined his head. "Lieutenant Anthony Robinson, Royal Navy, His Britannic Majesty's Sloop of War *Salamander*. And this is my First Lieutenant, Mr. Morgan."

"Your servant", said the darker man.

Akiwoya's gun banged again overhead, and Robinson looked toward the companionway.

"Lieutenant Gallant, are you firing on . . .?" he began.

Gallant's mind had been racing from thought to thought, the need for swift action speeding it. And now the wild scheme that had been but half-formed when he came aboard *Salamander* hardened into firm shape.

"The buccaneers, M'sieu' Robinson. Their boats."

"Their boats? But where . . .?"

Gallant shook his head. "Your guards and those in *Echo*, my vessel, have been disposed of. The pirates were inshore, making repairs to another prize they'd taken. We've been firing on boats they had out while we bring aboard the last of our shore party."

Robinson gaped. "Well, I'm damned!" he breathed.

Gallant stepped closer to him. "Listen to me carefully, Lieutenant. We'll see to your bindings in an instant." His gaze glittered into Robinson's eyes.

"You and I are at war, hein? We have our duties to perform in the face of that fact!"

"Of course. But . . . ."

"Let me finish. I believe, strangely, that you knew my mission. And that yours was to impede mine. Am I correct?"

Robinson's expression was guarded. But the flicker in his eyes gave Gallant the answer, and the marine plunged on.

"Very well. My task was . . . is . . . the pursuit and recovery of a vast amount of bullion, and a religious sculpture, all being the property of my King. You were sent to recover it, perhaps? Am I correct, Lieutenant?" He glanced up the open hatchway. "I beg you to answer, and quickly!"

Robinson was motionless for an instant. But then an odd spark kindled in his eyes as he looked into the intense and compelling gaze of this peculiar Frenchman. And he felt himself nod, heard himself say, "Yes. That is quite correct, in fact."

"Very well", Gallant went on quickly. "That hoard is now in the hands of those cutthroats, owing allegiance to neither of our flags, I may add, who have put us in this situation. They are a savage and bloody lot who have plundered vessels of both our nations, hein? And now they intend to make off with it, and finance Providence knows what new infamy with it!"

"Go on", said Robinson, fascinated by the predatory, killer light that shone in Gallant's eyes.

"They have a large ship, perhaps forty guns, and two consorts. And either tomorrow or the next day they'll sail with the plunder from the place they've hidden it thus far. Where it's been for years, if you count all they've taken!"

"Where is that?"

"Baie Mohone. A hard day's southward sail, at the minimum."

Robinson glanced at Morgan. "Damn, Tom! That's where we found Rand!"

Gallant started at the familiar name, but pressed on, the tone of his voice making Robinson tingle with a strange anticipation in spite of himself.

"Then listen!" he was saying. "I'm proposing a truce, Robinson, between us. The pirates are a filthy lot, and enemies of us both. They've made us both look like fools. And I've seen them do worse, much worse, ashore." Gallant's expression was grim. "To let them get away with what they've done hurts us equally."

And then Gallant struck.

"Join me, M'sieu' Robinson! Sail with me, here and now! Blast a way with me out past that buccaneer prize that's going to rake us stem to stern if we don't cut our moorings and sail!" Gallant's eyes bored into the Englishman. "Then let us crack on sail and trap that heinous lot; Salter, and the other one, Spooner, and their whole coven of . . . ."

"Spooner!" spat out Robinson. "Him?"

"I heard his name. He commands the consorts, it seemed, while Salter was to take the forty-gunner." Gallant was speaking with vibrant intensity. "Trap them, before they get to sea, and take back the damned gold and the sculpture before they put it to some foul use! And put their bones to rot on the seabed if we can!"

Then Gallant drew himself up slightly as he said his last words.

"Then, when we have the hoard secured and have done for the salauds, you have my word as a Christian gentleman that we will resolve our own competition in a fair and honourable way. Whether it be by fair ship action or the crossing of our own blades!"

Akiwoya's gun banged out again, the sound a dull thunder down through the sloop's planking.

Robinson looked round at Morgan, at the attentive and tense faces of his crew. *Salamander's* men had struggled upright and were watching the little scene under the companionway ladder.

"And if I refuse?" he said.

Gallant nodded. "You and your men will be released from your bonds and fed and cared for to the best of my ability. But I will press on with it all."

Robinson shook his head. "Damn me if a parliamentary approach isn't called for here, Tom!" he said in a loud voice. He looked round the gundeck's shadows. "What say you, lads? Would you fight alongside these Frenchmen? To have a good turn at the pirate bastards?"

There was a split-second silence that followed his words. And then a roar burst from a hundred and twenty English throats.

Robinson turned back, his own grin matching the one that was breaking across Gallant's features. He reached out his bound hands and accepted the marine's hand in a firm, powerful grip.

"By God, you have your truce, Gallant. And your alliance!"

Another roar burst from the watching *Salamanders*, and with his heart pounding in his temples Gallant turned to Garneau.

"Get them unbound, Garneau! Quickly! And then get back aboard *Echo!* As soon as we can set an axe to that stern line and break out the anchors, we'll sail!"

He spun to Robinson, who was tearing at the bonds on his wrists with his teeth, and with a flash of his sheath knife he cut the English officer free.

"The pirate's a small vessel, Robinson, what you call a pink. Close inshore to larboard. A small battery, but certain to broadside us in a minute after what we did to their boats! We're moored head to sea, bearing northerly. The wind's quarterly, west by south, and the tide's turned fair. I'll make sail, get under way and empty my larboard battery into him! Can you do the same?"

Robinson rang long fingers through his hair, shouting now over the tumult the freeing of his crew was producing. "Yes, if I can get into the magazine! But as to the ship's state, who knows what the buggers have done to her!"

Gallant shook his head. "She's fully stored, I'll warrant, Robinson. They were taking her to sea tomorrow. Bread, powder, water . . . she's likely victualled to the hilt!"

"Tomorrow! Then, at sea, they were going to . . . ." He did not finish. But his eyes met Gallant's.

"I think we understand the need for this, M'sieu' Robinson", said Gallant, nodding. He moved to the ladder. "I'll await your company off the headland!"

Robinson cleared his throat, watching Gallant leap lithely up the ladder.

By Jehovah, he thought. Allied with the man I was pursuing against pirates I refused to believe in.

"And what in hell will Mister Anson make of this, I should wonder!" he muttered. And then his voice rose. "Mr. Thomas! As the men get free see that the ship goes to Quarters! All but the cooks, who'll pass round bread and a piggin o' grog if they can find it! We shall have sail and gun action presently!"

And with the cheers of his crew ringing in his ears, he bounded up the ladder to the open night air.

When Gallant reached *Echo's* quarterdeck, Béssac was already there, his deep baritone cracking out orders in rapid succession. Around him the men of the after guard were feverishly reading sheets and braces for the making of sail, eyes turning to Gallant as he sprang up the ladder.

Béssac saw him and jerked a thumb forward. "That's it for the bow chase, capitaine. Akiwoya got off nine rounds."

"Sacristi, Béssac, what was he shooting at? They were out of his arc of fire before I went over . . . ."

"They didn't know that, ashore", grinned the mate. "He was throwing the shot high, over *Salamander's* 'sprit, just to make 'em keep their heads down. Christ knows where it landed."

"Damage?"

The mate cleared his throat. "Two boats sunk outright. A third damaged, but they were bailing as they pulled back."

Gallant nodded, moving to the waistdeck rail. "Very well. It's time to get to sea, old friend. That pink'll have a vicious little broadside, and for the life of me I can't understand why they haven't fired yet . . . ."

Béssac was about to speak when there was a sudden commotion aboard *Salamander,* and he stared dumbfounded as Garneau and his men appeared up the midships companionway, and were then followed by two English officers and a horde of burly seamen, who began sprinting away about the ship in a brisk and businesslike manner.

"What in blazes!" Béssac blurted out.

Gallant grinned at him. "Pass the word, Béssac! The Englishmen are with us in this one!"

"What!"

"We've had a gentleman's agreement, so to speak. We're going together against Salter and the rest of them, and trap them in their lair. And after that we'll resume our own argument."

"You're joking. They *agreed* to that?"

Gallant slapped the rail. "Damn it, Béssac, they're not fools! And they've a score to settle as much as we do!" He looked aloft. "Pass the word forward about it. And then let's make sail, old friend!"

It needed little effort to pass the word of this startling development through *Echo's* crew. Within minutes the seamen at their feverish work on deck and aloft in both ships were gaping in cautious amazement across at each other. And then there was a grin and a wave, and then more, and soon a chorus of hearty bellows back and forth between the ships.

There were almost simultaneous bellows from the quarterdecks of both ships that silenced the jocularity. Gallant looked over to near *Salamander's* wheel and saw Robinson grinning at him.

Béssac grunted at his side. "Ready to heave short, capitaine. And I've got Sainte-Juste coming on the wheel." He looked over at *Salamander*. "God, look at their topmen work! No wonder the bastards are wizards at sea!"

"Indeed", said Gallant. He was peering ashore to search out the dim form of the pink. Why had they not fired? "Let's hope that magic serves us in the next . . . ."

"Deck there!" The lookout's call rang down from *Echo's* foretop.

Gallant cupped his hands. "Deck, aye!"

"A boat, m'sieu'! Pulling out! It's ours, and they've got Lauzon and Robert!"

Béssac heaved a sigh. "Good lads! Thank Christ!"

Gallant spat expertly over the rail. "Bon! The lines holding us to *Salamander* slipped? Good. Have an axe at that stern mooring and heave her short, Béssac!"

"Oui, m'sieu'. She's on one bower, starboard side. Should be easy to break out."

Béssac strode forward, and under his orders the bars were slotted into the drum of the capstan. Thirty of *Echo's* crew slid in behind them. Then an axe blow sounded from aft, followed by a slithery splash as the line fell, and Béssac's voice boomed out anew.

The pawls clinked slowly, then faster, as the capstan turned. *Echo* crept forward slightly.

Gallant threw a look inshore. There was the boat, pulling strongly out. It would be alongside in seconds, and Gallant found himself hoping his clothes would be in it.

Sainte-Juste arrived, bright-eyed, to seize the wheel. "Course to steer, capitaine?" he said.

Gallant gave him a quick smile. "Dead amidships till we get under way, Sainte-Juste. Then listen like a hawk!"

Forward, there was a yell from a man watching over the bows, and the clink of the pawls stopped. Béssac was striding aft. "A-cockbill, capitaine! We're free!"

"Cut tackles, now, old friend! And I want her fished out of the way quickly!"

In a few more minutes Béssac was bounding back to the quarterdeck, while in the bows *Echo's* anchor was being firmly lashed against its pad.

"Sail, m'sieu'?" he said.

"Immediately", said Gallant briskly, "Spanker first! Then headsails and topsails! Leave the courses till we're clear of this damned bay! I'll want . . . ."

His ears humming, Gallant squinted inshore. He cursed. He could see nothing of the pink with his flash-blinded eyes. Fool, to have not shut your eyes! he swore silently.

Béssac arrived at his side, puffing with exertion and excitement. He thrust a pile of familiar clothing, shoes and a hat at Gallant.

"Your clothes, capitaine, from the boat! Did we hit him?"

Gallant wrestled himself into his shirt, glad of its rough warmth. "Damn it, Béssac, it's impossible to tell! Sainte-Juste, watch your helm, hein? You've fallen off too far!"

He spat as he clamped his hat on his head. "Bloody flash blinded me. Let's see if the next broad . . . ."

Gallant's face was illuminated suddenly by a flicker of light from astern, and as both men spun on their heels to stare, *Salamander's* larboard battery began to roar out, the rhythmic punch of the flashes and reports as regular as *Echo's* had been.

Gallant stared inland, and a surge of excitement flashed through him. "There she is, Béssac! And, Christ, look what the English are doing to her!"

The low shape of the pink was visible now, clear against the dark wooded shore. The water all around the vessel was leaping in spurts and splashes, and the vessel itself seemed to be shaking and trembling as the English shot smashed into her.

Béssac looked at Gallant. "Sacristi, they're smashing it to bits! One damned broadside, and . . .!"

Béssac's face was lit, along with the smallest detail of *Echo's* deck and rigging, even the close-packed evergreens at water's edge, in an eye-searing yellow flash of light, as if an instant's worth of midsummer noon daylight had been flicked on and then snuffed out. There was a rush of hot air, and then in the next instant a tremendous, ear-piercing concussion.

Recoiling, Gallant gaped inshore at the huge fireball that was rising from where the pink had lain, a hideous red cabbage that became swiftly laced with black fingers until it vanished into the mushroom-shaped cloud that boiled up into the moonlight. Bits of wood and wreckage, small globs of hissing metal, began to thwack and ping down on *Echo's* deck, and the water alongside lifted to little splashes under the rain of fragments.

"Sweet Mary!" blurted out Sainte-Juste. "She . . . she blew up!"

Gallant shook himself. The pink was gone, as surely as if she had been plucked from the water by a giant hand.

From astern, in *Salamander,* Gallant could hear cheering. And now his own crew were picking it up, the voices echoing and rebounding over the dark harbour waters through which the two ships slipped with ever increasing speed.

Beside him, Béssac was scratching at his beard stubble.

"What the hell did that, capitaine? I can guess at a lot, but . . . ."

Gallant shrugged. "Christ knows, Béssac. Mishandled rounds by one of their own men. An overturned lamp. A fire our own rounds may have started. Or one of the English shot, impacting right into the magazine!" He shook his head.

The Mate nodded. "Bièn oui. I'm just thankful it happened. He didn't get a round into us!"

Gallant looked seaward. On this heading *Echo* was drawing well and would clear the leeward headland with room to spare. In an hour she would be at sea, ready to turn against the wind and beat down to the final chapter of the chase she had begun.

He pulled on his waistcoat and shrugged into his uniform coat, conscious now of the shaking in his knees. Pulling on the coat seemed a symbolic act, in a sense: the end of the shore episode; the end of woodland creeping, and mosquito-crazed nights in smoky shelters; the end of knives and stealth and the smell of blood on wet moss; and the end of dying, beautiful Micmac women, their eyes closing in needless death as rain streaked over their cheeks, and as arms closed in helpless grief around them.

Gallant shook himself, as if to cast a shadow off his shoulders. "Thank God," he said. "Thank God, I am home again, where I belong. And where I can fight in a way I know. Where I must stay, if God will grant it."

And, settling his hat firmly on his head, he filled his lungs.

"Béssac!" he roared. "The courses, if you please!"

A trio of gun flashes flickered inshore to larboard, where the pink lay, and before the crash of a broadside echoed round the harbour there was the low, ominous hum of round shot passing close overhead. Three towering geysers leaped up, hissing, in the narrow gap between the French and English ships.

"Vite, Béssac!" Gallant barked. "They've opened fire!"

A thrill stirred in Gallant, the familiar and never-failing thrill, as *Echo* moved under his feet to the first pull of life from the sails. She was alive again. Alive, and his!

"Steady as you go, Sainte-Juste!" he said.

Sheaves squealed in their blocks forward, and as the humped figures of men sank in rhythmic hauling on the halliards the shadowy triangles of foretopmast staysail, jib and jib topsail stretched up their stays, the canvas rippling and crackling out to starboard with the breeze immediately. As the sheets were gathered in a gentle gurgle began to sound under *Echo's* counter. To Gallant is was the sweetest of all possible sounds.

There was a sudden bumping and hails along the starboard side, announcing the arrival of the shore boat. Gallant saw men scrambling over the rail, their arms loaded with clothing bundles and muskets.

"Tie the boat on aft, lads! Quickly! Stream it astern!" he called out, through cupped hands. "Topsails, there! Let fall and sheet home!"

A flash of gunfire winked ashore again, and as the guns' concussions slapped at *Echo* Gallant watched three more shimmering, delicate geysers leap with a hiss a half-cable in front of the slowly accelerating corvette.

Short, he thought. One over, one under. And then the third broadside . . . .

Yells of rage came faintly to his ear. Obviously the pirates could see *Echo* was slipping out of their fingers.

Gallant looked aloft at the foretopsail leech. "Two points to starboard, Sainte-Juste! Let her build some way. And we'll give our guns as good an angle as we can!"

"M'sieu' ", said Sainte-Juste tersely, eyes glued on the compass card. He spun the spokes gently.

Gallant strode to the waistdeck rail. "Akiwoya!"

"Oui, capitaine?" The African's voice boomed up the companionway from the gundeck.

"The next rounds'll strike us for certain! Can your guns bear on him yet?"

"Still too far on the bows for a broadside, capitaine! Can you steer to starboard?"

Damn! Gallant squinted ahead, as overhead the great topsails rippled and then thumped taut with the vagaries of the wind. *Echo* creaked and rolled slightly under his feet. Another two points to starboard might still carry them clear of the shoal water against the leeward shore. "Very well!" he called.

There was a cry from the mizzentop lookout. "Deck, there! The English've broken out their anchor! They're making sail!"

Gallant glanced aft, in time to see the pale spectre of a topsail drop into place on *Salamander's* foremast, the thump of its fall clear on the wind. Good!

He stepped to beside Sainte-Juste and squinted at the binnacle. "Starboard another point, Sainte-Juste. There! Midships! No further, or we'll ground for sure!" He cupped his hands. "Braces, there! Abbelly! See to that mizzentops'l lee bowline!"

Gallant sprang back to the rail. In a quick swing his eyes took in *Echo's* hissing wake back to the looming, moving shape of *Salamander,* astern; the dark masses of the wooded shores; and in the cove to larboard, the uncertain shape of the pink, ready, he was certain, to unleash another broadside. At this range, so close now, and if they had their guns trained and laid properly, *Echo* could be terribly hurt.

Heart racing, he cleared his throat and bellowed again, the tension making his voice hoarse. "Akiwoya!"

"Clear arc of fire, capitaine!" came the African's cry. Then his voice was rising in the bark of orders.

"Larboard battery, fire! As you bear!"

A split-second later the first gun fired.

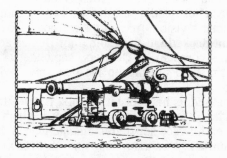

EIGHT

Suddenly, it was dawn, and a grey harsh light was streaming in through the stern windows. A whitecapped storm sea raged beyond, marked by *Echo's* wake.

There was a brisk knock at the cabin door. Gallant shook his head and rose, thrusting the pistols into the waistband of his breeches. "Come!" he said.

Béssac threw open the door, lurching a little to *Echo's* pitching as he stepped through. His seacoat was buttoned tight around him, and he was drenched with spray.

"You couldn't have timed it better, capitaine. Did you sleep?"

"Somewhat. Fell asleep at the desk." Gallant ran his fingers through his hair. "Where in Hades are we?"

"That's what I'm here for." The mate took a deep breath and launched into the litany of his report. "Ship's head is east sou'east, starboard tack, just like last night. The wind's east-

erly and damned near a gale, and looks to be worse. But I've
kept sail on her.''

Gallant felt *Echo* heave and pound down, heeling far to
larboard. "That's a powerful press of sail, Béssac. You trying
to drive her under?''

The mate grinned. "No. Just get us there on time. And I
think I have.''

"What? You mean . . .?'' started Gallant.

"Aspotogan headland's past the windward beam, capitaine,
and Tancouque's visible fine on the starboard bow.''

As Gallant ducked out the cabin door Béssac added, "I've
put the ship's company at Quarters, capitaine, as well. Akiwoya was finishing closing up his gun crews when I came
down.''

Gallant paused as his foot hit the first rung of the companionway ladder. "Sounds like you've got it all in hand!'' he
grinned. Then his face sobered. "*Salamander*. Where . . .?''

Béssac smirked. "Sacristi, capitaine, that rosbif could keep
station into hell if you wanted! He's about two cables off the
larboard quarter. Been there all night. You should see him!
Gunports open and awash, crews on every gun, sail cracked
on like a madman, and full of vinegar for a fight!''

Gallant nodded, resuming his climb. "Then there's just one
thing missing, old friend. The swine we're hunting.''

"Bien oui'', grunted the mate. "Well, we're near enough
to their lair to know soon!''

Gallant clambered out on deck. The howl of the rising wind
in the corvette's rigging was steady and sonorous, and the
planking underfoot was dark with spray. The sky had lightened
to a steely grey, but the wind still had a wintry chill to it that
made the marine shiver involuntarily.

Gallant looked out over the larboard quarter, and caught his
breath. There, lifting and driving prettily into the grey rollers,
spray tossing round her bowsprit, *Salamander's* sleek tan and
black hull rode under the press of her balanced and well-set
strained canvas. Her mainmast pennant streamed like a lance
to leeward, and the British ensign winging out from her staff
was such a brave sight, for all that it was a flag he fought,
that Gallant felt a lump suddenly in his throat.

Looking forward, he found he recognized the land off which
Echo drove almost instantly. Béssac was right; there was the
great mass of the Aspotogan Peninsula hard abeam, and behind
the low shapes of islands the broad face of Baie Mohone was

visible now. There, on the starboard bow rose the familiar hump of Isle Tancouque, and more than half the distance closer, the easternmost island of the diamond group to which Tancouque belonged. Hard on *Echo's* larboard bow there was white shoal water.

Beyond the shoal water lay the featureless low islet the English had already named Pearl Island, by all accounts. On this track *Echo* would beat through almost dead between Pearl and the low, flat island that formed the southern tip of Tancouque's diamond. A fair hunting ground indeed.

But would the prey be there?

"Deck, there! M'sieu'! M'sieu'!" The foretop lookout, his voice cracking with excitement, was shrieking down from his swinging perch.

"Deck, aye!" Gallant answered through cupped hands. A queer tingle shot up his spine.

"Ships!" came the electrifying cry. "Ships, three of 'em! Running out of the bay, past the big island! It . . . Christ, it's the big buccaneer ship, m'sieu'!"

"Sweet Mary!" hooted Béssac, punching a fist into a palm in glee. "We got 'em! Got the bastards!"

Gallant glanced at him. "Not yet, Béssac, not yet! We have to stop them, first!" His voice raised again. "You're certain? It's the black ship?"

"Oui, m'sieu'! The forty-gunner! Jesus save me, I can see her black ensign now! It's her, m'sieu'!"

"The consorts! What of those?"

Gallant could see the lookout leaning precariously out from the top, hair whipping in the wind, pointing as he called down. "They're ahead of her, m'sieu'! No more than a half-cable!" His voice broke again. "They're running for sea room!"

A thump sounded in Gallant's ear, and he spun to see a wisp of smoke whip aft along *Salamander's* side. The sloop had fired a warning gun, and her decks were alive with sudden movement. They, too, had seen the three ships. As Gallant watched he could see men out along the sloop's main yard, shaking out the line of reef points.

Now, M'sieu' Robinson, thought Gallant. We'll see how good a fighting team we can be!

He touched the pistol butts in his waistband and looked round at the nine-pounder crews, who were wild-eyed now with anticipation.

He forced his voice to an even calmness. "Keep a cool and

steady head, lads", he said. "And we may get that chance to hit 'em you want!"

"There!" said Béssac. "There they are, by God!"

Gallant's neck bristled. Out from the cover of the flat, southerly island of Tancouque's group, he was watching a low, black-hulled ship of sloop size under plain sail move into view, bound downwind on a dead run to seaward. Barely a mortar shot astern, it seemed, a second ship, virtually a twin to the first, followed, the water boiling under her bows a white slash under the black cutwater.

But behind them. . . .

"There, Béssac!" Gallant burst out, this time. "It's her! It's the *Pearl!*"

Out from the lee of the island the third ship was driving, its black shape huge and menacing on the heels of the little sloops. Ship-rigged and powerful-looking, a cloud of canvas set on her black masts and the black smear of her ensign rippling above her quarterdeck, the vessel moved like a sinister wraith across the grey waste of rollers out from the shelter of the bay.

Dear God, thought Gallant. What a fight this may be!

There was an oath of surprise, and the gun captain of the nearest nine-pounder was pointing forward.

"Look, m'sieu'! The lead ship! It's turning!"

Gallant narrowed his eyes. The hull shape of the leading black sloop had abruptly foreshortened, it was true. And now he could see dark ripples across the broadening faces of her sails as they swung under their yards, heaved round by unseen hands on braces.

Béssac clucked his tongue noisily. "She's worn round, capitaine. Damn me, but I'd say she means to intercept us!"

Gallant's heart beat faster. He glanced at the compass card and then aloft. "Steady as she lies, Sainte-Juste", he said tersely. "No course changes yet".

Gallant looked to leeward. Under the press, now, of her courses, *Salamander* had leaped ahead, and was now plunging along abreast of the corvette. Gallant could see a tall figure at her weather quarterdeck rail, staring across at *Echo*. His arm was pointing forward.

Béssac appeared suddenly, handing a brass speaking trumpet to Gallant. "Looking for this?" he said.

Gallant snorted. "Damn me, Béssac, sometimes I think you read minds!"

194

He swung up the trumpet. "*Salamander*, there! 'Hoy! Do you hear me?"

There was an answering wave from the figure at the rail.

Gallant raised the trumpet again. "The lead vessel is turning for us!" he bellowed, over the roar of the wind and the sea that heaved between the two driving vessels. "We'll engage her! Can you make for the other sloop?"

Robinson was waving his hat. It would have been useless for him to attempt to speak *Echo,* upwind.

"He's nodding 'yes' ", said Béssac.

Gallant filled his lungs again, only to stop his words in his throat as he glanced forward.

"Christ", he murmured. "The other sloop's turning to us, all right. But the *Pearl's* turning away!"

"*What?*" Béssac squinted through the glass. "You're right! She's running off, sou'easterly. Trying to escape, damn it!" He lowered the glass. "But why? Why would a ship with that weight of broadside run from us?"

Gallant had swung up the trumpet again. "The *Pearl* is trying to run for it!" he boomed. "Whichever of us can break free of her consorts must head her off!"

"He's nodded 'yes' again, capitaine. Now he's back at her wheel", he added, as Robinson's figure disappeared from the rail.

"All right", said Gallant. "We know what we have to do. Now where is . . .?"

Béssac pointed. "Starboard bow, capitaine. Christ, and running down hard! Look at her! She's no more than a league off!"

The black-hulled sloop of war was boiling down toward *Echo,* sails taut and drawing well, her lateen spanker winging well out before her hideous black ensign. A white flash showed regularly at her bows as she overhauled and crashed through the slate-grey rollers.

Beside the marine Béssac spat to leeward, and breathed an inventive obscenity. "That bugger means to fight, all right, capitaine!"

Gallant swallowed, his mouth suddenly dry. "That he does, mon vieux. But he's not raping a helpless merchantman, this time!" he said through tight lips.

He stepped quickly to the rail again, cupping his hands to bellow below at Akiwoya.

"A few minutes, Akiwoya!" he roared. "Your starboard

battery will be the first to bear!''

There was an answering roar from below, and Gallant was back in an instant beside Sainte-Juste, at the wheel.

"A bit nearer!'' he hissed. "Just enough to let her luff a bit. I want him to turn to his larboard. Bon! Hold her there, and no nearer! And for God's sake don't let her go aback!''

Sainte-Juste nodded silently, pale-cheeked. His fingers tightened with effort on the broad oaken spokes of the wheel.

"What are you doing, capitaine?'' said Béssac, looking aloft anxiously as the first rippling luff thundering through *Echo's* topsails shook the deck under their feet. "Hell, he's got the weather gauge, and if he uses it the way I would . . . .''

"That's the point, Béssac! I'm gambling, hein? A pirate goes for a hull-to-hull smash, boarders away, merchant crew on their knees in terror. And that, after a quick pass and a pattering of broadside, if anything! He's no damned man o' war!''

Béssac eyed the onrushing black hull. "And?''

Gallant pointed suddenly. "Look! He's bearing up a shade. He sees we're luffing and lolling, scared as a wench in her bridal bed! And that's what I want!''

At Béssac's uncomprehending expression Gallant pulled a pistol from his waistband and pulled it to half-cock. "Time enough to see what I mean, mon vieux!'' He pointed forward. "Here she comes. Be prepared for some rapid sail handling!''

Gallant looked quickly round *Echo's* weatherdeck as the corvette punched into another swell and staggered up, bows streaming. The nine-pounder crews were crouched ready at their guns. The sailhandlers were clustered at their lines, sheltering against the bulwarks, their eyes flicking anxiously between the onrushing pirate vessel and their officers on the quarterdeck. Behind him, Garneau and his marines fidgeted, muskets cradled and ready against their shoulders. And above his head, rippling out astern in cool, clean beauty, the pure whiteness of *Echo's* Bourbon ensign.

Ready again, by God, he thought. "Steady, lads! All of you! And remember what you've been taught!'' he barked.

Five hundred yards. The sloop rushed down, confident of its prey, coursing now to swing wide and spatter the seemingly labouring corvette with shot before wearing round to smash in for the boarding.

Gallant looked aloft. Sainte-Juste was doing his work beautifully, and *Echo's* canvas was flapping and shaking in horrendous, inexcusable chaos. That had to fool them!

Two hundred yards. The sloop surged up over a grey-bearded swell, and Gallant saw a knot of shaggy, bareheaded men clustering on her foredeck. Over the sea roar came a chorus of faint jeers and hoots.

Then suddenly the sloop was swinging her flank to *Echo's* bows. The first round was only seconds away, unless . . . .

Now!

"Hard a-weather, Sainte-Juste! Five points! Pay off and let her reach!" Gallant cried. "Ready, Akiwoya!"

Responding to the sudden pressure of the helm, *Echo's* sails snapped full with a ringing crack, and the corvette seemed to leap into sudden life. Borne abruptly away from the tossing and pitching to a reach, she knifed in breathless acceleration ahead, and the black hull was suddenly no longer sitting astride her bows, but was swinging abeam.

"Good man!" Gallant exulted. "A moment more . . .!"

In the black ship sudden shouts of rage and consternation carried clear on the wind. Then the pink flame of a gun flash licked out from her side, then two, and three, the thick gouts of smoke whipped into nothing by the wind.

The thump of their reports sounded in his ears, and Gallant winced, involuntarily. Then, beside him, Béssac was hooting, pointing at the toppling three geysers far to leeward.

"Hah! Nothing! Not even a near miss!"

"Our turn, now, Béssac!" said Gallant. "Ready about!"

Echo slammed into the shoulder of a last swell as Gallant threw a last look at the compass card and the yards aloft.

"Hard a-lee!" he barked.

Echo dipped and plunged round into the wind, the still sculpture of her canvas dissolving suddenly into thumping and whiplashing cacophony.

"Off tacks and sheets!" boomed Béssac.

The corvette pitched heavily as she met the eye of the biting wind, and aloft there was a ringing slap that shook the planking under Gallant's feet as the fore topsail went hard aback.

"Mainsail, haul!" roared Béssac. "Lively, damn you!"

Now *Echo* was almost round, and on her leeward bow the pitching stern gallery of the black sloop bore, naked and unprotected.

Just the sight I wanted to see! thought Gallant, and then he was leaping back to the rail as Béssac's stream of orders rang in his ears.

"Let go and haul! Quickly, lads! Trim her all sharp!"

Within seconds of his order and the frenzied hauling, *Echo* leaped ahead on her new track, now so far off the wind and so braced round that it was a thundering, heeling reach, the wind shrieking in from abeam. She roared on, swooping in on the stern of the sloop.

Béssac held on to his hat with both hands. "The bastard's wearing to starboard, capitaine! Trying to duck away!"

Gallant spat into the scuppers, a wild exultation bubbling in his chest. "Let him! It'll do him no good!" He cupped his hands. "A moment more, you gunners! Then give the swine what they deserve!"

In *Echo* raced. Holding his breath, Gallant waited. Thirty seconds more. Ten seconds more. Now!

"Now, lads! Fire! fire!"

Echo staggered, as if from the slap of a mighty hand. There was no regular, clockwork succession of reports as each gun came to bear. So eager had Akiwoya's gun captains been that they had handspiked their guns round constantly, training on the target moment to moment. And now, their teeth bared in savage satisfaction, they had fired the corvette's entire starboard battery of long nine- and eighteen-pound guns virtually at once, and at little better than point-blank range.

The effect was devastating. The sloop's stern gallery crumpled and shattered into winging halos of splinters and cartwheeling debris, and along her visible quarter whole sections of hull planking suddenly disintegrated. As the grey swells around her leaped with the towering geysers of the few shot that missed, the sloop's canvas shook and shivered on the yards. And then, splintering suddenly below the futtock shrouds, the sloop's mainmast buckled and toppled in a whiplashing chaos of writhing lines and obscenely ballooning canvas against the foremast with an audible crash.

The corvette's gunners worked at the guns in a frenzy, sponging, reloading, ramming in grim determination. The smell of the kill was in their nostrils, and they wanted it. *Echo* circled in, driven by Gallant's relentless commands and the straining efforts of her sailhandlers. Within moments she was tacking hard up again into the grey rollers, past the ghastly wreck of the sloop's stern, her gunports ready.

And again Gallant's order barked out. "Fire!"

The broadside was more regular and even this time, guided by Akiwoya's raging voice and quick movement. But again the shot punched home with deadly effect. Geyser after geyser leaped up, bracketing the stricken pirate hull. And again her remaining canvas, uncontrolled now, shook with the hammer blows. Lines and cables writhed like living things, and the sea face was peppered in the small splashes of raining debris.

Then Béssac was pointing, eyes goggling, and the gaze of all in *Echo* who could hear him followed his incredulous finger.

"Sweet Jesus' Blood! She's sinking!"

Gallant stared from where he stood, braced hard against the quarterdeck rail. The sloop had suddenly wallowed low in the trough behind a white-flecked swell, the water visibly swirling into her gaping gunports. Shrieks and cries carried on the wind to *Echo*.

Then in ponderous and unbelievable slow motion, the shattered stern sank beneath the grey water, and the sloop's bowsprit lifted smoothly like a finger toward the zenith of the glowering sky. And then, in a great, bubbling upheaval of wreckage and hissing foam, the sloop sank and was gone, the spot where it had been a moment earlier circled over by a lone, watchful gull.

Echo lifted and hissed down over a swell. Gallant, his stomach a cold knot, wiped his face with his sleeve and looked at Béssac.

"My God", murmured the mate. "We sank her. Like that."

Then Gallant shook himself mentally. This was not the time to muse on such total disaster, so total that it had touched for a moment their own inner seamen's fears. He craned to look downwind, past the snapping ensign, and his heart bounded.

The thump of gunfire faint across the water, *Salamander* was seemingly atop the hull of the second pirate sloop. From the latter sporadic gunfire licked out, but already Gallant could see loose sheets, and now the sloop's canvas was going hopelessly aback. But from *Salamander*, driving in taut on a broad larboard reach, and having already worn around from an earlier point-blank pass, the guns were barking in steady, deadly regularity. Even as Gallant watched he could see the black ship's rigging shake as round after round smashed home with deadly accuracy from the English guns.

Beside him, Béssac was whistling softly through his teeth. "Sacristi, capitaine! The rosbif's pounding the bugger to bits!"

Gallant nodded, awed. "And look how he does it, Béssac. Hull to hull, and banging away like a hammer on an anvil! No wonder they . . . . "

He stopped short, staring past the English sloop and its prey.

"The *Pearl!*" he cried.

Béssac stepped quickly to the binnacle and then looked up at the dark bulk of the distant forty-gun ship.

"She's still with the wind dead aft, capitaine. And no more'n a league away. Hell, half that! If we fell off onto a broad reach, starboard tack, we could . . . ."

Gallant slapped the rail. "Sacristi, you're damned right we could!" He spun on Sainte-Juste. "Take her off, Sainte-Juste! Your course will be . . . there! Sou'east by east!"

He turned back to the mate. "Braces and sheets, mon vieux! And quickly, or we will lose her!"

The mate flashed a grin and leaped down the waistdeck rail, bellowing orders. As he passed the midships hatchway Akiwoya was scrambling up through it, a wild look on his strong features.

"Holà, capitaine!" he boomed. "Did you see? Christ save us, we blew the bottom out of her!"

Gallant flashed his teeth at the African. "Well done, mon brave! And tell your lads that it was damned good gunnery!"

"God's Bowels, capitaine, I've already done that! But there's more, hein?"

Gallant looked up, staring forward over the bows toward the locked shapes of *Salamander* and her prey, and further to the black, spray-wreathed bulk of the *Pearl*. *Echo* was heeled over now, driving hard on the reach, racing across the steadily building wind that was now beginning to whip the crests from the tops of the swells. He knew what he intended to do, if he could catch the *Pearl*, and the awesomeness of it caused his stomach muscles to tighten into a knot.

He looked back at the gunner. "You may lay to that, Akiwoya, as the rosbifs say", he said grimly, half to himself. "You may lay to that!"

The Boutet pistol was still in his grip. He thrust it back into his waistband, turning his eyes again to the hulk of the *Pearl*.

The marine licked his lips. At *Echo's* turn of speed now the corvette was closing the distance quickly, the sullen roar under her bows and counter still building. The *Pearl* loomed huge and menacing before them, but again it was a measure of the hold Gallant's leadership had on them that it crossed no mind to falter at work or turn away from the prospect of a bloody and unequal encounter.

The potential disaster of that fate was all too clear to Gallant as he stood, feet braced, against the waistdeck rail. The *Pearl* would have seen the manner of *Echo's* fight with the sloop.

She would know that the desultory gunnery of a privateer was not called for, but the murderous and rapid volume fire of the ship-to-ship broadside. And, provided she was not crewed by poltroons, her weight of broadside was more than twice that of *Echo's*, her batteries higher set, her hull a fortress in contrast to the corvette's; fought well, she could destroy *Echo* in one minute-long flank to flank pass.

Gallant swallowed, clutching at the rail as *Echo* heeled and buried her bows under a sudden gust. But there was no other option open than that of attack. *Salamander* was abeam and dropping astern, still entangled with the other sloop. By the time the English vessel might have got free to join *Echo* in attacking the forty-gunner, the *Pearl* would be two or three leagues further to seaward. And with nightfall, she would vanish into the grey Atlantic wastes for good.

No. *Echo* had to fling herself in, a terrier against a bear, and hope to worry the *Pearl* into turning and fighting, or even to damage her. Either way, *Echo* had to purchase time until *Salamander* could enter the fray. Otherwise, the black ship, the plunder it likely carried, the Señora itself for all Gallant knew, would be gone. Gone, and all the effort, all the fighting and death, the sacrifice of *Wosowech*, all would have been for nothing. Nothing!

"She'll not get away. By God, she won't!" he said, through clenched teeth.

"Eh?" said Béssac. "What's that, capi. . .?"

He paused, listening over the sea and ship noise. Then the mate swung round, staring at *Salamander*, now well off *Echo's* larboard quarter. His face had a strange expression.

"They're cheering. Cheering! Capitaine, listen! The English are cheering us!" he said.

Gallant listened, and it floated to his ears, faint and distant. Voices raised in huzza after huzza, from the tiny figures he could see now clustered in *Salamander's* rigging and strung out along her yards.

They know, said Gallant to himself, a tightness suddenly in his throat. They know what we're going against.

"Deck, there! The pirate's turning, m'sieu'!"

The high-pitched call of the maintop lookout tore Gallant's gaze away from the English vessel to look forward. Beside him Béssac spat out a curse.

"Look at that! She's gybed, capitaine. Got the wind on her larboard quarter, now. Hell, he means to . . . . ."

201

Gallant grunted. "D'accord. He's turning to fight, Béssac!"

"Think he'll go for the weather gauge? At this distance off, he could still beat up for it. Force us to accept to loo'ard."

Gallant shook his head. "No. He'll hold her on a reach. He . . . there! Look now! He's not swinging her head further, hein? Bows on, and he's bracing up sharp. A reach, Béssac!"

Gallant could not look away from the narrowed shape of the *Pearl*. Heeling now to the beam wind, she was punching strongly toward the corvette, her ensign streaming black and menacing out over her quarter.

Béssac sucked a tooth. "He's not going to weather? Now, why in hell . . .?"

"He's confident, Béssac!" Gallant had an image of Salter's ruddy, grinning face in his mind. "He's got a broadside that'll blow us out of the water, and knows it, whether we're to loo'ard or windward!" Gallant smiled grimly. "He's challenging us, Béssac. Break off or come as close as you dare, is what he's saying."

"So? Do we take the challenge?"

Gallant studied the ever-closing distance, his mind working. "If we get to weather of him, there's greater chance his shot will go high. And if we get no nearer the wind we might go past him fast enough to make a poor target. There might, mon ami, even be a chance to turn hard off the wind and rake his stern. Maybe damage his rudder."

"So . . . ."

"So we hold this point, Béssac! Unless the *Pearl* alters course I want us down his windward flank, as close as we dare, and with this way on!"

Béssac brightened. "Mais, oui! Like going up to scratch with a big man, hein? Go in low, and quickly. And hurt as best you can!"

Gallant pulled his hat down over his eyes, wishing the fluttering in his stomach would stop. "That's it. We've got to buy time for *Salamander* to come up."

He moved to the waistdeck ladder. "I'm going to have a look at the gundeck. You can pass the word that we'll be on him in . . . ten minutes."

Béssac grunted assertion. Then his expression softened, and he said, "You don't need to say anything to the men, capitaine. They'll follow you, without question. Haven't they already?"

Gallant allowed himself a wry smile. "Peut-être. I won't flatter myself with that yet, Béssac. I want them to know what we're getting into." And he was gone down the midships companionway.

Beside Béssac, Sainte-Juste clucked his tongue. "You're right, M'sieu' Béssac."

"Eh?"

"What you said. There isn't a man in *Echo* who wouldn't follow the capitaine anywhere. We've never met a man like him, m'sieu'. Never!"

Béssac looked at the approaching form of the *Pearl*. "I know, Sainte-Juste. Neither have I", he said quietly. "And if he wants me to risk my guts for some damned statue of the King's, I'm fool enough to do it!" Then he laughed.

Below, Gallant spoke briefly with Akiwoya, hunched under the low deckhead beams, directing him to double-shot the guns and warning him of the point-blank encounter that was coming. And then with a wink of encouragement here, a word there, he moved as nonchalantly as he could along the guns, meeting at each one the nods and grins of the corvettemen.

As Gallant regained the quarterdeck he knew that he had won, in a sense, another kind of battle. *Echo* was efficient, well-trained and deadly. But most importantly, she and her men, whatever became of them, had *pride*. And the guns of the *Pearl* could never blast that away.

Béssac spat, hefting a nick-bladed cutlass. "We're ready, capitaine!"

"Very well". Gallant made a conscious effort to control his trembling knees and moved casually to beside Sainte-Juste.

"A light touch, now, matelot", he said evenly. "And pay attention to nothing but my commands, hein? Any wrong movement could finish us."

Sainte-Juste, his skin chalk-white, nodded silently.

"Bon."

Echo heeled again to a fresh, howling gust, her rigging humming. The pirate was under five hundred yards away.

"Akiwoya!" Gallant called. "Run out! Larboard battery!"

"Run out, larboard!" Akiwoya repeated.

From below Gallant's feet there came the squeal of trucks and a rumble as the long eighteens thrust their muzzles out through the ports. On the weatherdeck the nine-pounder crews heaved with brisk effort on their tackles. As the guns snouted out through the bulwark, the gun captains, portfires in hand, moved to crouch beside their guns' trails. Then all was still, save for the boiling rush of *Echo* herself across the whitecapped swells.

Three hundred yards. The *Pearl* dipped in a heel and then stiffened again. Transfixed by the sight, *Echo's* men stared as she loomed in. Gallant's hanger snicked out of its scabbard. "Steady, now, Sainte-Juste!" he hissed. "Graze her windward side!"

The sea leaping aside from their cutwaters, the two vessels closed with each other, now only a cannon shot apart.

Pearl towered up, huge and monstrous over *Echo's* bows, dipping and lunging. It was only a matter of seconds.

"Stand ready!" Gallant cried. His knees were shaking uncontrollably now, and he felt the nausea rising in his stomach.

"Hail Mary, full of grace, the Lord . . . ." Beside Gallant Sainte-Juste was praying under his breath. To Gallant's left he could hear the gun captain of the nearest nine-pounder mumbling the *Aperi Domini*.

"Here she comes!" Béssac roared.

Pearl was atop them. For a horrifying instant Gallant thought the ships were going to collide. Then, with a rushing, spray-tossing roar, the great wall of the *Pearl's* hull was rushing past *Echo's* cathead, and a shadow fell across the corvette's deck.

Béssac was bellowing. "Capitaine! Capi. . .!"

"*Fire*, Akiwoya!" Gallant shrieked.

With a crash the first of *Echo's* guns banged out at the black, rushing mass, the nine-pounders along the weather-deck leaping back on their breeching lines in almost split-second sequence. For an instant, as both ships churned on, the water between them a leaping white, it was only *Echo's* guns that were firing.

And then in the next instant *Echo's* guns were no longer audible. From the double row of gaping gunports in *Pearl*, the uppermost almost at Gallant's eye level, a staggering flash of flame and concussion leaped out in boiling gouts of smoke. The shock of the blast struck Gallant, and he staggered back, ears deafened, and fell to one knee.

The effect of the broadside on *Echo* was terrifying. The *Pearl's* guns, twenty-fours and eighteens, vomited their double-shotted charges into *Echo* at a distance of less than half a ship length. The corvette's hull bucked and shook in awful torture as ball after ball smashed through her bulwarks, ploughing into her gundeck and the spaces below. Men were pulped where they crouched into bloody, tumbling scraps of meat that left slick and scarlet smears across decks and gun carriages. The dark hell of the gundeck, already choked with the smoke of its own guns, rang like a farrier's shop as round shot after round shot smashed into guns, beams, tackles, eyebolts, ironwork, rearing and toppling gun barrels off their trunnions to crush down on the screaming, mangled men who a moment earlier had served them in quick, ordered discipline. Just abaft the trunk of *Echo's* mainmast an enormous hole the size of a longboat gaped open in the corvette's side, and the whining shot that had created it smashed on, surrounded by a flying halo of splinters that scythed down men in handfuls. Writhing men, limbless or blinded, their screams drowned in the horrible thunder, stumbled and fell through the gap into the boiling sea.

In rippling succession the wave of destruction passed down *Echo* as the *Pearl* surged past. Akiwoya, deafened by the din, stared as the gun in front of him cartwheeled back off its carriage and pinned the gun captain in shrieking panic against the midships grating. The splinters of the smashed carriage filled the interior of the gundeck, cutting down the men of the gun crew in a stroke. The African lunged over, stepping across a man rolling on the deck who was clawing at a pulped, featureless face. Then he saw that there was nothing left of the gun captain below the waist but a red mash of rags and flesh. He turned and fought his way forward through the wreckage-filled blackness, bellowing for his gun captains. He was answered by nothing but the repeating hammerblows of the pirate guns, and screams of agony.

On the weatherdeck above, the air seemed to be filled with clouds of black fragments. A shot smashed through the bowsprit foot, and with a grinding protest the bowsprit, pulled hard by the pressure of the forestays, canted suddenly higher, the snapped spritstay whiplashing like a maddened snake. A seaman who an instant earlier had been crouched with a rammer beside a gun was smashed into twitching, bloody fragments against the far rail, a gaping hole in *Echo's* bulwark and decking where the gun and crew had been. The headsails buckled and rippled, thundering in the unceasing wind with their new freedom.

In *Echo's* waist the hail of shot swept like a rake through dry leaves through guns and crews. Whole sections of rail and bulwark shattered into whistling, arcing pieces or cartwheeled crazily in whole sections to the far rail, and over. A punching impact at the foot of the mainmast shook the yards above with wind-spilling force, and with a rending crash and whiplashing of lifts and braces the main course yard smashed down, ripping through the damage net to the deck. The crews of three guns never saw the heavy, wreckage-snarled spar that crushed them like overripe fruit.

Gallant fought to his feet. The air around him was dark with smoke, through which an impossible rain of splinters, fragments, and bits of flaming wadding flew in all directions. He stared, horrified, as a man sprinting to aid another in the waist threw up hands to suddenly blinded eyes, mouth wide in a soundless scream, only to be cleavered in half by a whirring splinter. The upper half of the trunk thumped to the deck, arms still lifted in their last gesture of agony.

Gallant felt the bile surge past his throat. ''Sweet Christ!'' he moaned, through gritted teeth.

A splintering impact at Gallant's feet in the next instant sent him careening toward the binnacle, clutching at it for balance. A portion of the planking where he had been standing whiplashed up and away, a length of the starboard rail smashing with it off into the air, to splash into the sea.

''Ah! Ah, God!'' Sainte-Juste was screaming behind him, and Gallant spun round in time to see the helmsman stagger toward the shattered rail, his hands pressed over the pulse of blood from the terrible hole in his chest. Before Gallant could react Sainte-Juste had toppled over the planking edge, his wail as he fell snuffed out in the final roar of the *Pearl's* guns. The shot from those guns smashed in under Gallant's feet, *Echo* shivering and quaking like a horse under a quirt as they struck home.

Then *Pearl* was suddenly surging on, the shadow gone from *Echo's* deck, a rattle of musketry and jubilant yells and jeers sounding from the pirate's transom rail. Musket balls pinged into *Echo's* quarterdeck, and Gallant felt his hat snap from his head and spin into the sea.

The wind howled over *Echo* as she slewed round, stricken, in the *Pearl's* wake, her canvas luffing wildly, sheets and braces curling in the air under the writhing canvas. The hull pitched up and over a hissing roller, and from below came the crash and rumble of rolling wreckage, and the screams of trapped men.

Gallant looked round, his mouth dry. Not a man stood with him on the ruins of the quarterdeck. Below the snapping ensign, still somehow there although rent and holed, the gun crews lay in mangled horror on the blood-slick planking. The oaken ship's wheel spun loosely.

With a curse Gallant seized the wheel and spun it, squinting aloft at the thumping, booming sails. The chaos aloft was staggering. Lines snaked free everywhere, or trailed in the wind off to leeward. The maintopmast, wrapped in snarled line, canted at an angle to starboard.

Oh, God, Gallant thought. Don't, don't die! My *Echo*, don't die!

Then his heart skipped a beat. A whiff of black smoke curled out of the gratings, and was whipped off over the rail by the hungry wind. Then more smoke boiled up, the reek of burning cordage and timber touching Gallant's nostrils.

"Fire!" Gallant spat. "Béssac! Damn it, man, where are you?"

Béssac appeared abruptly, pulling himself up the quarter-deck ladder from the waist. His face and chest were black with powder burn, and blood flowed from a half-dozen cuts and wounds. His eyes stared at Gallant, dazed and full of horror.

". . . Ten men. Maybe fifteen, in the waist and fo'c'sle. That's . . . all, capitaine!" He shook his head as if trying to clear it. "Gun exploded in my . . . face."

Gallant reached out with one hand and shook the mate roughly. "Béssac! Get hold of yourself! We're on fire, man! Do you hear? *We're on fire!*"

Gallant threw a glance at the *Pearl*. The big forty-gunner was wearing slowly round to starboard to its original southward heading.

The marine spat in wild frustration. The smoke from the gratings was thicker now, curling in a black column out over the shattered, scarlet horror of the waistdeck.

He shook Béssac again. "Listen to me, mon vieux! You've got to get those men on their feet! And secure those sheets! She'll not answer her helm!"

Béssac's head lolled, eyes still clouded. "I . . . ."

With savage force Gallant put a backhand slap across the mate's face. "You have your orders, M'sieu' Béssac!"

For a terrifying instant a murderous rage flared in Béssac's eyes. Then, abruptly, he was staring at Gallant with the clear eyes of old, shaking his head as if waking from a ghastly dream.

"Christ save us!" he said. "All right. I'll see what I can

do. Jesus, that fire . . .!'' he did not finish.

"Capitaine!" It was Akiwoya, coughing and staggering, fighting his way up the ladder. The pall of smoke behind him boiled up into the sky, burying *Echo's* lower masts now, building and spreading as the wind drove it off, low over the water in an immense hanging cloud to leeward. So long had its dirty pall stretched off across the grey sea that in a few moments the *Pearl* would move into it . . . .

A wild thought flashed into Gallant's reeling mind. He was shaking uncontrollably, fighting for clear perceptions. The contest might not yet be finished, by God!

"Up here, man! Are you all right?"

Akiwoya coughed, rackingly. "I . . . yes. But, God, my *guns* . . .!"

"How many men?" Gallant barked. "How many still can . . . ."

"Fight? Stand?" The African spat. "Twenty. Maybe thirty. Damn it, how can I tell! The whole deck's a blood-soaked wreckage heap!"

"Get them up, Akiwoya! Arm them! Out of the lockers by my cabin, if they're still there!"

Akiwoya stared at him. "Capitaine, she's on fire! Christ, she's going to go like a tinderbox, any minute!"

"Get them up here, man!" Gallant roared.

Without another word Akiwoya had darted forward into the smoke, his voice ringing above the sea noise, the clink and scrape of the wreckage, and the ghastly moaning that still echoed from everywhere.

Gallant coughed. "Béssac, I want the foretopsail and the maintopsail drawing, and I don't care how! Quickly!"

Béssac was gone down the ladder, his hands reaching out to collar the first dazed survivors he found in the smoky murk that now enveloped the midships area of *Echo*. Now, only the quarterdeck and stern were free of it, the masts and bowsprit projecting in stricken grandeur above the billowing clouds. The corvette was beginning to wallow now, no longer light and quick in her motion. And that meant damage at the waterline or below.

Damn! Gallant knew it now. *Echo* was dying. But there was a last chance. A last chance that he could still use her as a weapon, in a last desperate effort to stop the *Pearl*. He squinted downwind. The *Pearl* was just entering the great cloud of *Echo's* smoke now, enveloped to the maintop. If Béssac would only hurry!

"Capitaine! We're sheeting home both the fore and the main topsails! But the maintop lifts will give any second! It's the best we can do!" Béssac's shout carried aft from the smoke-shrouded waist.

With a curse Gallant spun the wheel, and aloft the two topsails arched, buckled, and then arched again into hard curves. *Echo* heeled slightly, creaking, filled with the crash of shifting debris and new screams of pain.

God help me, Gallant thought, his eyes brimming with tears. There is nothing I can do for them. Nothing!

He forced the wheel hard over, and *Echo* shuddered round until she began to run down into her own smoke, its wall boiling out of her and enveloping the *Pearl*. With a gurgle under the counter *Echo* began to slowly accelerate.

Béssac was at the ladder foot, a small knot of men at his back.

"Capitaine! What now?"

"Lash 'em, Béssac! Sheets and braces both! Lash 'em hard, and then get those hands of yours forward to the fo'c'sle!"

Béssac stared, eyes white. "Wh. . . what?"

"Get up there, Béssac! You'll know in a moment!"

There was a new clump of feet up ladder steps, and Akiwoya and his gunners emerged from below, staggering under arm-loads of weapons.

"Good!" Gallant barked. "Get up there with Béssac on the fo'c'sle! Quickly!" He spat in exasperation at their uncomprehending stares.

"We're sinking and on fire, lads!" he roared, fighting the wheel as *Echo* wallowed over a breaking swell. "You want to die like that? No! And neither do I! Get for'rard and get a hand on a weapon! And think about taking a pirate bastard with you!"

Akiwoya's eyes widened. He spun round to stare forward. To stare at the *Pearl*, shrouded and blinded to her tops by the corvette's smoke as the stricken *Echo* slowly accelerated toward her.

"God damn my soul! You're going to . . .!"

"Ram!" Gallant roared. "You're damned right! And in two minutes more, Aki! We'll board her over the bowsprit!"

With a ragged cheer Akiwoya and his gunners struck off forward through the smoke, ducking over the wreckage until they had scrambled on to the fo'c'sle with Béssac's men.

On *Echo* drove. Alone on the quarterdeck, Gallant wrestled in savage effort with the wheel as *Echo's* wounds dragged the little ship ever deeper, working to slew her around.

Not yet, my girl, Gallant cried silently. Not yet!

And then suddenly, abruptly, the *Pearl's* masts were towering ahead, their yards bearing men who clung to the footropes and pointed at the sudden apparition out of the smoke, their shrieks of warning to the cloud-blinded deck below unheard.

Echo drove into the *Pearl* with a rending crash, the bowsprit sliding up and over the forty-gunner's rail, its remaining lines and stays snapping, spritsail yard ducking and disintegrating in a brushwood sound of snapping spars and splintering woodwork and cordage. With a horrid, low moan, *Echo's* cutwater ground against the pirate ship's side, and aloft, the *Pearl's* canvas shook and rippled, luffing violently as the locked hulls began to slew around to the press of wind and sea.

A wild eagerness boiled in Gallant. He leaped down into the smoky horror of the waist and fought his way forward until he stood astride the whiplashing foot of *Echo's* bowsprit, the acrid smoke swirling about him, the wild-eyed faces of Akiwoya, Béssac and the men crouched behind him. He whipped out his hanger and pulled one of the pistols from his belt.

"Come on!" he shrieked. *"Echo! Echo!"*

At that instant the sun, dropping its golden islets of light randomly over the grey sea, chose that moment to shaft down on Gallant's figure on the bowsprit. Licked round by the swirling smoke, his hanger blade gleaming overhead and the pistol pointed forward the *Pearl's* deck, his face and its wild look of fearless attack was lit by a stunning wash of sunlight.

It was too much for *Echo's* men. With a wild cry, all caution gone, they vaulted onto the bowsprit and flung themselves after him into the billowing smoke and down to the deck of the *Pearl*.

Gallant landed hard on the planking, slipping to one knee. The air around him, almost opaque with smoke, was filled with rushing, struggling bodies, the grindings and snappings of *Echo's* bowsprit, and everywhere hoarse shouts, yells and screams.

The marine fought to his feet, only to duck away almost by instinct as a wiry, bearded man in a bandana and leather seacoat swung viciously at him with a huge cutlass. The man's swing bared his armpit for a split second. Grunting with the effort, Gallant plunged his hanger into the opening, burying it to the middle. The bearded man twisted violently and fell back twitching to the deck as Gallant wrenched his blade out.

There was a flash and blast next to Gallant's right ear, and he heard one of *Echo's* men behind him gobble before his body slumped past Gallant to sprawl on the deck, a gaping hole between his eyes pulsing blood. Out of nowhere Akiwoya was leaping forward, roaring, cutting down the man with the pistol with a vicious blow.

Gallant glanced wildly around, a red haze across his vision. Everywhere, there were the forms of desperately struggling men, lurching back and forth in the smoky murk; so confused was it all that he no longer knew friend from foe, *Echo's* man from pirate. Screams, yells, hoarse cries of rage or pain, the ring and clash of weapons, the bark of pistols, filled his perceptions.

Suddenly a huge, swarthy man loomed up in front of Gallant, his beard filthy and matted, a brass ring gleaming in his nostrils. The man's chest was glistening with sweat and streaked with blood, and as Gallant's eyes widened he lunged at the marine with a wicked-looking half-pike.

Gallant twisted, feeling the pike rip through the loose front of his coat. The black-bearded man's face, twisted in a fearsome grimace, pressed into Gallant's in foul-breathed horror, and with a heave of his muscled torso the man bodied Gallant backward, to stumble and fall to the deck. As the marine fell, he saw the pirate lift the pike for a killing thrust. Gallant thrust forward the pistol and jerked the trigger. As it spat out, the pirate screamed, hands clawing to his face, and then whiplashed with an audible thump back to the deck.

Gallant rolled, fighting to regain his feet, only to be knocked down by a tumbling, grappling pair of bodies. The pistol spun from his grasp, kicked instantly by a running foot into the scuppers.

Then Gallant froze where he crouched. From there, through the smoke and the struggling, locked legs of the battling seamen, he could see the door that led aft under the *Pearl's* halfdeck to the great cabin.

And opening it and slipping in, face grim and desperate, was the hatless, shirt-sleeved figure of Nicolas Morin.

"Morin!" Gallant bellowed, heedless of the chaos surging around him. "Morin! Damn your eyes!"

Morin's head snapped round, staring and wide-eyed. He had heard. Then the door banged shut.

A fury of hatred exploded in Gallant's brain, and he sprang to his feet, smashing away with one savage punch the clawing form of a barehanded pirate who died the next instant, impaled on one of *Echo's* pikes. Gallant fought his way to the door, and with wild force kicked it open. A dark ladderway gaped before him.

Gallant plunged down, landing off-balance with a crash and a wrenching of his ankle at the ladder's foot. Breath coming in heaves, he snapped his head up in time to see a sudden movement.

"Sacristi!" he swore.

A hulking figure, hatless and in shirtsleeves, the blood streaming from a headwound down over a florid face to stain the shirtfront, had burst from a cabin door. It reeled across the narrow passageway and crashed against the far bulkhead. The eys, wild and blue, swung on Gallant, and the gore-tipped cutlass in the man's hands came up. He was beginning to laugh, a low, chilling, insane laugh.

"Salter!" gasped Gallant. "You!"

Salter's voice was like a bucksaw against iron. " 'Tis yew! Ye . . . ye've ruined me! Aye, ruined! Yew an' that damn' cockle of a ship o' your'n!" He was levering up now, moving. "I'll kill ye fer that! Kill ye, y' damned dog!"

The words dissolved into a wild animal bellow, and Salter lunged hugely, the cutlass blade arrowing for Gallant's chest.

But Gallant was ready. The uncaring, savage killing fever still boiled within him, and with a powerful slap of his free hand he swept the blade aside. He planted his feet.

The words were tumbling from his lips. "You vicious, cowardly, murdering bastard . . .!" With all his weight behind the thrust he buried the hanger in Salter's shirtfront. Salter stopped in his tracks, toppling up on tiptoe. A horrid shriek burst from his throat, and he was clawing, goggle-eyed, at Gallant's sword hand.

Then, with vicious force, Gallant jerked the hanger free. A rattle sounding in his throat, Salter toppled stiffly forward and crunched to the deck.

"It was too easy for you, Salter!" Gallant heard himself say at the corpse. "Too easy!"

He plunged aft along the dark passageway, oblivious to the noise of desperate fighting that rang on deck above his head. "Morin!" he bellowed.

Then it was before him: the panelled, low door in the partition that led to the great cabin. Without missing a stride, Gallant lowered his shoulder and bulled into it. The door splintered away with a sharp crash, and Gallant leapt through to drop into a ready crouch, the hanger tip circling.

The cabin was huge, in comparison to Gallant's own in *Echo*. From the broad windows sunlight was streaming now across heavy oaken furniture, across jumbled books, charts, and clothing, across an exquisite Turkish rug that covered the deck.

And it streamed across the glowing, beautiful sculpture that stood in golden glory in the middle of the broad desk near the stern windows. An achingly lovely, gently wrought image of a robed woman, stunning in its simple grace, fully as high as Gallant's hanger was long. The sunlight caught and twinkled in the jewels inset in the figure so that it seemed to be lit by its own inner radiance.

"The Señora!" Gallant breathed.

"Exactly, my dear Gallant", said a cold and sneering voice to one side.

Gallant spun with cat speed. There, waiting in the shadows against the larboard bulwark, under a great oaken knee, was Nicolas Morin.

A mocking grin creased the pallid mask, and the point of his sword, a slim sliver of steel, extended in readiness toward Gallant.

"Persistent bastard, aren't you?" said Morin, a strange tremor to his voice. "I should have had you killed when I had the chance!"

Gallant's eyes burned into him, his breath raw in his dry throat. "Where is it, Morin? The bullion? Is it in this ship?"

Morin's blade began to swing in a shallow circle, and he cocked an ear to the desperate sounds of fighting that still rang overhead.

"Bullion? Hah! You'll be shark's bait in a clock's tick, you fool! You and those would-be heroes of yours. You don't ask such questions!"

Gallant edged closer, his heart pounding. He licked his lips. "We're taking your ship, Morin! Strike! You're finished!"

Morin whinnied, eyes crinkling in amusement. *"Strike?* Don't make me laugh, Gallant!" He sneered. "We're doing for you and your crew in a clock's . . .!"

He stopped. Gallant stared, then started as the *Pearl* jolted to a sudden, crunching impact that shifted the very deck beneath their feet. From on deck there came the rippling blast of a volley of musketry, followed by a powerful roar from the throats of fighting men. A roar that was followed by the thunder of boots and running bare feet, and the crash and ring of blade against blade.

Gallant listened, unbelieving, as a booming voice echoed down the open companionway. A voice whose hearty English bawl could not be mistaken.

"Salamander! Salamander! At the buggers, lads! Don't let the Frenchies get 'em all! Huzzah! Huzzah!''

Gallant spun on Morin, a wild exultation in his chest. "The English, Morin! They've boarded! You're finished, Morin! Finished!''

Morin's face twisted into a hideous grimace of hate. "Damn you!'' he shrieked, and lunged.

Almost too late, Gallant met the lunge with a ringing parry, only to cut viciously at Morin's head in return. But the pirate turned away, kicking aside a chair as he spun. Gallant was after him like a panther, and round the cabin the two men fought in grim silence, their blades sliding and ringing over the heaving gasps of their breathing.

Out of one ear Gallant could hear the fighting sounds above dying and fading. Christ, had the *Pearl's* cutthroats prevailed? And boots were clumping down the companionway ladder.

"Now, you meddling fool! Now, you die!'' Morin snarled. With a sudden reserve of strength he smashed in at Gallant; once, twice, three times, four times, his licking blade worked in, brushing Gallant's parries aside. Pressed back, Gallant caught a heel in the rug and fell heavily to one knee, teetering off balance.

"Hah!'' Morin cried. "Now!'' And his blade levelled for the killing downward thrust.

"No!'' Gallant cried. With every ounce of his strength he twisted into a desperate thrust upwards, hard and deep.

The blade sank into Morin's belly, to the hilt, with a horrid thunk. He froze, immobile, where he stood, staring with unbelieving eyes down at Gallant. His sword clattered from his fingers and he staggered back, turning toward the gleaming figurine on the desk, reaching for it.

Then he crashed to the carpet.

Numbly, Gallant rose to his feet, staring down at the still form.

The debt is paid, Morin, he said to himself. For Wosowech, for my poor lads in *Echo*, for them all. Paid in full.

There was a scuffle of shoe leather at the door, and Gallant turned to see Anthony Robinson, sword in hand and a handful of bayonet-armed English marines at his back, step in over the door lip. They stopped, staring down at the body with the bloody blade protruding from its back, and then at Gallant.

Robinson grinned boyishly. "Thought you needed us down here as well. Seems you didn't, what? Is he . . .?"

Gallant nodded. A great tiredness had risen from nowhere within him. "Morin, the key man. That's Salter, in there. One of his partners. There . . . There was the other. Spooner."

Robinson nodded. "We got that bastard, in the sloop. Died with one of my bullocks' bayonets in his guts."

Gallant shook himself, trying to clear the daze in his head. "My men. *Echo*. Is she . . .?" he began.

Robinson's face sobered. "Your lads put up one damned fine scrap, Gallant. Never seen the like. They'd carved themselves a bloody stronghold, if you please, 'midships, when we came aboard. Surrounded by dead, all six of 'em. Damn me, we had to keep out of their reach for a few minutes or else they would've gone at us!"

Six! An ache gripped Gallant's chest. Six men, out of the whole company!

Robinson was going on. "The black and the mate of yours had accounted for a score, by the look of it. Real hellions, Gallant!"

"My ship. She was burning . . . ."

"Yes. We . . . we cut her adrift, Gallant. It was that, or lose all three ships. She's drifted off about a cable to loo'ard. Won't last long. Took a damnable beating, eh?"

Gallant nodded, silent. He turned to stare at the Señora, and gently laid a hand on the immaculately carved drapery. It was cool and smooth to the touch.

Robinson sheathed his sword and turned to his marines. "Carry on, sergeant. Get these lads back on deck. Mr. Morgan will likely need help in herding the pirates below."

He moved to Gallant's side. "So that's the . . . er . . . Señora, is it?"

"Yes. Beautiful, isn't it?"

Robinson clucked his tongue. "Aye, it is that. But we're not going to have the bullion this time round."

"What?"

"Oh, there's some in this ship. The lads had found a half-dozen chests before we found you. And there was some in the sloop we took.''

"But . . . ."

Robinson took off his hat and wiped his sleeve with his cuff. "Spooner. Before he died he told Morgan that they'd left most of the ingots and coins back in their 'hideyhole', as he called it. Somewhere in that mass of islands inshore, there. This statue's the biggest piece, for weight." He shook his head and replaced his hat. "So we've only part of the haul. The bastard died laughing. Thought it was a great prank on us."

Gallant let out a long, shaking breath. There was nothing he could say.

A seaman thrust his head in through the cabin door, knuckling his forelock. "Mr. Morgan's respects sir, an' he says t' tell you the French corvette's sinkin', sir."

Gallant drew himself up. "I must go see her, Robinson", he said, his voice hoarse.

Robinson stopped him with a touch on his arm.

"You've no ship, and no crew, now, Gallant. Our agreement can't be carried out in full. I'm afraid the sloop and this ship, and what bullion in them, are my prizes."

Gallant nodded. He had been prepared for that.

"But there's what you did back up in Spaniard's Bay. You saved my life. And those of my men. And my career. I . . . well, I shouldn't have this prize, were it not for you."

Gallant managed a smile. "I shall console myself with the thought that you would have done the same thing, Mister Robinson." He squared his shoulders. "Now, if you please . . . ."

"Wait!" Robinson's gaze was earnest and direct. "There must be a way. A way I can repay you."

Gallant met his gaze for a long moment. And then, almost of their own volition, his eyes turned slowly to the glowing figurine on the desk.

Robinson was silent for a moment. Then he said, "Yes. You're right. It has to be her." He coughed. "Very well. Consider it done."

The Englishman walked over to the desk and touched the jewelled diadem atop the figure's head. "I shall no doubt be taking these prizes to England, Gallant, rather than the Boston prize court. I intend that my report will list this figure as . . . 'lost'. I would hope that yours would make no mention of this."

"You have my word", Gallant whispered.

"Done, then", said Robinson. "She's yours, Gallant. Christ knows you earned her." He sniffed. "And I'll see that you're put over the side in a boat with your men . . . and her . . . when we're in safe distance of the French coast, homeward bound." Robinson paused. "I want you to know, Gallant. For me, it will always be your lads that stopped and took this ship. Not mine. She'll always really be your prize." His eyes were full of a warm light. "God strike me, I never saw a braver thing!"

Gallant was unable to speak. But he reached out his hand, and the Englishman took it. The grip was long and firm.

"Never", said Robinson, quietly.

When the two men gained the upperdeck, Gallant caught sight immediately of Béssac, Akiwoya, and four others. They stood, the bodies of their fallen shipmates at their feet, staring out at the drifting, smoke-shrouded form of the corvette.

Without a word, Gallant moved silently to their side. All round the little knot of corvettemen the boarders from *Salamander* watched in silence.

Beside the marine, Béssac's cheeks were streaming with silent tears. Overhead the wind whistled, lonely and cold, through the rigging.

A cable-length away, *Echo* sank lower and lower, her masts and yards still defiant and high above the billowing smoke. From her stern staff the white ensign still rippled, brave and forlorn against the gunmetal sea and sky.

And then, with a rumbling roar and a cloud of hissing steam, *Echo* lifted her bowsprit to the sky and sank easily and slowly away, until there was nothing to mark her passing but a few fragments tossed on the moving face of the sea.